A GIRL NAMED CRICKET

PETER J. MANOS

1

Cricket

My parents hurriedly undid their harnesses and arose, their heads just missing the low overhead curvature of the fuselage. Mother turned to me, releasing my harness, but I remained seated, arms tightly folded across my chest. My terror of a fiery meteoric death had subsided, replaced by that familiar rancor rising in me again like bubbles of fetid swamp gas. How could I ever forgive them?

"Come, dear heart. We must go," she said in our whistle/click language.

"English, please," admonished Father. "Even when we think we are alone." His words reverberated with fear, but I was indifferent. I did not wish to speak in any case, no matter the language.

"Come, dear heart," repeated Mother, ignoring him.

When I did not move, she knelt beside me and touched my shoulder. I tightened my hold on myself.

Father placed a hand on the door. Cabin and atmospheric pressure equilibrated with the faintest hissing. As the door opened fully, fresh cool air wafted in and a panoramic vista appeared. I could see the stars! That was not right!

"There is no ceiling out there. No ceiling!" I objected.

"Parts of the planet have no ceiling," said Father.

Alien. That was the word for it. Sassatha was largely decked with low orange clouds. Nor was the landscape here in any way familiar, much less reassuring. Although we had been prepared for some of this, it was still frightening. Father recognized more of these phenomena than either Mother or I and could even name them in English.

Bushy plants, spaced ten to twenty feet apart, covered a vast tract of land. About our height, they were covered with thousands of leaves smaller than a fingernail. Why I thought they must be poisonous, I do not know. Just irrationally fearful, I suppose.

Scattered among them were growths like enormous hands protruding from the ground as if giants, buried from here to the horizon, were trying to escape from their sandy graves. They stood twenty or thirty feet high, with straight, stubby fingers. An indifferent pale moon illuminated the macabre landscape and cast Father's shadow against the wall behind him.

A few yards away a white, winged animal with a flat face and surprisingly large eyes, shocked into flight by our raucous landing, came back to its perch atop one of the giant hands. A furred animal with a hairless tail, frightened into skittering motion, became visible and vulnerable. The predator spotted its prey, took flight, and a moment later snatched the little animal with remorseless claws.

And I could see all this! Our metamorphosis to human form—or transmogrification as I thought of it—had enhanced our auditory and visual acuity.

Doubtless, Father saw an omen in the death of the little animal, but after a moment of motionlessness, he sighed and began to work. From the storage compartment at the back of the plane, just past the galley and the toilet, he removed three transport boxes that carried our tools, instruments, and supplies. One by one, he took them by their straps, walked down the narrow aisle carrying them before him, stepped out of the craft, and rested them against the fuselage.

"Come now, my heart," said Mother for the third time. "We must go."

When he was finished with the first chore, Father approached and leaned over me.

"This demonstration of your displeasure is pointless and stupid," he said. "Furthermore, you are endangering our lives."

"Don't," said Mother. "She's been through enough."

"*She's* been through enough! Had I not experienced it myself in close quarters, I would have believed it impossible for a person to whine continuously for two weeks. Juveniles are so blazing—"

"Don't," repeated Mother sternly.

"...juvenile."

He turned back to me and, continuing to ignore his own admonition, spoke in our language, quietly and intensely.

"Let me tell you what will happen if they find us here, seething silent one. First, they will bind your wrists together. Then they will push you into a cage in the back of a vehicle and drive to an airport. They will fly you to a laboratory where they will put you into a cell and strip you and search you and scan you, prod you and poke you and prick you. Again and again, they will ask you to demonstrate the workings of our devices. For the rest of your life, they will question you. And they will do the same to us, probably in separate cells."

"Dear one," said Mother, touching my shoulder once more, "one day you will understand how sad we are about the subterfuge that was necessary, but you know that we love you. We will not leave without you, but if they find us, it will be the end of...of...us."

My silence chilled them. I finally stood, hissing. I stepped from the vessel onto the sand while eluding Mother's attempt to hug me. She followed and stood next to me, abandoning gestures of affection.

"Isn't the air sweet?" she said.

I turned away, but was immediately distracted by the endless, roofless expanse above me. But I could only look at that for a moment before fear stopped me. I looked at the odd textured surface under my feet and kicked at it, but the minuscule sand storm provided no gratification.

To avoid the catastrophe of discovery by some errant low-flying airplane pilot or itinerant after-dark herpetologist, camouflage was necessary, but as Mother felt the need to watch over me, the task was entirely Father's.

Before covering the rocket-turned-glider plane with vegetation and as much sand from the dune as he could, Father used the fierce white flame from our Sassathan blowtorch to destroy our machines, manuals, instrument panels, food—anything that, if found, would surely trigger a hysterical "man hunt" for the owners of the plane. To the native eye, the fuselage and wings would appear oddly shaped, but not necessarily extraterrestrial. Things that could not have been made here were reduced to amorphous puddles of metal, vitreous slag, and ash. He worked with as much energy as he could muster, but was soon exhausted. Two weeks of weightlessness and only fragmented sleep had taken their toll on each of us. In the end, the vessel could not be completely hidden.

Mother knelt, touching a hand to the ground as if to convince herself that we had indeed arrived. A more familiar type of animal, green-and-yellow-striped and scaly, not a yard away, scampered from its hiding place.

Mother let a handful of sand sift between her fingers.

"Silicon dioxide," said Father. "Mainly."

"I know what it is," said Mother.

Finished with the blowtorch, he lifted a transport box, helping Mother slip her arms through the straps and rest it on her back. I allowed him to put one on my back. Mother helped him with his.

We walked single file, my parents periodically exchanging places at the lead, the second in line keeping an eye on me, though I followed closely behind.

My eyes traced a sine wave. Up towards the galaxy, down towards the ground, up towards the galaxy...This was the most unusual surface I'd ever walked on, at times soft, at times hard, at times rippled, at times smooth. Unpredictable.

"Pay attention, please." Father was currently in charge of my supervision.

"I am paying attention."

"Your head is bobbing up and down as if mounted on a spring."

I retreated into silence.

As we were tired, and our legs weakened by the weeks of weightlessness, we took the shorter routes even if they occasionally brought us in contact with the bushes, which exuded a subtle pungent scent and which I was convinced were poisonous.

As otherworldly as these things were—the flora, fauna, landscape, and sky—nothing was as otherworldly and frightening as walking on the *surface* of the planet—not safely underground. Might we not be torn to pieces by blast winds, burned by rain, or poisoned by air? Indeed, my lungs had begun to tingle, increasing my anxiety, but I could as easily have sought my parents' reassurance as I could have asked to ride on their backs. I kept looking up, each time startled that there was no ceiling there, no clouds.

The straps of the boxes bit into our shoulders. Never in my life had I lifted anything so heavy, much less carried it on my back. Indeed, my original body would have been incapable of lifting this burden. These new muscles were thicker and stronger than my original ones. And although I had exercised, I'd never walked for more than eleven or twelve yards at a time.

Weaving in and around the bushes had become tedious. We were relieved to come to the sandy shoulder of a little-used unpaved road.

This surface proved firmer than the naked ground and more even. Eventually we arrived at the transition from unpaved to paved road and a little further on, to the outer perimeter of the town.

"An abandoned abode," noted Father unnecessarily, stopping for a moment, probably because his legs were tired. "Note the boards over its apertures."

The squarish structure was approximately five to six times Father's height. The two halves of the top were pitched upward and met at a ridge. The whole thing seemed like a blemish bursting forth from the earth.

"It is like a blister," I said. "Repugnant. Why should anyone wish to live in it?"

"It is rare," responded Father, "to find a person who combines dermatological acumen with architectural criticism—alien architectural criticism at that. Fascinating. Now, shall we resume walking?"

I persisted. "It is constructed entirely of flat two-dimensional surfaces. The wind could blow it away. A ridiculous structure."

Disappointed in both of us, Mother shook her head. "Desist, please."

A little further on several more abodes appeared. Before them lay the rusted carcasses of boxlike conveyances.

"Defunct motorized conveyances," said Father, pointing.

"My dear husband, you cannot help yourself, can you?"

"I am attempting to be helpful."

We continued to walk.

Why were these oxidized conveyances here in the first place? Were they on display? Or had they been destroyed by acid rain where they now lay? Had the poisonous downpour driven off the inhabitants of the blisters? I felt unwell.

Primitive lighting fixtures high up on metal poles illuminated sections of black road. Hard as these roads were, the flanking strips of white stone, upon which we now walked, were absolutely indurate and unyielding. A fall here would abrade the skin or break bones. I adjusted my stride and footfall lest I send shock waves through my spine.

Why would anyone make such a dangerous thing? Where was common sense? Had they not yet invented cushioning?

My parents had been observing me closely.

"It is a relatively young civilization," said Father.

We came to a section of town whose one or two level structures were in better repair, though a clustering of giant blisters was more distressing than a single one.

A twisted, glowing red glass tube read, "Prickly Pear Gas and Auto Repair". I could read the individual words—my neural net transducer was still working after the landing. But what of the meaning? Was this a place to purchase vapor-exuding thorny fruit and treat one's injuries oneself, perhaps with that very same thorny fruit? I would soon learn to scan the airwaves for a more accurate picture of things.

2

Cricket

"How do I look?" asked Father, adjusting his wig, which had taken up a precarious position towards the back of his head. I turned away, looking back into the desert for signs of dust storms or clouds.

"I must pass," he said.

"You are not going in there alone," said Mother, adjusting the straps of her carrying box and touching her own wig. "We all must pass."

This was an argument he could not win, so he told us to stand behind him and to remain as mute as the moon. I was relieved to be getting out from under this exposure to a frightening, fathomless sky.

Two seven-foot-tall canisters, each with a single, long, flexible tube-arm reaching into a pocket of sorts, stood side by side, watchful. Behind them stood an elongated building with a red metal roof.

Just as I was eventually to learn what things were and what they were called, I was to learn people's names and characteristics, some in more detail, some in less. In Prickly Pear, where everyone talked about everyone else, one had only to listen to learn about its denizens.

We were about to make first contact with humankind, in the

person of one Jerry Riggins, of whom, of course, we knew nothing at the time.

From various people, we later learned about the attendant, a cranky, twenty-five-year-old high school dropout, simple, superstitious, easily offended, and unscrupulous, though not formally yet a criminal. We would tempt him along that path.

The white t-shirt tucked carelessly into his jeans read "Boys will be boys." He'd slicked his hair back with a greasy substance like motor oil, but was not entirely successful. With an aquiline nose and thin limbs, he resembled a hawk in need of rest.

Behind a short, black plastic counter, he appeared to be looking at a naked woman displayed on a small glowing screen he held in his hand.

Next to the counter stood a stand displaying two types of oil for engines. The office windows faced the canisters—pumps. On the back wall hung a calendar featuring shiny conveyances on which sat scantily clad women. Why they sat on the conveyances instead of in them, was a mystery. And why so little clothing? And why were their tops and bottoms so tightly bound in cloth that their flesh was overflowing the rims of their attire?

As we, the oddest blond threesome he'd ever seen, came through the door, a buzzer sounded and interrupted Jerry's reverie. I couldn't help but imagine what he saw or thought he saw:

A man in his forties wore a faux, brown deerskin jacket with tassels; white, snap-button cowboy shirt; green string tie; blue denim pants; and green imitation alligator boots. With his prominent cheekbones and jaw like an icebreaker, he must have looked like one of those puffed up comic book superheroes, though he was of normal build and just under six feet in height. With his worried eyes scanning the small room, his demeanor was anything but heroic.

Standing behind the man was a woman of about the same age and height, also blond, wearing a long-sleeved, belted white dress patterned with blue forget-me-nots and yellow buttercups. It dropped to her ankles, covering the tops of her black lace-up boots. A matching bonnet, tied under her chin, covered her head. Her otherwise attractive oval face had slipped into a worried frown, eyes narrowed, eyebrows pulled together.

The sixteen-year-old girl wore the same style dress, boots, and bonnet as the woman, but was shorter than the adults, about five-foot-seven inches. She, too, had high cheekbones.

"Good evening," said Father, as Jerry put his small device into his back pocket.

"Yeah? What's so good about it?" said Jerry Riggins, looking around at the three of us.

Father paused for an inordinately long time before speaking.

"Your...our moon is bright tonight, shining on a poor traveller's path, nor is there precipitation...The air is clean. At the macroscopic level, it is peaceful and peace, you will surely agree, is good. The night is warm. I imagine beautiful flowers can be seen during the day. It is great good fortune to have a night like this..."

"Oh, stop. I'm getting sick."

Again a pause longer than the last, before Father spoke again, drawing on the repertoire of what he thought would be valuable societal facts, names, and references in which he had steeped himself on our journey. However, some were hundreds of years out of date, nor could he always use them appropriately. Many would simply be incorrect.

"You are ill, young man? I am so sorry. Perhaps you should take some Bayer aspirin or Alka Seltzer and go to bed. Drink plenty of water. Do you have a thermometer? Have you taken your temperature?"

"Are you kooky, or what?"

Jerry Riggins glanced out the window, presumably to see what kind of car this weirdo was driving, but there was no car.

"Where's your car, man?"

"Ah, you see the problem. How astute of you. Have you attended the University of California at Los Angeles? Or at Riverside, perhaps?"

"No, I don't see the problem, and I don't see as how my education is none of your frigging business. What do you want?"

"I would like to have some money, if you don't mind," said Father,

The crime rate in Prickly Pear, California was lower than the state average, though the Heaven's Hoods from East Los Angeles occasionally made one of their prominent pilgrimages to the desert north of town for a little camping, drinking, and debauchery, with some incidental speeding, shoplifting, and aggravated assault. Gentle Father, with his neatly trimmed, short blond hair and tasseled jacket, would not have appeared to be a member of a motorcycle gang, but he was at this moment reaching into his pocket for what Jerry Riggins could only imagine to be a gun.

He froze in fear.

Instead of a gun, however, Father removed from his pocket a block of gold about the size of a sugar cube and placed it on the counter

"Would you be so kind," he said, "as to take it in hand and heft it."

Jerry Riggins was so relieved, he laughed.

"It is not, as you say, a joke. That is pure unalloyed gold. Would you perhaps consider purchasing it from me? At the current rate of exchange, it is worth eight to nine hundred dollars at a minimum. I do not have the latest quotes, of course."

Mr. Riggins picked up the golden cube.

He tossed the cube from hand to hand. He nodded to himself. Then, with his pocketknife, he scratched it.

"You want me to buy this?"

"Yes, I would be grateful if you would."

Mr. Riggins scratched his head. He must have been thinking this some kind of confidence game, but this cube looked, and felt, and acted like gold. He pressed his lips together, moving them from side to side.

"What the hell," he said. "I'll give you twenty bucks for it."

"Bucks? Oh, dollars. No, I'm afraid I must not part with it for twenty dollars because twenty dollars is less even than a fortieth of its value. Believe me, young man, when I say that you would be delighted if I sold it to you for four hundred dollars as that is less than half of its worth."

When Father turned up his palm, Riggins returned the gold.

"It was delightful meeting you. Good night," said Father, turning to leave.

"Tell you what," said Riggins, "I'll give you seventy bucks for the thing. Come on, how do I know it's gold? It could be...I don't know...something else."

The interspecies haggling went on for a while. Father must have been quite tense because when I emitted a brief whistling sigh, he whipped around to face me.

"Hold your tongue, literally if you must," he said in English.

His harsh tone with me set Mother off. Jerry Riggins heard a rapid fire, high-pitched back and forth of whistling, chirping, and clicking as both Father and Mother briefly lost control and reverted to our language. Then, simultaneously, both touched their thumbnails to their temples and were silent for a moment before Father spoke in English.

"Wait for me outside," he said.

"No," said Mother, also in English. With her hands on her hips and her feet spread apart, she was the proverbial immovable object. Recognizing this, Father snorted and turned back to Jerry Riggins, whose jaw had dropped.

"It appears then we are unable to agree on a price," said Father.

Mr. Riggins's eyes, however, were now on me. I was to learn that my appearance at least, if not my behavior, was appealing, though my eyes and mouth struck me as overly small for my face, my nose overly large, and my figure overly curved. But I was comparing this body with my original.

Jerry Riggins smiled admiringly at me. When I grimaced, he must have thought I was smiling back at him. He glanced for a moment at my prominent new bimodal chest before speaking.

"This is the screwiest night I've ever had. You're lucky I just got paid." He was still looking at me when he agreed to pay $475 for the gold.

"Thank you," said Father when the exchange had been made. "Now I wonder if you might tell us where we could find a room for the night."

Jerry Riggins gave directions to a motel.

Back on the street, Father swore at Mother, curses rather like English four-letter words. Before he began working on the Colony ship, he'd been sweet-tempered, playful, would even carry me around the module on his back in a game we called Hunting in which Mother was the hunter and I the hunted, though they often switched roles. But my bitterness now held sway over my sadness. They had themselves to blame for the rending of their harmony.

"Purulence! Decay! We have only just arrived, and you expose us. You spoke our language before that man? What were you thinking? "

"Do calm down," said Mother. "In my irritation at you I said a few words. A mistake, I admit, but warranting no such harsh tone, neither before the young man, nor in private. You are acting like a short circuit, sparks flying. It would have been easy enough to tell that man that your wife is a naturalist and that she enjoys making bird calls and can he guess what bird I was imitating."

"Forgive me for not seeing the humor in this but—"

"I am not being humorous."

"You certainly are not."

I had to speak up. "Father, you are being absurd. Were I to go back inside, tell him where we are from, and sing the epic poem *Ognim in Search of Water*, what would he have done? Called the authorities? Called a doctor? Wrestled me to the ground and tied me up? What would he have done, Father? What?"

"Daughter, I—"

"I'll tell you what he would have done. He would have shaken with laughter and asked my name. You are overwrought. No one here will believe anything but what they see before them."

"How glib you are. And when they see before them the craft half buried in the sand? What will they think then, oh, clever disrespectful one?"

"Stop this, both of you. I am tired," said Mother. "Let us find a bed. No more arguing tonight."

3

Cricket

The long, low, pastel pink Still Waters Motel, one indistinguishable green door next to the other, faced a nearly empty parking lot.

Before entering the office, marked by a green sign flashing the word "vacancy," Father made us promise to allow him alone to do the talking. To be precise, he extracted this promise from Mother, my silence taken as acquiescence. I foreswore speaking to these human beings, to my parents, or to anything else for that matter. However, unlike oaths of silence taken by the members of some religious orders on this planet, I could ignore mine at will.

I was relieved again to have a ceiling above me and walls around me, even if they were just flat planes.

A shabby sisal carpet covered the floor of the small office, its furniture of an equally shabby rattan. (Looking back, I find it remarkable that I was eventually to learn not only what sisal and rattan were, but also how they were derived.) The walls, fittingly, were sand colored, hung with a few subtly lopsided pictures of those giant hands against impossibly blue, cloudless skies.

Everyone in town knew the manager and half-owner, Miriam

Gaylord, a big chatty woman with short brown hair and sequined eyeglasses. "She always wears a black dress covered with red roses," they told us later. They would not be reluctant to tell us about her woes. On that first encounter, of course, we knew nothing about her, just as we'd known nothing about Jerry Riggins.

She had owned the Still Waters Motel in Seattle before escaping the continuous drizzle to settle here, where the sky was reliably cloudless. The sun, while not curative, did much to relieve her rheumatism, though her joints still gnawed on themselves from time to time.

She and her brother Buddy, an inveterate alcoholic, had invested their life savings in this motel after the mayor assured them, in his hypomanic style, that Prickly Pear was destined to become a booming tourist town. They'd get more business than they could handle.

At 12:06 AM, Miriam Gaylord, fifty, divorced, arthritic, and failing at business, was soundly asleep. Looking back, I imagine her dreaming about a fight with her brother.

On a dark wood countertop, next to a guest book and business card holder, perched a shiny little call bell with a button on top. To the rear of the office, behind a door marked "Private," slept the proprietress.

Glancing from Mother to me, Father shrugged, read the sign that said, "Ring bell for service," and rang. Ping! With self-discipline, he waited a minute before ringing again. Ping! Ping! Another minute. Ping! Ping! Ping! Impatience fired my ire at them. How long must I wait for this linear progression to become exponential? For gentle tapping to become violent pounding?

"Perhaps if you rang with some enthusiasm," said Mother.

"Enthusiasm? The decibel range of the contraption is limited. It is not even amplified. I am as enthusiastic as the next person after two weeks of sleepless nights while being accosted by the whining of a hysterical teenager—," he said loudly, speaking our language.

"Don't," said Mother. She eased Father to the side to take charge of the bell.

Most people would exclude motel call bells from the vaunted family of percussion instruments, but only because they had never heard a desperately tired, particularly musical, Sassathan using a desk bell to try to rouse a sleeping motel owner. Under Mother's direction, the lowly bell now issued as never before (and never again) a remarkable medley of cheerful musical improvisations varying in pitch, volume, and rhythm. It had become an elfin creature singing its heart out. But, still, no one came to the office to assist us.

After less than a minute of this, I walked from the entrance doorway to the counter, took the bell from Mother, and hurled it at the door marked "Private". It gave its own death knell and exploded into shrapnel.

"Black bile and vomitus!" cursed Father. "What are you doing?"

"I'm tired," I said not bothering with English, picking up the glass business card holder as if to throw that as well. Later, when I was calmer and had time to think about my behavior, I was deeply ashamed of myself.

"Stop this madness!" said Mother. "Put that down now! Immediately!"

"Then do something effective. I have a headache. That ringing little monstrosity was—"

A rustling from behind the office door. Silence superseded our squabbling. The door opened and a large, groggy woman in a pink terry-cloth bathrobe emerged. We froze. She looked at us and then around the room.

"Where are the birds?" she asked.

We understood the words of the question, but what did she mean?

"We saw no birds as we entered," said Father. "Were they perhaps extremely small, passing us unseen below knee level as we opened the door?"

"How would I know what they looked like? It sounded like the room was full of them."

Suspecting that further engagement in the conversation would only complicate matters, Father performed his well-rehearsed shrug. An instant later we understood. It was either the bell ringing or our musical speech that sounded to her like birds.

"Oh!" said Father. "There were no birds. We whistled to get your attention."

"You should have used the bell."

"I'm afraid my daughter broke it by mistake." He pointed to the pieces on the floor.

Miriam Gaylord looked at them and then at me.

"You must pack quite a wallop, young lady."

"We will pay for it, of course," said Father, pulling a wad of bills from his pocket.

"We'll worry about that later. Let's get you folks checked in."

As Ms. Gaylord and Father began the process, Mother and I removed our travel boxes and settled into chairs. There was nothing for us to do and we were exhausted.

"License number?" asked Miriam.

Father shrugged.

"Don't know your license number?"

"Oh, you mean for a car," said Father.

"You didn't come in a spaceship, did you?" said Ms. Gaylord.

"We come in spaceship. Yes," I said.

Horrified, Father and the Mother whirled around to look at me, and then, holding their breaths, turned back towards the owner. These humans must be far more intelligent than the colony ship's computer had assessed, for this ordinary woman, just awakened from sleep, and presumably lacking any advanced academic degree in exobiology, had spontaneously asked if we'd come in a spaceship. And now, I had confirmed it.

"You rented a car, didn't you?" said Miriam, ignoring me. "That's why you don't know your license number, right? Well, it should be right there on the tag on the key."

"We have no car," said Father. "We walked."

Miriam looked at the packs.

"I'll still need to see some ID. Driver's license is fine."

"Would my birth certificate suffice?" said Father.

"Well, what I really need to know is where you folks live. How I can get in touch with you if I need to. You know, problems with your credit card and such."

"We have no credit cards."

"We alien creatures," I said.

Mother popped from her chair. Beginning in our language, but promptly switching to broken English, she scolded me. I arose and walked over to stare at one of the pictures of the giant hands. Mother followed.

"I just love Joshua trees," said Ms. Gaylord.

I returned to my chair. Mother followed.

Father pulled the wad of money from his pocket again.

"May I relieve you of your concerns by paying now?"

Miriam Gaylord appeared embarrassed at having displayed mistrust of us poor, tired, if odd, hikers.

"Don't worry about that. Just fill out the registration." She removed a yellow registration form from a drawer beneath the counter and handed it to Father along with a writing instrument. He placed the form on the counter and attempted to print his name on the top line. When no marks appeared, he took the instrument in hand, examined it, pressed on the clip, turned the barrel, and only then pushed the button on top. He completed the form slowly and placed it on the counter facing Ms. Gaylord.

With her elbows resting on the counter, she leaned over to read it.

She read our new names aloud. "Do I have that *right*?"

"Yes. Is anything wrong?"

"No. No. It's just that they're uncommon names," she said, the shadow of a frown passing momentarily over her face.

"Are they?" said Father. The colony ship's supercomputer, which was to have given us humdrum, forgettable names, had bungled the job and bungled it badly.

"Maybe I'd better look at that birth certificate after all. Then we can finish up."

Father took from his breast coat pocket, where he'd put it with forethought, a modest but official looking document, entitled State of Hawaii Certificate of Live Birth, which listed Kapiolani Maternity and Gynecological Hospital in Honolulu as his birthplace.

"My," said Ms. Gaylord, "you're a long way from home."

"You have no idea," said Father, in a momentary fatigue-induced lapse.

"How long do you plan to stay?"

"Until the end of our days," said Father.

Mother walked over to him, temporarily abandoning guard of her pouting and erratic daughter. As Father and Mother faced each other, she touched her left thumbnail to her temple, whistling for a fraction of a second, and then said in English, "Not talk that front of child."

"My wife has a speech impediment," said Father. Again Mother touched thumbnail to temple, her eyes narrowed. Returning to where I sat, she dropped into her chair.

"Well," said Miriam, ignoring the peculiar little spat, "how 'bout we just sign you in for the night?"

"Excellent," said Father.

She re-examined the registration form. Quirky names for a quirky family, she must have thought, but Father had insisted on paying for three days *in advance*. She couldn't complain about that. The Still Waters Motel was, after all, losing money. Only a few tourists stayed here on their way to the Mojave National Preserve. And when the Heaven's Hoods stayed at the motel, the cost to repair broken windows and doors, not to mention burnt mattresses, swallowed any potential profit.

Miriam and Buddy had been forced to lay off staff. Now they changed the sheets, did the laundry, vacuumed the rooms, and took turns on night duty. The obdurate absence of a buyer prevented them from selling the place. But tonight, they had guests who paid in cash. Even if they were strange guests.

Before showing us our room, Ms. Gaylord said she liked our outfits, and asked if perhaps a western was being filmed in the area, and if we were actors in it. Father, at a loss, finally just said no, that we just liked to dress this way.

A large bed and a cot took up most of the floor space. Faded pictures of yellow, indigo, and red desert wildflowers, always accompanied by Joshua Trees, hung on beige walls. By the window, whose dark brown shades were drawn, sat a sad little writing desk and mismatched wooden chair. An oval mirror hung over a dresser on the opposite wall. The cramped pink bathroom contained a toilet, sink, and slender shower stall, huddled together in solidarity against the callous guests who mistreated them. Three off-white towels hung on a rack.

"I hate this room," I said. "Everything is flat and straight. No arcs, no parabolas. How primitive they are."

"If you insist on speaking Sassathan," said Father, tired of arguing, "speak softly unless you wish that woman to return looking for birds."

Exhaustion finally held sway. Arguments ended. Silence descended. Father took thirteen gold cubes and put them in the top drawer of the dresser.

"These should be enough for some time," he whispered to himself. Then what, I wondered. We got under the covers. After minimal repositioning, my parents fell asleep, their concerns, for the time being, fragmenting and drifting away.

I was tired. More tired than I had ever been. But I lay in my sagging cot fully awake, unable to stop reliving our plunge to Earth.

At 300,000 feet the wing tips began to glow, the temperature in the cabin to rise, and the wind to roar like a monster angry at our trespass. Would the orange glow spread to the fuselage and through the walls? Would the instrument panel bubble up, droplets of melted glass igniting as they fell? Would our clothes burst into flame around our crisply baked bodies? As dispirited as I was, I didn't want to die. Gripping the armrests, I had braced for the end.

Our craft assumed a nose-up tilt, increasing drag to slow its descent. Refashioning itself from rocket plane to glider, it jettisoned its fuel tanks and engine so they tumbled into the Indian Ocean. It flew over the South Pacific, over the North Pacific, and banked over Baja California heading north. Here on the nighttime side of the planet, bright asterisks of cities shone further north and east, but not where we were headed.

On touchdown, the craft mowed down a hundred bushes, which screeched against the fuselage and wings like sentient creatures tortured. Uprooted or sheered off, they bumped over the wings and fuselage, or were violently flung into the air. The hideous banging, thumping, and jolting stopped abruptly as the craft plowed into a sand bank only ten yards before it would have struck a Joshua tree, a hand raised in warning, "Danger. Go back."

I writhed in bed. I scolded myself. This rumination is pointless! You have landed. You're alive. No fire. No explosion. I must quiet my mind, I thought, or I would be awake the entire night and even more miserable in the morning.

So I began to focus on the sensation in my odd articulations, moving from ankles, slowly up to knees, then hips, wrists, elbows, shoulders, and neck. How remarkable my ability to walk or manipulate objects with these unusual joints. And how sensitive the skin to the lightest touch. How easy it must be to puncture, more like a bubble than integument. But these were not new thoughts. Eventually, the weight of my fatigue sank me into unconsciousness.

The next day, each of us took the most luxurious shower of our lives, indeed the only shower of our lives, extending it to a profligate two minutes. Lest my parents feel their catastrophic decision to leave home validated in any way, I suppressed all expression of pleasure as the stream of precious water washed over my head, eyes, tongue, and the setae-covered soles of my feet and palms of my hands.

4

Cricket

We awoke very hungry, having consumed the last of our scout ship rations two days before arrival. I was surprised then, that instead of immediately starting out in search of food, Father recounted a dream.

"I was standing before the colony ship's computer which eons of cosmic radiation damage had changed into Big Bird, a confused, bumbling seven-foot-tall yellow bird from an American children's television program. I recognized it from my study of the culture."

"Symbolizing?" asked Mother.

"Unreliability. The computer had indiscriminately gleaned from the airways a hodgepodge of words and images from films, videos, television, and satellite transmissions, and confounded them with each other."

"Father, there is a growling in my stomach."

"It's called boborygmi," said Father. "A message from the mammalian gastrointestinal tract that fluids and gases are in motion, suggesting hunger."

I touched my palm to my abdomen and reassured it that I'd heard its message. "Be still. My father will not let you starve. I am almost certain of it."

"Dearest husband, perhaps we could hear the rest of your fascinating dreams later. We have a big decision to make now."

"That is correct." He was hovering around the heavy transport boxes. "To paraphrase Shakespeare, to take or not to take, that is the question."

"Borborygmi and now Shakespeare." Mother arose from the chair near the window. "Indispensable words. I look forward to employing them at every opportunity."

"Forgive me my vocabulary. I will try to simplify it, or as they say here, dumb it down a bit."

"I am sorry. It is the hunger speaking."

"Forgiven. Now, should we, or should we not take the boxes with us as we venture out in search of food? On the one hand, we might look like hikers if we wore them. On the other, the packs are quite heavy."

"We will be facing the indigenous intelligent species en masse for the first time. Many eyes will be on us. We cannot afford to stumble, either literally, or figuratively."

Remarkably, all I had to say was that I did not want to carry the transport box and the discussion was over. We left our packs in the room.

Miriam Gaylord told us we could eat breakfast at Rosita's down the street, a Mexican restaurant that also served an American-style breakfast. On a Saturday morning, with only one other restaurant in town, it would be busy. We would need to be careful.

We had extensive knowledge of the culture of southern California, but because of Big Bird's damage, this knowledge was patchy, irrelevant, incorrect, or grossly incorrect. We knew who Walt Disney was, for example, but not what a pancake was, or a French kiss, or a pussycat. Father spoke fluent, though not idiomatic English, and now believed that the polite response to "Good day," was, "What's so good about it?" Mother and I spoke considerably less well and may have sounded to some as if we were from Eastern Europe.

We peered through the plate glass window. Were we more

frightened of entering this crowded restaurant than we had been of entering coffin-like canisters that for eons would hold us in suspended animation as our bodies changed form? Would the natives recognize us as other? Would they stand and swarm us?

"I think I've lost my appetite," said Father.

"We have survived centuries in deep space and a crash landing on a new world. We will survive breakfast," said Mother softly. Her optimism and cheerfulness were lifelong, but I gave her no credit for them, even now when we needed them. Everyone knows temperament is congenital. And I blamed Father for his anxiety.

"Unless some madman bursts in firing an assault rifle, as happens now and again as I have been given to understand," said Father. Humans had atavistic tendencies. We'd been advised to keep watch for them.

———

With trepidation, we entered and stood fidgeting at the reception counter. Father, Mother, and I, in our respective deerskin jacket and ankle-length dresses and bonnets, despite our presumably "normal" features, could not but appear peculiar. Big Bird had styled our clothing on the costumes of Hollywood movie stars portraying early nineteenth century pioneers.

If every head in the place did not turn toward us, every eye did. And some necks twisted, and some children stood on their seats to get a better look at us before their parents pulled them back down explaining it was impolite to stare. But this being Southern California, our outlandish dress was insufficiently novel to sustain much interest. The breakfasters soon returned to their breakfasts.

The restaurant's decorations were not reassuring. Full-bosomed maidens in low-cut white blouses pleaded with feather-bedecked, bare-chested, knife-wielding priests, to spare them from sacrifice— phosphorescent paintings on black velvet. Big Bird, despite its blunders, appeared correct about these peoples' atavism.

"Do they still do these things?" I whispered.

"You will note," whispered Father in answer, "that no one here has feathers in their hair, or strings of animals' teeth around their necks."

Rosita herself seated us, Mother and Father together, I opposite. A middle-aged, full-figured woman in a white cotton dress embroidered with red and yellow roses, she wore her graying black hair in a tight bun under a net. Her skin was like smooth brown stone. I thought her eyes kind.

"Buenos días." She gave us menus. "It is very busy this morning. Forgive me. I will be right back."

Surprisingly, we turned not immediately to the menus, but to the remarkable bas-relief carvings on the booth's high wood walls.

Two intermingling streams of reptiles flowed through each other from opposite sides of the panel. Individuals grew larger towards the middle, diminishing in size as they approached the opposite wall. Broad plates of cacti seamlessly filled the interstices.

How pleasant to see animals of such form. I was about to turn to the menu when Mother's eyes began to twitch rapidly from side to side. Safely seated with her family in the booth, she felt secure enough to scan the Internet, though scanning might leave her vulnerable under other circumstances. It also had some risks. She had as little experience with scanning as did I, though I had begun experimenting, focusing on animals to start, and law enforcement, but also letting my searches take me to unexpected places.

"You are about to hear an edifying lecture, this time from your mother." Father smiled wryly.

"Can she not wait until we have eaten?" I said as if she were not present, which, in a sense, she was not. But then she found what she wanted. Her eyes stopped their oscillations. Lightly, she brushed her fingertips over the bas-relief.

"The artist who carved these came to this country undocumented." She spoke quietly.

"There is a lesson for us in this?" asked Father.

"I need sustenance," I whispered.

"Let your mother finish."

"My borborygmi protests."

Father put a thumbnail to his temple, temporarily silencing me.

"He'd crossed the border illegally and was in danger. Rosita and others hid and cared for him until he moved to a big city where his life-sized sculptures of laboring Mexican men and statuesque women made him rich. He carved these booths to express his gratitude to Rosita and he paid for the construction of the high school. His bronze statue stands out front."

Before Mother could say more, Rosita returned to our table. "You like Quintana. No?"

I had no idea what she meant. Father, too, was baffled. Mother surprised us.

"Pablo Guzman Quintana. Yes. We like."

Lost for a moment in thought, Rosita touched the surface of the carving, then in some mysterious way fortified, smiled brightly.

"Coffee?" she asked.

On board the Colony, during intermittent periods of consciousness, Mother had learned only a little English, preoccupied as she was with her overwrought daughter. Now was her chance to practice one of the few English phrases she was comfortable with.

"What you recommend?" she asked.

"Pardon me?" said Rosita.

Then I, as angry and anxious as ever, but hungry, demonstrated my own pluck. "We fresh here. What are coffee?"

"What *is* coffee," corrected Father, glaring at me. And then, remembering himself what coffee was, decided we'd better try it here and now, because we would be faced with this question for the rest of our lives. "Coffee?" was, in fact, the most frequently asked question in North America.

"Three coffees, please," he said, proud of himself.

Rosita must have thought us odd beyond our poor English. On the basis of no evidence whatsoever, she decided we were Russian. Russians in Prickly Pear! "Asombroso," she muttered to herself. She brought cream and sugar to the table without even asking if we wanted it.

"Everyone in town knows Rosita and Rosita knows everyone, but I don't know you," she said. "You are tourists, no?"

"We not tourists," said Mother. Father scowled. Though she

understood his warnings grew from fear, they piqued her. He'd never acted like this before, but on the other hand, we'd never been on a different planet before.

"We are not tourists," said Father. "We are new in town."

"Where do you live?"

He explained that we'd just arrived and were staying at the Still Waters Motel. Rosita nodded and said, "Hmm," a word none of us knew, then gestured at the menus.

"Take your time," she said. She was halfway across the room when she turned to look back at us.

Whether from fatigue or impatience, Father read the menu aloud in Sassathan, but spoke so softly that only someone with the auditory acuity of a bat could have listened in, and even then bat-ears would have heard only soft whistling as if he were surprised by what the menu offered.

"No insects?" I asked. "These people are primitive beyond belief. Almost as bad as my parents."

"You are not going to ruin my breakfast, Miss Bad Mouth," said Father. "Keep your mouth closed if you're not putting food into it."

"Darling, don't—," began Mother.

"People are staring. Please examine your menus," ordered Father.

Instead, I examined the inhabitants of the four booths across from, and parallel to ours.

Nearest the door sat two women, one in a black short-sleeved shirt and slacks, a seven-pointed silver star on her chest, and a San Bernardino sheriff's patch on her shoulder. Young, slim, her bobbed brown hair reaching her chin, she struck me as delicate despite a belt hung with handcuffs, sinister pouches, and a gun.

"That woman has a gun," I said. "Big Bird was correct about something."

"Do not stare," warned Father, dismissing my unease.

Her left hand rested on the table while she sipped a coffee in the other.

The woman's plump companion was about the same age, and seemed her antithesis in cargo pants and a pressed men's dress shirt. Her severely short dark blond hair was as flat on top as the facet of a crystal. She spoke of the classes she taught with a deep, confident voice.

A handsome dark-skinned family occupied the next booth. The mother, a woman in a bright green dress, looked like an athlete. She was engaged in animated conversation with her lithesome teenage daughter, whose hair was a rich black nimbus of corkscrew ringlets. The girl glanced in our direction, smiled, then turned back to her mother. The father, a grinning black Atlas with a ball of curly, graying hair, we learned later, was Hoppy Jones, owner of Prickly Pear Gas and Auto Repair. Next to him was his son, a teenage version of himself. While mother and daughter conversed, father and son ate.

Then came a family of three: a stout man, whose baldness contrasted with an exuberant mustache, and a girl about my age, wavy black hair to her shoulders, in blue jeans and a tight red tank top restraining a squirming five-year old girl in a white dress.

"We'll go in a minute, Annie," said her father. "Settle down."

"Stop being a brat," said the older girl.

A man, woman, and boy occupied the last booth I could see from where I sat. Until now, my eyes had not lingered on anyone for long. But the lithe, brown-skinned teenage boy caught my eye and held it.

A cowlick stood stubbornly at the back of his thick, black head of hair. His nose and jaw were prominent. A sinewy right arm extended from his blue shirt. The empty left shirtsleeve hung like a limp banner on a windless day. I gazed too long, and he saw me. His hard brown eyes challenged me. I turned away.

Something ineffable unsettled me. His face, his carriage, his physique, his gaze—all contributed. Unsettling me further was my confusion. What was I feeling? I could not find a name for it. I had never felt this way in my original body. I adjusted my bonnet, retying the bow several times beneath my chin. I turned to the menu for distraction.

Eggs. We knew what they were, though we'd never seen one, of course. Hard-boiled, soft boiled, scrambled, sunny-side up, poached, over easy, or deviled? Would I be able to stomach them?

At the top of the list of breakfast choices were: two eggs, any style. So they must be large. Hash browns. No idea. Bacon or sausage.

This was meat from higher animals and out of the question. Toast and butter; something that has been burned and smeared with animal fat. Disgusting. Huevos rancheros. Incomprehensible.

Rosita returned.

Mother, peeved at Father's showing off his English, was the first to order.

"I have two eggs, any style. I have hash brown. I have toast and butter."

"You want me to choose how to cook the eggs?" asked Rosita puzzled.

"Yes," said Mother.

"Bacon or sausage?" asked Rosita.

Mother hesitated. The only meat we'd eaten at home was from insect-like creatures raised for food.

"No, thank you."

Father chose a different style for each of us: sunny side up for Mother, deviled for me, and poached for himself.

We observed how the other diners held knife, fork, and spoon. Need I say the food was utterly foreign, that we took each bite—and a small bite at that—with trepidation. We tasted samples of each other's food. It was all strange, but palatable, a testimony to the accuracy of our gustatory transformation. Coffee was good, especially if sugar and milk were added. Water with ice cubes was fabulous. Ice cubes!

Others in the restaurant lingered over their coffee, some glancing at us occasionally. Father and Mother kept their voices low. They reviewed foreseeable daily expenses. Unless another cube of gold was exchanged, we would soon run out of money.

"And you had better learn English," Father told Mother and me. "And you had best stop glancing at that boy," he added. Was I still doing it? I was embarrassed.

———

We were surprised when the bald, cannonball of a man with the excessive mustache appeared at our table. He wore white pants and a loose white cotton shirt. His girls remained in the booth, the eldest with her arms around her squirming five-year-old sister who was struggling to free herself.

He swept the top of his head with his hand and was about to speak when the little girl broke loose from her sister, sprinted down the aisle, and hid under the table with the policewoman. Her sister jumped up and went after her.

"Damn," said the man, turning away. "Annie, stop it!"

He approached the table, but the girl escaped both her father and sister, popping out from under the table, and dashing into the kitchen. A moment later, Rosita came out with the girl held firmly in her arms.

"She almost knocks a pot from the stove," said Rosita. "Wild child."

"She's rambunctious, not wild," said the man.

"I want my mommy," said the girl.

When Annie was returned to the arms of her sister, the man returned to our table.

"Good morning, and welcome to Prickly Pear. I'm not usually the welcoming committee," he said, "but we don't really have a welcoming committee. I'm the honorary mayor. Clyde Cummings, at your service. Rosita tells me you folks are Russians. That so?"

Mother and I closed our mouths and held our breath after issuing involuntary peeps. Since Father was unsure what "that so?" meant, he used a phrase he'd just learned.

"Pardon me," he said.

"Are you folks from Russia?" said Mayor Cummings.

"Ah, no. We were born in Hawaii."

"Well, I'll be danged. Rosita said you were Russians."

"That is a common mistake," said Father, ad libbing. He took the folded document from his breast pocket. "Many people take us for Russians, but we are as American as...apple cake."

Why thousands of images of an American president's Hawaiian birth certificate should have been broadcast around the globe, inevitably radiating into space, was a mystery, but it provided the template the computer used to forge us authentic-looking birth certificates with ease. Money, it was unable to counterfeit because of the special paper required.

Father unfolded the document and handed it to Mayor Cummings, who appeared puzzled even before reading it. He squinted at Father as he handed it back.

"Watson Sminth. That's an unusual name."

"Is it?" said Father, stopping before inadvertently confirming that it was not just his name that was unusual.

"You folks on vacation?" asked Cummings.

"No, we are not on vacation. We have moved here."

"I can't remember the last time anyone moved here. But we're going to turn this place into a tourist hot spot, a boom town. I'm working on it. You're getting in on the ground floor, so to speak."

He slid his thumb under his shirt between two buttons, tugging slightly when he wanted to emphasize something he'd said.

"People would rather go to Disneyland, or the beach, than way out here. But you'd think we'd get some tourists. Maybe we don't have rodeos, or grand canyons, or gambling casinos, or what have you, but we've had more than our share of flying saucer landings, let me tell you. I've seen them myself, by golly. Roswell's got nothing on us. The creatures litter the desert with stuff because it's broken or something. Fascinating. I collect and sell it."

As hunger was alleviated with this strange breakfast, anger at my parents reemerged, amplified by anxiety at being surrounded by these humans. But I was tired of fighting, so I did not tell Cummings that we too were alien creatures and had littered the desert "with stuff." I disliked him. Perhaps it was his domineering manner, his skeptical eyes, the cast of his mouth, or that awful mustache.

"Anyway, I just came over to tell you that a bunch of ruffian motorcyclists may be riding through town today or tomorrow. Best to avoid them, especially you young ladies. They like to grab pretty girls and take them on joy rides. Not much joy for the girls, though."

At this, the boy with the missing arm clearly turned toward us— toward me. Before I could stop myself, I returned his gaze. Had he been listening to our conversation? Who was he?

"We thank you for the information, Mayor Cummings," said Father. "Don't mention it."

After Cummings returned to his table, Rosita came over to ask if everything was "okay." Father complimented her on the food.

We were about to leave when two men marched through the front door and straight into the kitchen. The words "POLICE" and "ICE" were printed in white block letters on the backs of their black jackets. Breakfast chatter hushed. We heard Rosita's angry voice from the other room, though her words were indistinct. The officers emerged from the kitchen with their handcuffed prisoner in tow, a frightened young man wearing a long white apron. Rosita was right behind them. They paused near our table.

"Where are you taking him?" she asked.

"Mira Loma detention center in Lancaster," said the soft-spoken, heavy-set man in loose clothing. A large round bald spot crowned his head. He looked like a monk.

"Sorry about this, ma'am, but he came here illegally."

"Which I'm sure you didn't know," said his partner, a thin, nervous, weasel of a man with small eyes, nose, mouth. As if hoping to find someone else to arrest, he scanned the restaurant. His searching eyes settled on us. Doubtless bemused by our outfits, he shook his head slightly as if to say, "What some people won't do for attention."

The monk handed Rosita a card.

"You can call to speak with him. You leave a message and he'll call back. He's charged for the calls, so you'll have to set up an account for him. You can send a money order from the post office. Again I'm sorry, but he broke the law."

The young man took off his apron and handed it to Rosita.

"*Muchas gracias, Rosita,*" he said.

"*Te voy a llamar, Jose. No te preocupes. Consequiré un abogado.*" She hugged him. Both had tears in their eyes. "*Vaya con dios,*" she said.

Cummings approached the officers, holding Annie in his arms.

"Good morning, Mark, Wendell. That was fast," he said quietly.

"Thanks for the tip, Clyde."

Rosita stood there, frozen in place. The slender policewoman who'd been watching the drama, arose to take part in it.

"You didn't tell me anything about this, Cummings. Jose's been here for over a year."

31

"And what would you have done if I had, Vera?" They expelled each other's names as if they'd been stuck in their throats.

"That's irrelevant. If you think someone's breaking the law you should speak with me about it."

Cummings shook his head.

"It is relevant."

The woman looked around at the customers, now members of an audience.

"I'll speak with you later," she told Cummings.

Chatter slowly resumed as the police and their charge left and Cummings and the policewoman returned to their respective booths.

"Undocumented alien," whispered Father in English. "You see I do not exaggerate."

———

Tom

So I was sitting in Rosita's with my folks, just trying to eat breakfast without spattering food all over the place. My left arm ached because it was too damn stupid to know it had been incinerated or buried months ago. What do they do with amputated limbs? I should have asked for it. Buried it in the backyard to see if anything grew. An arm bush, maybe. With these creepy thoughts, phantom pain, and all, I was only half paying attention.

"Yeah, Dad. Sure. We'll find a way. I just don't want to hear any more about it right now, okay?" Right now? Hell, he kept up this pep talk day and night. They both did. Just trying to make me feel better, but it made me feel worse. There's no way I was going to college now. Gymnastics scholarship down the drain. Borrow the money? Forget it. Couldn't ever pay it back. Get a job? Yeah, as what? A roulette croupier? Only need one arm to rake in the chips with that hooked stick they use. Fat chance.

Damn it. Slip-sliding away. Like everything else in my life. Hold still, you miserable piece of toast.

"Tom, let me butter that for you."

"Mom, give me a break. You going to feed me for the rest of my life?"

"Sorry."

I wondered if Claudia was going to come over and say hello. Not that it would make one bit of difference between us, but I'd sink to the center of the earth if she saw my mother feeding me. Be a man, Martinez. Go over to their table and say hello like nothing ever happened. She said she'd go to the Halloween dance with you. Use that as a starter.

I was brooding with such gusto that my parents had stopped talking. We're gloomily munching away when—holy barracuda!—these people walked in, right out of Hollywood. Or a Las Vegas show. Or a Quakers meeting. They were a little bedraggled and scanned the place like escaped cons.

Everyone in the place took a gander, but then got back to breakfast. After they'd settled in their booth, the girl sat facing in my direction.

Dad said, "Maybe that's their Sunday go-to-meeting clothes."

"They're a handsome family, don't you think, Oscar?" said Mom.

"I suppose so, yeah."

The girl was nice-looking, which irked me. And I didn't even know why. With renewed intensity, I went at my breakfast like it's hand-to-hand combat. And of course I'm at a disadvantage with only one hand.

I told myself not to look at her, but my eyeballs had their own ideas. It was hard to read her expression, especially since I only looked for a few seconds at a time. She looked tired. They all looked tired. Then I saw, or imagined I saw, her looking at my arm. I mean where it used to be. That's it. I didn't look at her any more.

Before that family left, the police arrived to arrest poor Jose, the hardest worker in town. Going to jail because he doesn't have papers. How down on your luck can you get? But he's got both arms. Knock it off, crybaby.

———

Cricket

F or the tourists who never came, the paper placemats at Rosita's were maps of downtown streets. Running North/South were Prickly Pear, Main, and Sandstone Street. Running East/West were the streets Rosebush, Quintana, and Arroyo. Everything in Prickly Pear was within walking distance of everything else.

Curlicues of paint peeled off the facades of the one- and two-story shops on Main Street. Vintage Duds, a secondhand clothing store, displayed colorful t-shirts and jeans in an unguarded window, but metal bars covered the window of The Tequila Tabby Cat.

"What is so valuable it must be protected by steel?" asked Mother.

"Ethyl alcohol, their favorite intoxicant." Father turned to me. "And you are forbidden to use it unless at home with us."

We passed Dawn Bakery, Danny's Market, and Colby's Hardware. Good News, a print shop, produced brochures, most of which were about where to stay, what to eat, and what to do in Las Vegas, though some were about the Mojave National Preserve. A few of the buildings were partially clad with sheets of aluminum.

We passed a storefront window displaying a "for rent" sign.

"This is what I want," said Mother. She could not, of course, practice medicine here, but she could set up a little business in medicinal herbs, spices, fragrances.

Father shook his head. We walked on, but twice she looked back at the empty window.

The only three-story building in town, the unfinished town hall, stood on the southwest corner of Sandstone and Main. No one climbed the narrow staircase to an "observatory platform" on the third floor to catch a glimpse of the "landings." A railing had yet to be built around the platform.

A few fan palms grew along Main Street, but were rare in the residential areas.

The sign over one store read, Cummings's Alien Artifacts, but Cummings's Sundries was faintly visible beneath the new paint. Displayed in the window in cardboard gift boxes were glass pieces the size of salt and pepper shakers in which were embedded filamentous wires and tiny colored squares. "Found near alien landing site, 12 October 2013" read one of the labels. A faded newspaper clipping reported Mayor Cummings' chance encounter in the desert of "an alien craft." A picture taken at night showed the spaceship, remarkably like an upside down pie pan, resting snugly on the desert floor. Also displayed were clothes, including souvenir t-shirts printed with pictures of pointy-headed gray aliens and captions like, "Kiss me. I'm from another planet," and the like.

"They think they have had visitations by extraterrestrials?" said Mother. "How likely is that?"

I snorted.

The residential districts were an easy walk from downtown. Cacti, rock gardens, and dead thumbnail-sized brown lawns fronted pastel, stucco, and clapboard houses. Having been born on a planet that had long since run out of naturally occurring potable water, we marveled at the extravagance of lawns, even tiny and brown as they were. California had restrictions on water use. Perhaps the lawns were only watered in winter.

Flooded with impressions and sated with food, we started back to the Still Waters Motel when a rumbling arose along Main Street to the south. People were moving away from the curb, some even into the shops. A few cars sped away.

———

Tom

I was browsing in the sci-fi section of Hashimoto's, a secondhand bookstore owned by one of the teachers. I didn't want to do anything anymore except read. I'd go to the school library or this little hole in the wall and load up on sci-fi, thrillers, mysteries, etc. And books on self-defense. I looked at YouTube videos, too, and practiced some moves in my room. But if I pictured Barker standing there, I'd feel queasy.

Melissa was at the cash register. I'd just paid for a dog-eared paperback copy of *The Hitchhiker's Guide to the Galaxy* when I heard that unmistakable rumble. I stiffened like I was about to be hit. I made myself go to the window.

Melissa said, "Good thing they're not much interested in books."

"Yeah."

Across the street, those three quirky strangers were standing on the sidewalk instead of ducking into the store behind them. Damn it! Didn't they know anything? Barker would not pass by that girl without stopping.

Judging by the sound, the gang was still about an eighth of a mile away. Plenty of time for me to get across the street to warn the idiots. So go! Now!

I forced myself out of the store, but stayed on this side of the street to hear what was going on. As I waited, I remembered my first encounter with Barker.

I was walking downtown with Claudia and Annie, who'd been acting up as usual. We were going to have an ice cream.

"Let me go. I'm not a baby."

So Claudia let go of her hand. The sound of motorcycles grew louder. A moment later, as the gang headed our way, Annie decided she wanted to look at a doll on display in a window across the street. She darted out. Barker, in the lead, swerved and braked. He just missed her. He parked. The gang parked behind him.

Annie stood in the middle of the street in shock at the close call. We ran out to her. Claudia took her in her arms. We went to the window with the doll in it. Annie was still.

Barker came over and bawled at Claudia.

"Why the hell aren't you watching the little girl?"

"She got away. I'm sorry."

"I could have killed her."

"You're right. I'll be more careful. Thank you."

By this time, townspeople and a couple of gang members had gathered around us.

"You're the mayor's kid, right?"

"Yes."

"What's your name?" he demanded.

"Claudia."

Annie's arms were wrapped around Claudia's neck, her legs around her waist. She started to cry.

"It's okay, kid. Don't cry," said Barker, his voice shifting from hard to soft. "Next time stop, look, and listen before you cross the street. Use your eyes. Use your ears. Then use your feet. Got it?"

He must have learned the rhyme in Kindergarten.

Annie kept crying, but more quietly.

"Hey, Barker, are we going, or you wanna babysit?" asked a wiry young man with a scar on his face.

Barker ignored him.

"So, Claudia, to make up for almost maiming the kid and cracking up my hog, why don't you come for a little ride with me? You can give her to your boyfriend for safekeeping."

"I...I can't. My parents won't let me."

"You ride with this guy," he said, pointing at me. "I've seen you. So don't lie to me."

I wanted to do something, but I was intimidated. He was built like a refrigerator and must have be six-two or -three.

"I mean," said Claudia, "they won't let me ride with someone I don't know."

He grinned.

"Not a problem. I was born in LA. I got a kid sister looks a little like the girl there you're not taking care of. I like tamales, but they only make the really good ones in San Isidro during the tamale festival in December. Okay? We're acquainted now. Come on. We'll go for a little ride and I'll bring you right back."

He'd kept his voice down since reciting the rhyme and Annie had stopped crying.

At a loss, Claudia turned towards me, her eyes pleading.

"She can't go," I said. "It's nothing personal."

"Who the hell do you think you are, her father?" A second ago he was purring; now he was snarling. Annie started crying again.

There was no point arguing. I took a step closer to Claudia.

"I think you should take Annie home."

Barker growled, "I think you should shut up."

"Go home, Claudia." I repeated.

Barker grabbed my t-shirt with his left hand and waved his beefy fist in front of my face.

I was a mix of fear and fury.

"Let go of me."

"Shut up and I will." He lowered his fist, but still had a grip on my shirt.

"Let him go," said Claudia.

For a second, I overcame my fear. I placed my hands on his chest and thrust him away. He must have already loosened his grip because I freed myself. The crowd that had grown around us murmured and the man with the scar on his face taunted.

"Hey, Barker, the kid needs to show you a little more respect, don't you think?"

Frowning, Barker grabbed my shirt again. "You do need to show some respect, jackass."

"Claudia, go home," I repeated.

"I said shut up," he bellowed.

"That's enough, Mr. Barker," said an angel of mercy stepping through the crowd.

"Officer Camacho," said Barker still holding my shirt. "Am I glad to see you. This guy was causing a lot of trouble. Someone might have gotten hurt."

"I'll take care of it then. You can let him go."

Before he released me, he leaned over and whispered in my ear.

"I hope you're not this reckless on your motorcycle."

———

Cricket

A cloud of dust appeared in the distance long before twelve men of various ages dressed in black, each astride a sleek, mechanical beast, came roaring up the street towards us, one behind the other. The leader, seeing us standing at the curbside in our theatrical outfits, gave a signal with an outstretched arm. The riders pulled to the side of the road, quieted the thup-thup-thupping of their machines, and sat, legs straddling saddles, feet on the ground.

We can never fully know ourselves, I realized in this instant. Despite the reputation of these men, here I was peculiarly taken with the motorcycles: their streamlined gas tanks of glinting metal, the dip and curve of their silhouettes, the front tire thrust forward on chrome forks. I was already becoming accustomed to clean air. How bracing it would be to rush through it on one of those machines. Wait! Was I mad? Was I absolutely mad?

The tall burly man at the front of the troop dismounted. He was in his mid-thirties, like most of the others, dressed in black, though he wore a white leather vest. A Greek cross with flared ends adorned his helmet. I suppose some might have thought him handsome. He had a short beard, like a mountain goat. I was not yet confident in the reading of human facial expression, but his smiling eyes and mouth appeared cynical and salacious.

He strode up to Father and smiled more broadly. A nude woman, inked in red, with horns and a tail peered at us from his right forearm. On his left, two gamboling kittens.

"Good morning, cowboy," said the big man in a brash voice.

Father, of course, realized that we should have retreated into a store like everyone else, but that it would be considered rude to do so now. He sought the proper response, something an ordinary person, doing ordinary things, on an ordinary day, might say, and then it came to him.

"Yeah, what's so good about it?" he returned in an equally loud voice. Then his tongue flicked in and out for a few seconds before he got it under control. It meant nothing to us, of course, it was just what tongues did.

The big man's smile was gone. He examined Father with the deliberation of a lumberjack deciding where to make the first cut.

"So, you're a wise guy."

"And you, too, are a wise guy," said Father, returning the compliment, or so he thought.

Sitting on their motorcycles, the men close enough to hear the exchange, roared with laughter. Cautiously, like frightened cats emerging from their hiding spaces, a few people came out of shops to watch the show. Mayor Cummings came around the corner now, but his pace slackened, and he came to a standstill when he saw the line of motorcyclists along the curb.

"Hey, Barker," called a baby-faced, wiry young man whose cheek was marked with a sickle-shaped scar, "You letting that doofus make a fool of you?"

Turning toward the heckler, Barker spat on the sidewalk. "Can it, Billy Bob," he growled.

Billy Bob smiled. "Make me."

When Barker turned toward him, Mother and I each grabbed one of Father's arms and pulled him away. We started down the street, but a moment later Barker came up from behind. He put a big hand on Father's shoulder, stopping him forcibly. Caution aside for a second, Father, in our language, asked us to release his arms. He turned around to face the man.

"What's the hurry? We was just getting acquainted," said Barker.

Though we had grown eyebrows and long eyelashes, our nictitating membranes long since resorbed, we still blinked infrequently, unless we wished to. This unblinking gaze was unnerving to some.

Barker did not hold Father's gaze. He turned to me and grabbed my hand.

"Want to go for a ride, sweetheart?"

What should I do? I'd been asking myself this question since this barbarian had, in essence, assaulted us. But now that he'd touched me, I did something I'd been told I must never to do. To my surprise, Mother and Father joined me. Spraying a mist of saliva in the process, we hissed like three cobras about to strike.

"Jesus!" said the man, releasing my hand.

The police officer who'd been at the restaurant appeared at our side. Wide-eyed and small-boned, her bobbed brown hair in bangs, she appeared too delicate to deal with this mountain of gristle. Despite her vexed mien and a hand resting on her hip above the butt of her gun, she must have seemed as imposing to him as a kindergarten teacher. Her name tag said Camacho.

"Any trouble here?" she asked of no one in particular.

"Yeah, seems we got some snakes dressed up as people. Shit, man, they ain't normal!" He spat on the sidewalk, swiveled around, and began to walk back to his motorcycle.

"Mr. Barker," said Camacho. "Would you mind talking with me for a moment."

"Yeah, I'd mind." He mounted his motorcycle.

"If there's any trouble this time, I'm going to have to detain you."

"Yeah? You and what army?" He turned the key. The machine belched, coughed, and roared into life. With a motion of his arm, like a war lord waving his troops forward for the attack, he lead the gang back onto the street and out of town into the desert where they would camp and hold their bacchanalia. Camacho watched them disappear around a corner, then dropped her arms to her sides, but her hands remained clenched. She shook her head.

"You folks just passing through?" she asked.

Were we passing as humans? She couldn't possibly mean this, could she? Father looked at Mother and me, hoping we would not complicate matters by trying to respond to a question we did not comprehend, as he himself did not comprehend it. He took the fallback position.

"Pardon me."

"How long will you be in town?"

"We am in town one day," said Mother.

Exasperated at Mother, but controlling himself, he said we had just arrived, but were planning to stay. The desert air would be good for our health. He made no mention of what our particular maladies might be, nor did he remove his birth certificate from his pocket.

Clenching and unclenching her fists, Camacho looked in the direction of the riders. She swallowed, then turned back toward us. I needed no experience interpreting facial expressions to read hers. She'd been publicly humiliated by that savage, seemingly not for the first time.

Why was she policing Prickly Pear alone when it was clear she needed a partner or two? Because, despite its good reputation, the San Bernardino County's sheriff's office was forced to reduce its size due to a poor economy and reduced budget. The department couldn't even replace some of its rattletrap equipment, including its black and white police cruisers, much less adequately patrol the county's scattered small towns.

Camacho was without backup. Thus prudence was even more important for her than for officers working in teams.

"It's a nice quiet town most of the time. I'm sure you'll like it here," she said, adroitly avoiding mention of the gang. After chatting briefly with us about the weather and reminding us that school would be starting soon, she said goodbye and left.

"We are attracting far too much attention," whispered Father. "Let us quickly...."

We were just starting back when the one-armed boy tramped across the street toward us.

"What is wrong with you people?" he demanded, glaring at us. "'You're a wise guy, too.' That wasn't too smart. And that hissing business. Were you trying to provoke him or what? Are you street fighters? Damn!"

For once, Father was dumbfounded.

"You don't just stand there gawking like idiots when you see them coming. You disappear." He pointed a finger at me. "You especially."

He shook his head angrily and then turned to go. As he was crossing the street, he kicked one foot and then the other high into the air. What a species I thought. Each individual unbalanced in his or her own peculiar way.

Dismayed by the morning's events, we walked wordlessly back to the Still Waters Motel.

An airplane from Edwards Air Force Base breaking the sound barrier boomed over our heads. The pencil-thin contrail slowly thickened into a ghostly meandering worm in the blue sky. The sound rattled windows and it rattled me. Those primitives on their machines had unnerved me.

And so had that boy. What was he so heated about? Why so disrespectful to my father? Yes, I would avoid the hoodlums, but I would avoid that boy as well. I repressed my ambivalence about him.

The warm mid-morning air was on its way to hot, and my head had begun to ache. When we returned to our room, I threw myself on the bed and cried. What a horrible place this was! Not here two days and I already found most of the natives repellant. I ignored Father's questions and Mother's attempts to console me.

———

We spent the rest of the day in the room, having explored enough for the time being. Father obsessively unpacked, tested, and repacked our devices. Mother practiced the manipulation of her implanted transponder for deeper scanning of the Internet. I could tell because of the rapid oscillations of her eyes.

Sulky, bored, tired of lying in bed, and made dizzy by my scanning, I turned on the television and began flashing through cooking shows, Spanish language soap operas, reality shows, cartoon shows, religious shows, and more advertisements than there are scavengers in a garbage dump. I stopped at an image of a man waving his hands before a blue map of North America over which were superimposed images of streaming cloud banks.

The scene switched to a desk behind which, each in their own swivel chair, sat a woman in a dark suit, almost like a man's, and a man in a dark suit, exactly like a man's.

"Well, Jim, the scientists are completely baffled, but apparently the president has called the Russian and the Chinese presidents. They deny any knowledge of the event."

"That's right, Pamela. A huge explosion hundreds of thousands of miles beyond the moon. No one has the slightest idea what it was...."

We had expected this, and yet its impact was no less for that foreknowledge. We watched, transfixed. One lucky astronomer, his or her telescope pointing in the right direction, had actually made a video of that enormous blossoming fireball.

"Goodbye," said Mother.

Father looked grim, but said nothing.

Turning away from the television to look at my parents, I recalled my discovery of their duplicity. We would have a once-in-a-lifetime opportunity to view Sassatha from space, they'd told me, though I'd never heard of space tourism. I believed their vague explanations because I wanted to. We were privileged to be going on this excursion. I must talk to no one about it. Oh, how they emphasized secrecy. I should have suspected that something was amiss.

I remembered my surprise on seeing the ship as our shuttle approached it; an enormous, irregularly shaped vessel, a quarter of which was a rotating torus providing centrifugal gravity to those inside. Knobs, spiky towers, and conical antennae studded the silvery surface like aggressive parasites.

"It's monstrous," I said, as the Colony came into view.

"It is quite large," said Mother in an odd, hesitant tone. She looked at Father.

"Yes," he added unnecessarily. "It is large, isn't it?"

After a few more of these inane exchanges, I had become suspicious that something was being kept from me.

"You said that two hundred forty-eight people were going on this tour. That giant could hold ten times as many and all their belongings as well."

"Tour. That's a comforting way to put it," said a fidgety passenger across the aisle. "It's reassuring. Just a tour. Yes, I must think of it that way."

As our shuttle had approached, the door to the Colony's docking bay slid open. Our transport craft slowed, entered the cavernous space, was directed to the landing spot by an electromagnet, and touched down with a jarring bump. An airtight passageway with handholds, attached to the shuttle door, lead us to the auditorium. Within the torus, we were able to walk.

I was ill at ease even on the shuttle. I'd never been in the presence of so many people and the auditorium held so many more, none of whom I knew.

The leader of the tour, as I ignorantly still thought of it, welcomed us, but wasted no time with pleasantries.

"We will be going directly to the dormitory after everyone's hydration has been assured," she said. There were indeed water bottles by each seat.

"Dormitory? We have just arrived. Aren't we going to the bubble rooms to look at the planet?"

Mother, apparently charged with my enlightenment, began to reveal the shocking news.

"Daughter, as you know Sassatha is dying. Furthermore, our air, water, food, and waste disposal systems are beginning to fail..."

People were leaving the auditorium, but we remained seated. When she finally explained why we were here—that is, when I finally understood what she was saying, the details of it, the enormity of it—I was shocked into silence. When they stood, I robotically stood with them.

As we entered the dormitory, as it was euphemistically called, my knees grew weak from fright. Resting on the floor so they could easily be entered—and presumably exited—lay four rows of suspension canisters, rather like clear plastic sarcophagi. Beside each was a box for clothing.

I cannot find the metaphor or simile to describe my state of mind, for I was mindless with fear, oblivious of people shedding clothing, entering the canisters, pulling the hinged lids down over themselves. I do remember Mother helping me into mine.

"It will be all right," she said, and stroked my cheek. "We will see each other soon."

And there was the first awakening after a few hundred years. The eeriness of walking among my fellow "sleeping" compatriots was heightened because they now all looked human. Seeing myself transformed, but being only slightly alarmed was also bizarre. I could do nothing but what my parents asked of me, including reentering the canister after a time.

Even during our multiple awakenings, I could not believe what was happening.

I found my voice again only after we had boarded the scout ship landing craft and headed for Earth. They had lied to me, must even have rehearsed their lies. I would never again see my friends. I had not even been permitted to say goodbye to them. Yes, as we left the Colony I found my voice.

The people on board had been strangers. I remember exchanging not a single word with any of them. So seeing the explosion on the television was painful, but not as painful as it could have been.

Lower needs top higher needs, specifically hunger tops contemplation, even mourning. By the next day, we found ourselves again at Rosita's with roaring appetites, reflection on hold. Taking no chances, we ate exactly what we'd eaten the day before and returned again for lunch and dinner.

After three more days, Rosita considered us regulars. She brought coffee in the morning before we asked for it and knew we drank only water with lunch and dinner.

It seemed to my parents a good omen, though if questioned they denied believing in omens, when Rosita asked Father if we would be interested in renting a house she owned on the outskirts of town.

"My sister lived there, but she moved to L.A. a year ago. It's not much and it needs a lot of fixing up, but my son Hector can help. He's got a truck and can get you some furniture and appliances, too, if you want."

Father gratefully accepted the offer, sight unseen. That night he returned alone to see Jerry Riggins, who by this time had learned that he had greatly profited or "made a killing"—a particularly vulgar phrase—when he'd bought that previous cube of gold. He quickly agreed to buy a second for the same price.

5

We walked to our rental house-to-be each day to help Hector pull the plywood boards from the windows, sweep out the sand and the insects, wash the sinks and toilet, dust the shelves and kitchen counter, and carry furnishings from his pickup truck into the house. A couple of neighbors even came by to introduce themselves.

Inside the house on the first cleanup he said, "We'll leave the geckos. They eat a lot of bugs."

"We are more pleased to have them than you can imagine," said Father.

We returned to our motel room the evening before the big move to discover that the gold cubes neatly and naively stored in the top drawer of the dresser were gone.

"We have been burglarized," announced Father, shaken.

Yet transport boxes containing our medical instruments; metallurgy, chemistry and biochemistry sets; tools; and computers, had been left untouched.

"We must report this immediately," said Mother. "Perhaps Ms. Gaylord can help."

"Oh, yes. Very easy," began my agitated father, "Mrs. Gaylord, twelve cubes of solid gold have been taken from our room. Nothing else...Why yes, we always travel with gold bullion. Doesn't everyone?"

"If you do not tell her, I will tell her."

While they stood arguing, I lay in bed and covered my ears with my hands lest the fear in their voices only amplify my own. This place teemed with criminals. I thought of those motorcycle riders. And now a burglary. There had not been a burglary on Sassatha for four or five hundred years, indeed the word was archaic and only found in stories. Without currency we would become homeless, another archaic word. I supposed I too frequently used the word "hate," but I could not help myself. I hate it here I thought.

Father told Miriam Gaylord that we were missing a few items, among which was some gold, which his wife fashioned into jewelry. Ms. Gaylord said she'd look into it and within half an hour was knocking on our door.

"Jerry Riggins was here and told that fool brother of mine that he'd lent you a wrench and that his boss needed it immediately. Riggins gave him a bottle of whiskey. Buddy let him into the room. I'll call the police."

Father asked that she not call. He would first like to speak with Mr. Riggins. He left for the garage and returned shortly. Riggins had left Hoppy Jones a note. "My mom's sick. I have to leave town. Sorry." Father told Mr. Jones what had happened. "I always had my doubts about that kid," said Jones, "but help is hard to find."

So the next day, near penniless after having given Rosita even more money for secondhand furniture, sheets, blankets, knives, forks, spoons, plates, clothes, etc., we glumly moved into our new home.

Neither Father, nor Mother were glum for long. He immediately began working on his solar power station and other devices.

He gave Mother and me metal bracelets.

"They will function when I am finished on the roof." He gave us instructions but warned us to use the bracelets only if our lives were threatened.

"Once the results of their use is seen, we will be intensely scrutinized. Need I add that they will suspect us of the worst?"

I paid only half-hearted attention to his instructions, something I would come to regret in the worst way, but unable to care about in my misery.

Mother converted the garage to a laboratory and tool storage area and, though we did not have the money for it, inquired about renting the empty store on Main Street.

I fretted about school. I'd never been to a school. I disliked the very concept.

Miriam Gaylord had reported the burglary to Officer Vera Camacho who reintroduced herself. Mother invited her in, almost immediately asking, "Coffee?" She didn't want any.

The four of us sat in the living room while Camacho asked Father awkward questions. Father fabricated answers.

"What we were doing with gold ingots?"

"My wife makes jewelry from them."

"How many were there?"

"Three." Telling her that we had possessed ten thousand dollars worth of gold seemed unwise.

How big were they? Was nothing else even looked through? Why had the ingots not been hidden? How had Riggins learned of them? Occasionally during the question and answer period, Father glanced at the open bedroom door where some of our devices were exposed. He must have appeared suspiciously edgy.

Though still puzzled, Camacho ended her questioning, arose, and bid us good day. As she was about to leave, she turned to me.

"Remember, school begins in two days. You'd better register. You wouldn't want to be truant, I'm sure."

"I'm not going to school," I had told my parents repeatedly, but in the end, of course, I had to go, lest someone come to investigate my truancy.

6

Prickly Pear High School was situated at the corner of Prickly
Pear and Quintana streets, four one-story, red-brick buildings
forming a quadrangle, within which stood four stately eucalyptus
trees, one at each corner of the quad. During lunchtime or recess
students congregated to sit on the shaded benches under the trees.

Despite the principal's zealous patrolling of his beloved
eucalyptuses, students had carved initials, hearts, and arrows into the
trunks. I had no idea what the symbols meant but to me arrows were
yet another indication of these people's primitiveness, not to mention
their carrying around instruments sharp enough to do the carving.

To say I was terrified of being thrown into a menagerie would be
to exaggerate, but I had been unable to eat anything that morning. I
had done some preliminary scanning so I would not be completely
overwhelmed, but scanning made me dizzy so I did not pursue it.

Reddish brown Mexican tiles covered the office floor. Mother,
Father, and I stood in front of the pale wood counter. Behind it stood
the officious Mrs. Heather Hughes, who combined the roles of school
secretary, registrar, and cerebrum to Leo Bloom, the principal.

Behind her, Melissa, the cheerful willowy black girl I'd seen at
Rosita's, flitted between file drawers and computers like a sprite. A
wreath of interwoven dandelions crowned her head. A silver stud

pierced her nose. A yellow butterfly brooch perched on her green blouse. She smiled at me, but I did not smile back.

"How may I help you?" asked Mrs. Hughes.

"Our daughter," began Father, glancing at Mother for a second to be sure she would not complicate my registration by speaking, "was a sophomore at her last school when she became ill. Consequently, she may have fallen a little behind."

"Our teachers will be sensitive to that." Mrs. Hughes gave me a smile that entirely failed to mollify me.

Later during the process, Father supplemented my dossier by adding, "She has a speech impediment. She does not talk much."

When the paperwork was finished, the registrar expressed the usual surprise that our family, rumored to be Russian, had moved from Hawaii to live in a little desert community.

"Forgive me for asking," said Mrs. Hughes, "but why did you move from Hawaii?"

"Uh...the pineapples," free-associated Father. Realizing his answer made no sense, he added, "Allergies."

"Pineapple allergy? I've never heard of that one. It must have been awfully bad for you to move all the way out here."

"Pineapple allergy is the scourge of Hawaii."

"Is that so? And which one of you has the allergy?" asked the woman.

"The girl."

"I see. Well, be sure to have her transcripts sent from her previous school."

"I will do that," said Father.

Mother and I were completely still.

When Mrs. Hughes offered to have someone show me around on the first day, I shook my head.

"You're a confident one, aren't you?" she said. "Well, that's fine." She gave me a schedule of my classes and a map of the school.

I know I should have said, "Thank you." But I just nodded.

Melissa smiled at me again and, with the slightest fluttering of her fingertips, waved. I ignored her.

I was still not fully accustomed to being "outdoors". I still checked the strange blue sky for gathering toxic storms. The moon was still ghostly. The flat-sided and edged buildings still wrong. My lungs still tingled from the otherworldly air. And though I understood that I had been conditioned to accept this new body, I was amazed that it did not frighten me to look at it in the mirror. And of its dictatorial hormones and its emotional repertoire, I still had much to learn.

Now I faced a large open space. Clumps of excited students crisscrossed the quad, heightening my anxiety.

So here I was, a sixteen-year-old "girl" on the first day of school, mute as the sand dunes, my yellow hair artificial, my sinuous body covered in second-hand blue jeans and a t-shirt that were too tight. But this was the style and I had to fit in. The girls, it appeared, some of them, felt obliged to display the contours of their bodies. This behavior had evolved to attract mates. Attract mates!

Was it out of anxiety that I put my hand in and out of my jeans pocket to feel the material, which was unlike any material I'd ever worn before? Or did I just like the sensation?

As I tried to orient myself amid the streams of students, a girl with a provocative bounce and swaying walk, wearing a short red-plaid skirt, came up to me. Spirals of glistening black hair reached to her shoulders. I recognized her from the restaurant.

"You're new here, aren't you? What's your name?" asked Claudia, but when I told her my name, she laughed.

"Cricket? You're joking."

I'd never been in a crowd before and now here I was unprotected under an open sky among hordes of humans. I was on edge. I was going to speak but what emerged was "tssss."

"Well, *excuse* me."

She turned and walked away shaking her head. Unfortunately, Claudia and I were in the same mathematics class as was the ubiquitous one-armed boy. Beverly Hardy, the stout young woman with her hair cut in a flat top was the teacher. She still wore loose khaki cargo pants and an immaculate, pressed, men's long-sleeved dress shirt. Standing stolidly before her desk, she took attendance. At the back of the class, I raised my hand when my name was called. Claudia and a few of her friends tittered. Hardy frowned.

"I will not hesitate to send anyone making a disturbance in my class to Mr. Bloom's office."

Thereafter the class was quiet and attentive. After discussing the curriculum, class rules, and what she expected of us, she began a review of geometry at a level so basic I had learned it when I was five years old. She paced in front of the blackboard asking questions. When she asked me a question, I shook my head. She had the good sense to ignore this rather than to make a fuss. Nor did she ask me to stay after class.

As I stood for a moment just outside the room to orient myself, Claudia and two of her friends walked by.

"That's the bug lady," she said.

They laughed.

My next class was American History with Mr. Hashimoto, a short, thin man in his sixties or seventies, with a nubbin of a nose, bushy gray eyebrows, and a full head of slicked back gray hair. He wore dark slacks and a short-sleeved shirt.

Again I sat in the back of the room, which quickly filled with fifteen other students. The second bell rang, and Mr. Hashimoto asked that the door be closed. He took roll call, pausing before reading my name.

"Cricket Sminth. Am I pronouncing that correctly?"

I nodded, trying to ignore the giggles.

A moment later the door opened and that confounded boy carrying a dark bulbous helmet ambled in. His t-shirt revealed the distinct muscles of his right arm. His nose, jaw, and cheek bones appeared even more prominent than they had when he was sitting across from us at Rosita's or confronting us in the street. This is all I need, I thought.

"You're late, Martinez," said Mr. Hashimoto, making a mark in his roster. He finished the roll call, then stood, welcoming us to American History 1865 to the Present, and began talking about the end of the Civil War, writing dates and names on the blackboard. The phrase "forty acres and a mule" brought to my mind images of peasant farmers with wide-brimmed straw hats. I had seen this image during my cursory study of human history.

Meanwhile, the Martinez boy furtively turned the pages of a

paperback book resting on his lap, but not so furtively that Mr. Hashimoto did not see it.

"Put that away, Tom." He did so.

After about fifteen minutes lecturing at the blackboard, Mr. Hashimoto began walking back and forth in front of the classroom, asking questions requiring that the information he'd just presented not only be remembered, but assimilated.

"Melissa," he said to the girl I'd seen in the principal's office. "What was the purpose of Reconstruction?" Today her hair was adorned with a bright orange flower, her nose by a tiny crescent moon stud, and her ears by pendulous orange earrings, which swayed when she spoke.

"It was supposed to help the southern states govern themselves again...and to let them send people back into the congress, I guess."

Mr. Hashimoto turned from Melissa to a boy named Eddie, who, I'd noticed earlier, wobbled like a duck when he walked.

"What other problems did Reconstruction deal with?" asked Mr. Hashimoto.

"Uh, to free the slaves?"

"To free the slaves?" said Mr. Hashimoto. "Just a minute. Who won the war?"

The class muffled a laugh.

He turned now to me.

"Cricket, can you tell our shaky historian here"—he pointed a finger at Eddie, whose face continually twitched—"who won the war?"

"Pardon me," I said, using one of my parents' favorite expressions.

The class found this even more amusing that Eddie's answer.

Mr. Hashimoto raised his voice slightly.

"Who won the Civil War?" he asked again slowly.

By now all heads had turned towards me. Since Mr. Hashimoto had asked me a question that everyone in the room could answer and asked it loudly and slowly, the class now assumed I was a dimwit. I would, in their eyes, shortly confirm it.

Big Bird, as my father referred to the bungling computer, had transferred to us an enormous amount of information. It had used holographic imprinting on the gossamer neural net implanted over our brains, electrically and pharmacologically enhanced audiovisual techniques, subliminal methods, and multiple-choice questions. But even Big Bird could not assemble a complete understanding of world history, and even if it could have, we could not have learned it all. Besides, centuries of radiation damage had scrambled many of Big Bird's circuits. It had confused and conflated many disparate facts. So my answer must not be taken to mean that I had been a poor student.

"I'm just asking who won the Civil War, Ms. Sminth. No tricks."

I was unable to squelch a short string of chirps before saying, "Mao Tse-tung."

For a second, it was as if every student was enclosed in a soundproof bubble but as the bubbles burst the room was filled with a rising tide of laughter.

"All right. All right," said Mr. Hashimoto when he'd overcome his own surprise. "Settle down."

He lectured for the rest of the hour and then as the others were leaving, asked to speak with me.

"Ms. Sminth, I know you were trying to be funny, but...." He sighed, unsure if indeed that's what I was trying to do. "You're an attractive young lady. You'll get plenty of attention, believe me. So behave yourself, all right?"

I nodded.

The first day of school and already I am marked as an insect and a dunce. But should this matter to me? No! In fact, I should welcome it. Keeping these simple-minded people at a distance will be effortless.

My self-talk failed to calm me, though, and during the mid-morning break before chemistry class, dispirited and at a loss, I wandered around looking into empty classrooms whose doors had been left open. A distressing high-pitched chirping arrested my attention. A six-inch-long, speckled green gecko was locked in small steel cage at the back of a biology classroom. I walked in and carried the cage out. Many saw what I was doing, including Claudia, Melissa, and that Martinez boy. I walked to the back of the school, liberating the animal into a sandy lot, and returned the cage to the room.

Only Melissa spoke to me about this.

"I don't blame you one bit," she said. "Wish I were that brave. Now if Bloom calls you into his office, don't argue. Just agree with everything he says even if it's stupid and it won't go that bad. He's a softy, really. He hasn't even kicked Martinez out of school, so you know you're safe, right?"

She waited for a response before saying, "Well, see ya."

Chemistry was next. Black lab benches formed a horseshoe around the room. During roll call my name again was met with chuckles, which I had come to expect. Claudia was in this class. So was Martinez who was repeatedly squeezing a small black rubber ball. The muscles in his forearm bulged.

After he took attendance, the young teacher, Pedro Gonzalez, briefly spoke of a few safety rules and demonstrated the use of the emergency shower should someone set themselves aflame and the emergency eyewash fountain should someone get something in their eyes.

"It can be a dangerous place," he said.

Now he filled a balloon from a blue tank marked HYDROGEN, tied it off, and released it so it rose to the ceiling. As soon as he lit a candle attached to the end of a yardstick, I held my hands over my ears. Gonzalez saw this, raising his eyebrows for a second, recognizing that I knew some chemistry. He lifted the candle towards the balloon. With the sound of a cannon shot it exploded. Cabinets rattled. The class was jolted.

"Ah, I see I have your attention now, Martinez," said Gonzalez. "Since this may be the one and only time, let me tell you a key to understanding chemical reactions. This is so important, you should write it down: Breaking chemical bonds requires energy. Forming chemical bonds releases energy. More energy was released when the bonds formed to make water than was required to break the hydrogen and oxygen bonds."

No one turned to look at the boy, which I thought strange. Were they afraid of him? He put the ball into his pants pocket and put his hand on top of the lab bench.

"What is this type of reaction called, one that releases energy?" asked Mr. Gonzalez.

Claudia and a few others raised their hands. Mr. Gonzalez pointed at her.

"Exothermic," she said.

"That's right, and what is a reaction that needs energy called?"

"Endothermic."

"Right again."

"And why is hydrogen the fuel of the future?" he asked.

When Claudia shrugged, he asked Melissa.

"Because when it burns it makes only water. It doesn't pollute the atmosphere."

"I have a room full of future chemists. Great!"

He asked more questions, talked about the large periodic table that hung in front of the room, assigned us lockers where our flasks, beakers, and other lab equipment were stored, and then asked us to choose lab partners. Students quickly sorted themselves into pairs. I looked around for a partner but Melissa—the only person I would even consider—was already paired with Claudia. Martinez made no effort to find a partner. In the end, by default, we were paired with each other. Martinez pressed his lips together and scowled at me. I scowled right back at him.

No laboratory work was scheduled this first day. At the end of the class Mr. Gonzalez gave us the keys to our lockers. Martinez paid me no attention, but had Claudia's eyes been lasers, I would have been badly burned.

I had not been prepared for lunchtime, so despite having been given a few dollars, I did not go to the cafeteria, but sat on a bench under a eucalyptus tree from which arose a subtle aromatic, mildly piquant scent. Back home in the module, the air had been scrubbed clean. Any smell was a danger signal. I tensed up even more.

Perhaps half the student body sat outside with brown paper bag lunches. Across from me was another eucalyptus, also framed by a square of four benches. Eddie Driscoll sat alone on one of them eating his lunch, his face writhed at times as if its muscles wished to escape. Two tall boys wearing basketball jerseys numbered 14 and 8 approached him. A moment later they pulled him off the bench and sat on it though there was enough room for all. He tried sitting at the edge of the bench, but they pushed him off. Eddie walked away.

A moment later Martinez faced the two. After a few words, number 8 pushed him. Martinez balled his hand into a fist and punched number 8 in the chest. Number 14 punched at him, but Martinez stepped back, blocked the punch, and then landed one on 14's cheek. The boys were soon on the ground wrestling with each other. A crowd formed around them blocking my view. I was disgusted with them but also with the onlookers. I had not exaggerated in thinking of them as barbarians. Mr. Gonzalez stopped the fight and dispersed the crowd.

I was in a particularly bad mood for the rest of the day. Melissa approached me once more, but I didn't speak with her.

During the next few days at school I heard snippets of conversation about me:

Melissa: "She's just shy, that's all."

Claudia: "You wouldn't recognize stuck-up if it stepped on your toes."

Sarah: "You're both wrong. She's autistic."

Nicole: "No, I think she's just afraid of people. Maybe she was abused."

Claudia: "Well, you've got a point there. What kind of parents would name their child after an insect. Poor bug lady."

7

Tom

So here he is. Martinez the gimp. Back at school. Come on. Stare at him. Ask him how he's doing if you could use a punch in the nose. Jeez, what a jerk I am.

I was thinking like this in May when I got out of the hospital, and the whole summer hadn't changed me.

I remember lying in that damn hospital bed. I'd never given sleep much thought. No thought at all actually. Not until they put in those torture tubes. Tube in my arm. Bad. Tube in my nose. Worse. Tube in my penis. The worst. No matter which way I turned, one tube or another would give me a little tweak, a pinch, a nip. Sometimes two or three at once. I might find a semi-comfortable position and doze off for a few minutes. But it was like they had a warning light at the nurses' station. "Danger. Patient Asleep." A nurse's aide would pop in. "I have to take your temperature," she'd say. Or "I need to check your IV." It was impossible to sleep. I felt like I was collapsing into myself.

So I developed a definite opinion. If someone says sleep deprivation is only "enhanced interrogation," not "torture," I'll tell them they're full of it.

Even getting out of bed was an ordeal. I couldn't do it without help otherwise I might pull out one of those damn tubes. And pulling the catheter out of my penis would be really, really bad news because there's a little inflated balloon inside the bladder to keep the catheter from coming out. If you pull the tube out without deflating the balloon it would feel like pulling a railroad car through your pecker. Not a good feeling. I didn't want to try it.

Funny, I remember the tubes and the disturbed sleep more than the pain. They were pretty good about controlling that. Except for the pain in my throat from the tube that kept my stomach empty. My bowels were on strike.

The garrulous guy in the other bed was a middle-aged truck driver named Joe who'd had emergency hernia surgery. I now know more about hernias than I do about motorcycles.

"Middle of the night, I tell ya. Middle of the night. I tell my wife, like, 'I got a bellyache, Dottie.' 'You think it was the chili?' she says. Never felt like this before. 'Let me look at it.' My wife, the doctor. But she does feel around and says, 'I think something's wrong.' And she calls 911."

"So some of the bowel pushed through where I'd had my appendix out when I was nine. And then it got kind of strangled by the muscles in my belly. And that cut off the blood supply so a couple of inches of bowel died and they had to take that out. For a hernia like this, most of the time they put in mesh, but they couldn't because of where they'd operated on my appendix, but I'm going to be okay. I've got a great surgeon."

"What happened to you, kid?"

I grunted. Pointed to my NG tube. Told him I couldn't talk, which he knew was a lie since he'd heard me talking with the nurse. I just didn't want to get into it. Then, of course, my folks arrived and I had to talk.

Mom kissed me on the cheek. "How's my baby?"

I shook my head slowly twice. Once because I didn't like her calling me baby and once because I felt rotten. But I should have said "pretty good." That would have been the sensitive thing to do. My mother was worried enough as it was.

"Good morning, Tom," said my dad. "Get any sleep?"

"A little."

"We brought you some things," said Mom.

Would you believe it: a collection of Superman comics that had been in my closet since elementary school? A box of chocolates I couldn't eat. And the latest copy of *Popular Mechanics* with the cover, The Future of the Flying Car.

"What about *Easy Rider* and *Motorcyclist*? They were in the closet next to the comics."

Mom and Dad looked at each other. I got a bad feeling.

"We'll bring them next time," said Dad.

When I thought Joe wouldn't see me, I signaled that they should pull the curtains between our beds as if that would stop him from hearing what I knew was going to be an argument.

"You said that yesterday."

Mom sighed and put her hands on the handrail, leaning close to me.

"Motorcycles are the last thing you should be thinking about now."

I knew that was coming as sure as a concussion if you got hit in the head with a brick. I'd prepared my response but didn't get a chance to deliver it.

Apparently, they'd stopped at the nurses' station on the way in and asked to speak with Dr. Li. Even for an orthopedic surgeon he was a big guy. Most orthopedic surgeons were athletes in college. Athletes like I used to be.

"Good morning, Dr. Li," said Mom.

He greeted them and then me.

"How are you feeling?"

"Okay," I lied.

"Pain?"

"In my throat."

"Yeah, those NG tubes are no fun, are they? The nurse tells me it's not draining much, and you've passed gas. We may be able to get it out today. The catheter comes out too, but the IV stays until we're done with the antibiotics. You'll be home in three days."

"When can he go back to school?" asked Dad.

"Nothing stopping him, really. He'll be weak from loss of blood so he'll have to take it easy."

Dr. Li turned to me.

"You've been a trouper."

And then he left.

I lowered my voice, but didn't whisper, and tried matter-of-factly to say, "I'm not going back to school." But it came out slowly with a pause between each word, like I was talking to a couple of idiots.

"Why not? There's over a month of school left," said Dad.

"You can't miss more school, Tom," added Mom.

"I said I'm not going."

Dad looked at the curtain between the beds, then at me, then at the door, and back at me.

"This is not a discussion. You're going to school and that's that."

I was ready for this. I wasn't going to lose my head. Losing my arm was enough. Ha. Ha. And I sure as hell wasn't going to cry.

"Sorry to sound like a kid, Dad. But you can't make me. Think about it. What are you going to do? Frog march me to school each day?"

Joe called across the room, the curtain having no effect.

"Give the kid a break."

"Even he understands," I said.

————

C laudia came to see me a couple of times. The hospital was pretty far away, and she had to get her father to drive. He'd always give us some time alone.

My parents and I decided not to tell anyone what had happened unless I changed my mind and decided to go to court. So I had to make up a simple story. I was going too fast, swerved to avoid some road kill. And that was it.

Claudia was grossed out by my arm. I mean by my having one less. She couldn't hide it. I wasn't sure if I held this against her or not. We'd been dating. Well, on and off. She liked Rick, too. And one day she came at eleven in the morning and he came at eleven forty-five. They left together. I never did figure out if they'd planned it that way.

As soon as I walked in the door at home I repeated that I was not going to school. I convinced my parents I was serious by remaining in bed two days straight. At that point they were ready to make a deal.

It was my father's motorcycle, but our understanding had always been that if I could use it, I would take care of it, which meant making repairs. I'd managed to make enough money with part-time jobs, especially during the summer, but now the bike needed expensive repairs and I couldn't ride it anyway because of the controls on the left handle bar.

After I swore that I would not leave town on the bike, that there'd be no desert jaunts, that I'd scram if Barker was anywhere to be seen —as if I'd seek him out. Jeez!— my parents agreed to have the bike fixed, including a reconfiguration so I could control the bike with one hand. And two legs, of course. I'd shone them the YouTube video of one-armed motorcycle racers.

In return, I agreed to go back to school.

"You drive a hard bargain, son," said Dad.

Going back to school was still scary, the stage fright of an unprepared performer.

I just wanted to be left alone. And except for my parents nagging me to study while giving me pep talks and the teachers doing the same, people did leave me alone. My face must have been like a road sign saying, "watch for falling rocks."

During the summer I did some weightlifting, reading, martial arts, and practiced riding with one arm when the bike was ready.

I really would have spiraled into a black hole if my folks hadn't transferred the left-sided handlebar controls to the right.

Back at school now, the first day of a new year, I held my helmet by the straps, so it doubled as a school bag. No schoolbooks in it at the moment. Just a spiral notebook, pens, pencils, my paperback, and lunch.

One of my big worries was that my shoelaces would untie themselves. Retying them would be half an hour of hard labor. And getting pissed off at anyone for looking, especially if they asked to help.

Before classes began, I went around back just to be alone. Thinking about gymnastics. Never again. How 'bout tennis? Sure.

Tennis or bowling or ping pong. Weren't things bad enough without taunting myself? Jeez!

I turned to go when I saw the new girl. She'd just made a fool of herself in history class. Either that or she was angling to be class clown. Warning. Disturbed attention seeker ahead. What was she up to now?

She carried a small metal cage to the edge of the vacant lot. As soon as she opened the little door, out sprang the lizard they kept in one of the bio labs. It scurried away with no second thoughts. The sight distracted me. I was grateful for that. On the other hand, I didn't want anything to do with that girl. Of course not. I didn't want anything to do with anyone.

To top the day off I got into a fight with Rick and Dave. I don't want to be in school anymore.

8

Cricket

Despite my still unfamiliar, oddly jointed mammalian legs, I walked with remarkable ease back to our terrestrial abode—I couldn't call it home. Two blocks east on Quintana Street and six blocks north on Sandstone, into our run-down neighborhood. The sun had passed its zenith, moving slowly westward across the sky, looking down on me with pity.

The pitched roof of our dilapidated, gray clapboard house was out of kilter, rising noticeably higher on the left than on the right. Would the whole structure fold up in a high wind? What a miserable place to have to live. And so ugly.

Heaped in back of the house, like the broken shells of gigantic prehistoric mollusks, were the remains of two ancient automobiles, which Father had already started cutting into pieces to make enormous parabolic mirrors. Mother had begun working in the garage, now a plant breeding area, though she'd hidden her medical instruments there as well.

The pebble path to the front door complained in crunching protests with each step I took. It disliked being stepped on and so did

I. I would put on a little demonstration of my displeasure for Claudia the next day.

My parents were seated at the peeling yellow kitchen table our benefactress had provided.

"Sit down, dear heart. Tell us about school," said Mother. Then my Father asked. Then Mother again. Then they asked together. Thus began an unvarying pattern. Each day after school my parents, using uniquely parental pressure, forced me to tell them about my day at school. Father's incessant study of the culture had revealed a secondary benefit of such interrogation. It was what good parents did. It was what normal, just plain folks did: asked their normal, just plain children what they'd done at their normal, just plain school after a normal, just plain day. More than anything in the world my parents wanted to be seen as normal, just plain folks and anything I did that diminished their verisimilitude, not only annoyed them, but frightened them as well. They were always listening for that knock on the door, when the familiar question would have a different emphasis, "Where *are* you folks from?"

"It was repugnant and grim, rather like a herd of tragaloons confined to a small space. Just as welcoming. Just as violent. But tragaloons are extinct, unlike these unspeakably stupid people who are very much alive."

Even Father was shaken by my outburst and felt sympathy for me, even empathy. He put his arm over my shoulder. Before I could leave the room, before I even knew what was happening, I was sobbing, heaving, my nose and eyes running as if exposed to a poisonous gas. Then my mother put her arm over my other shoulder. My sobbing, already loud, grew louder. As angry as I was at them for lying to me about our interstellar emigration and for the loss of all that was familiar and dear to me, I must compliment them for simply holding me and remaining silent. Only when my sobbing had ceased, only after I'd washed and dried my face at the kitchen sink and was again breathing normally, did they ask if there were something they could do.

"Yes," I said. "I need a container to collect some insects in."

"Oh, a school project," said Mother hopefully.

"You could say that."

―――――

S itting on a bench underneath my eucalyptus tree at lunch the second day of school, I waited nervously, the jar clutched on my lap. As Claudia and her friends walked by, I held the jar up to my face as if engrossed by its contents. When I was sure I had their attention, I made a big show of emptying the contents into my right hand, six black and yellow Jerusalem crickets, *Stenopelmatus nigracapitus*. Although they were not true crickets, they served their purpose. I popped them into my mouth and began chewing. Claudia shrieked.

"Yuuuk!" blurted a companion.

They quickly turned away from me. The term for what they were at the moment, I learned later, was "grossed out."

By eating crickets, I had asserted that I was not one myself. I had cautioned them. Don't call me a bug. Don't trifle with me.

This foolish act, however, and my release from the biology laboratory of that heartbreaking captive gecko, led to an interview with the principal on school day number three, immediately neutralizing the empathy my parents had demonstrated for me on school day number one.

Mr. Leo Bloom, resembling Albert Einstein, with a high forehead and gray hair standing out as if electrified, was, unlike Einstein, rumored to eat pan-seared kidneys for breakfast right there in his office every morning. He welcomed my parents into the room where I had already been sitting at a small, round conference table for a very long five minutes. Portraits hung on the wall behind his enormous, boat-like desk, labeled with the people portrayed: Aristotle, J.K. Rowling, James Joyce, and others, presumably people he admired. I knew none of them but examined each closely to stop imagining myself trapped, like a fly in a spider's web.

"Leo Bloom," he said, extending his hand.

"Watson Sminth," said my father shaking his hand rather more heartily and longer than necessary before relinquishing it to my mother for her to shake. When they were seated, Mr. Bloom tried to learn something about the parents of the odd teenager who had remained mute during his preliminary, unproductive questioning of her.

"So where are you folks from?" asked Bloom.

"Hawaii," said my father, my mother nodding so vigorously that her concurrence must have seemed of great importance to her.

"Really? What brings you all the way out here? Don't get me wrong. This is beautiful country and all, but this *is* the desert. Hawaii, though, what I know of it, is supposed to be a kind of paradise."

"Pineapple allergy," said my father. "My wife and daughter's. I myself can eat pineapple all the livelong day."

Not wishing to delve further into the unusual nature of our ailments and probably thinking of nothing else to say, Mr. Bloom described the reason for the meeting, gently chastising me face to face before turning again to my stiffly seated, masked-faced parents.

Mother, now primly dressed in a black polka-dot dress and tire-rubber-soled huaraches, a yellow bandana tied tightly over her head, began to speak, but as she had not learned the language near as well as my studious father, she came to an abrupt stop after uttering a few involuntary whistles. Father, dressed in his white cowboy shirt, jeans, and boots, continued where she'd left off.

"Dear Mr. Bloom, I'm afraid our daughter was born with several inconvenient, shall we say, congenital...ah...disorders, among which is a speech impediment and a place to the left of the bell curve of intelligence of your.... What I mean to say is that she is a slow learner, impulsive, and emotionally brittle, but we will have a good talking to with her and I assure you there will be no more...no more disturbances."

"No need to be harsh with the girl. My last job was in east L.A. In a graffiti-pocked school where the insolence of some of the students was astounding. One even threw an egg at me once. Your daughter's behavior isn't all that bad."

Fortunately, they confounded my tears with sadness and contrition rather than with what they actually expressed—suppressed rage. I only experienced sadness later when I recalled the fear I'd heard in Father's voice and seen in Mother's agitated head nodding.

"Now. Now," said Mr. Bloom. "It's going to be all right, Cricket." He reached into his pocket for a handkerchief, which I grudgingly accepted. How callous he must have thought my parents, calling me stupid in my presence. He had the good sense to bring the meeting quickly to a close. He'd ask Tom Martinez to take me under his wing and show me the ropes. He had his reasons.

Tom Martinez! *Black bile and vomitus!* Mr. Gonzalez had already paired me up with that intemperate, disinterested anti-intellectual. *Take me under his wings and show me the ropes!* I saw a birdlike boy leading me around on a rope. My crying renewed, I stifled it.

―――――

A t the back of the mathematics class on school day four, I seethed like water in a teakettle just before it begins its piercing whistle. My parents knew perfectly well that, even by their standards and not those of these hopeless primitives, I was not stupid. But because I had not spoken a word, because I was to be shepherded around the school by Martinez, and because I ate bugs and released geckos, the word was out that whatever else I may have been—stuck-up, abused, autistic—there was one thing I was for certain: simple-minded, if not outright imbecilic.

Plump Beverly Hardy, in her signature immaculate khaki cargo pants and white shirt, marched back and forth in front of the blackboard, peppering everyone in class, except me, with questions. I pictured Mr. Bloom sitting at a conference table with my teachers, urging forbearance, as I was, obviously, a dodo brain.

"The Pythagorean Theorem, Ms. Hardy," answered Claudia, sitting at the front of the class in a short skirt and frilly blouse. She flounced her hair and looked back at me, contemptuously holding my gaze for a moment, before turning around. "We already studied that last year."

Ms. Hardy put one hand on her hip, holding a piece of chalk in the other, and nodded.

"So prove it."

No one spoke. Hardy pressed her lips together and, holding her hand outstretched before her, offered the chalk to any taker. "Well?" she said.

Looking back on it, I cannot call my behavior impulsive, though the decision was quickly made. Weighing the pros and cons, I simply preferred the immediate pleasure I would experience now over the inevitable censure I would experience later. Was I putting my family at risk by demonstrating my knowledge of the most elementary mathematics? That seemed unlikely, though I could not dismiss out of hand my father's seeming exaggeration of the dangers to us that these easily frightened people represented. And, in any case, the subtle squirming of my classmates behind their wooden desks and Claudia's disdain was all the flame necessary to set the kettle whistling.

I stood abruptly, scaring the girl next to me, strode up to Miss Hardy, took the chalk from her, glared at Claudia, and started writing. I drew a large square, pressing the chalk so firmly against the board a piece snapped off. Within the large square, I drew a smaller square turned forty-five degrees so it looked like a diamond. Each of the small square's corners touched the larger circumscribed square, thus forming four identical right triangles at the corners of the large square. I labeled their sides, a, b, and c. The hypotenuses of these triangles formed the sides of the small square so that its area was c^2. The length of a side of the large square was $(a + b)$.

The area of the four small triangles was $4(1/2ab)$. Since their area plus the area of the small square filled the area of the large square, their summed areas equaled the area of the large square, that is $4(1/2ab) + c^2 = (a + b)^2$. Simplified, the equation was $a^2 + b^2 = c^2$, thereby proving the theorem. In less than a minute I was finished. I handed back the chalk, but before returning to my seat I hissed at the class. I shouldn't have done it, I know, but it just happened so perhaps I was impulsive after all. Yes, impulsive, a slow learner, emotionally brittle. Black bile and vomitus! I didn't care.

Ms. Hardy thanked me and was about to say something more but I shook my head slowly and unmistakably, so she changed her mind and went on with the lesson. After she dismissed the class, she asked me to stay for a moment.

"That was very impressive. I have a feeling that geometry is familiar territory to you. Each year I chose a few special students to help those having trouble with the material. Would you like to be a tutor?"

I shook my head.

"Well," sighed Ms. Hardy, "let me know if you change your mind."

I had further alienated myself—alienated, of course, the perfect word—from my classmates. They would certainly leave me alone in peace, if not in tranquility, which in turn should make school attendance tolerable. The teachers would also keep their distance. My mood improved an iota. I might be able to avoid unruliness.

9

That night I was pulled into the back yard by the stars in the crystalline sky. In contrast to Prickly Pear's, Sassatha's skies were muddy. But as my eyes moved along the Milky Way, I was not making comparisons.

What was I doing? Not searching for our star, I knew that much. It was visible only in the Southern Hemisphere. Was I searching at all? Searching up there for something inside me? I was confused, but not agitated.

Mother came out to join me. I considered walking away in a huff. She had, after all, allowed Mr. Bloom to shackle me to the Martinez boy, not to mention her complicity in the biggest offense of all—my abduction. But the panoply of stars held me.

"All truly intelligent beings are awed by the sight of the stars," she said.

"And all truly dunce-like beings?" I had become a contrarian. Whatever mundane observation my parents might make, I felt the urge to deny or turn it upside down.

"When I look through the galaxy's disc," said Mother, "I think of the billions of planets teeming with civilizations."

"After the three of us die, ours will be extinct."

"Is that what you're thinking about?

"No. I am not thinking about anything."

Empathy with my parents I did not wish to feel. They were unhappy that I was unhappy, and they knew it was their doing.

"If you are not thinking," continued Mother, "you are feeling."

Did she really expect an answer to that implied question?

Before long, Father joined us.

"Magnificent beauty we could not enjoy at home, the fiery forges of the elements, the givers of light and life."

"You are spoiling my tranquility," I lied. I was not tranquil.

"Forgive me." He walked away from me to a corner of the yard. Mother joined him. I could not hear what they said.

I went back inside.

Saturday morning sunlight revealed clouds of dancing dust particles whirling in agitation as Mother drove them from their resting places on the floor with her heartless broom. Mopping would follow sweeping and window washing follow that. She moved from room to room, using a cheap plastic dustpan to collect and dispose of the sweepings.

She whistled while she worked, but as her whistling was otherworldly, Father disapproved. What if the neighbors should hear? Noticing his furrowed brow, she tried reassuring him. "I am fulfilling my role as housewife and mother. Oh, that the neighbors may notice how ordinary I am, how ordinary our broom."

"The day you are ordinary," responded Father, is the day I grow a third ear."

"Ah, that you might better listen to my song."

"Should the authorities drop by for a visit, may I suggest you hum rather than whistle? Or chew gum."

"Gum?"

"I am going up on the roof," he huffed, careful to close the door quietly behind him.

Restless but at a loss for what to do, principally because I wanted to do nothing, I sat painfully idle in the living room. Images from school flitted through my mind like buzzing insects, but trying to swat them away only attracted more insects. Mother's housekeeping irritated me. It seemed that whichever planet we lived on I was doomed to live under a storm of dirt, either outside our domicile or within.

I opened the front door and was about to leave when I saw a woman coming up the walkway. Rude as it was I shut the door.

"Mother, someone is coming."

The next door neighbor, followed by a wobbly, sandy brown cocker spaniel, came up to the door carrying a white ceramic bowl. A prematurely stooped woman in her late forties, she wore a dark green plastic sun visor, bearing the word Luxor, which, we were to learn, she'd obtained in Las Vegas. Her shorts were pink, and a pink flamingo was printed on her t-shirt, also obtained in Las Vegas.

The dog found a bit of shade near the house and lay down. Throughout the visit it made no sound.

I would not say that I was interested in this person per se. However, my boredom was gone. I would observe events from the somewhat tattered wing chair Father preferred.

Mother was at the door in an instant.

"Hi, I'm Cindy Penny. I brought you this. Put it in the oven at three fifty for forty-five minutes and—voila—dinner is done."

She handed over the casserole dish

"Thank you much. My name Crick Sminth."

This gave Cindy pause.

"Sorry. Would you say that again?"

"Crick Sminth."

"My, what an unusual name, if you don't mind my saying so. What was your maiden name?"

"Pardon me?"

"What was your name before you got married?"

Clearly it was pointless to warble her real name to her neighbor.

"My name Crick Sminth that time." Mother motioned me over. "This daughter Cricket."

I extended my hand, which Cindy shook.

"You come in?" asked Mother.

Hot lava! If Father heard that a human was entering the house he might fall off the roof. Nor was I enamored of the idea. I sat down again, gripping the arms of my seat, and held my breath.

Mother showed Cindy to a place on the couch.

"Coffee?" she asked.

"Oh, no thank you. I'm trying to cut back. Makes me a little more jittery than I usually am. Not good when I'm driving, that's for sure."

Mother now sat on the couch with her.

After a brief discussion of the weather, which we learned was the safest gambit in beginning a conversation with a stranger, Cindy asked a familiar question

"So where you folks from?"

"Hawaii."

"Oh, really? Quite a change."

Ms. Penny made no observations about the strangeness of the move, instead telling Mother that she'd moved here for her health, because of her asthma to be exact. She was originally from Columbus, Montana.

"Used to be called Sheep Dip, then Stillwater, then Columbus."

Whatever its name, the winters were far too cold and after her divorce there was no reason not to move. With little money, places like Palm Springs were out of the question. She liked it here. You could walk anyplace. It was cheap. She'd had her children young, so they were all grown up now. They visited several times a year, but complained there was nothing to do here.

"This is a nice place. People generally mind their own business. Well, with a few exceptions. Live and let live, that's the motto to live by."

Montana did have its advantages, though. In the summer you could grow anything because there was usually enough water. California's drought had been severe and prolonged. People were conserving water because it was the right thing to do and because it had been mandated. Water was increasingly more expensive.

"But it reduces your choices. Are you a gardener?" asked Cindy.

Mother said she was. When Junior, the cocker spaniel, appeared at the door, presumably looking for its master, Cindy got up to leave.

"Wait. I present you," said Mother. From the kitchen she emerged with two pea-sized purple seeds in a tin that had been used for breath mints at one time.

Cindy took the tin in hand and held it up to her eye.

"Not pot, is it?"

"Pardon me?"

"They're not marijuana seeds, are they?"

"No. Good plant."

Mother told her that they could be grown indoors or out, bore fruit early, and that perhaps Cindy would find them tasty. At least she tried to tell her these things.

"Well, thank you. Hope you enjoy the casserole. It's noodles and cheese with some green chilis."

Cindy walked back to her house. Junior followed, limping.

As soon as he observed Cindy leaving the house, Father must have scrambled down the ladder as if the house were on fire. Although he walked through the front door instead of running, he was taking big breaths, either from exertion, or to calm himself, lest he bark at Mother, which would be unwise under any circumstances.

"Was that woman in the house?" he said, as if asking a shoplifter what was in her pocket.

"I sense an interrogation in the making. May I tap into my clairvoyance and answer your questions before you ask them, except for the first one, of course, the answer to which is 'yes.'"

By this time, I had stood, yielding Father his wing chair. Mother sat opposite him on the couch.

"Yes, I invited her in. Yes, I spoke with her. No, she was not overly inquisitive, nor suspicious, hostile, or devious. My dear husband, we are here to stay. We must become members of the community. She brought a welcoming gift. I gave her a pair of rylnin seeds."

When he heard "rylnin seeds," Father's composure evaporated.

"Either I hallucinated the word 'rylnin' or the heat has denatured the proteins of your brain! Please tell me I am hallucinating." His voice was far too loud.

"Your anxiety and tone of voice are uncalled for. Desist!"

The rapidly increasing heat of the argument frightened me,

particularly Father's part of it. "Please, both of you, be civil. You're upsetting me." My plea softened Mother's tone, but not Father's.

"Because we can enjoy rylnin does not mean they can enjoy rylnin, perhaps not even tolerate it. How cavalierly you dispense with common sense."

"I am a physician and an herbalist. I believe your anguish is uncalled for. Even were you correct, I could not ask for my gift back. Please calm down. I dislike seeing you suffer like this. For your health, for my health, and for our daughter's health, please calm down."

"You are correct," said Father. "I will leave the house. Perhaps I will walk to the gasoline-dispensing establishment to see if Mr. Riggins has returned.

I craved distraction. I asked to go with him. He did not object.

As we strolled along, Father took the opportunity to express his emotions, which these new bodies, like high-powered amplifiers, heightened. Originally, we'd been slow to excite, more cerebral. Indeed, I could recall no episode at home on Sassatha when I'd been "emotional." This emotionality was, of course, as new to Father as to me.

"Your mother is impulsive at times, but she means well. It is just that I worry that...Perhaps my reaction was excessive. I am sorry that my tone upset you."

Compared with the thought of having to return to that nest for the schooling of *Homo stupidensis* on Monday, my parents' loud voices upset me not at all.

I did not wish to add to Father's distress, but I made no effort to silence myself because, I too, had need for emotional expression.

"I have said it before, but I must say it again. I can never forgive you and Mother for having lied to me. If you have any affection at all for me, you could partially atone for the crime by extricating me from a yoking to that boy."

The sidewalk was cracked in places, but no less unyielding for that. I was dressed more normally now except for my high, black, laced boots. Someone at school had called me commando Cricket. I knew Father would dismiss my request about Martinez, but perhaps he'd assist me in getting new shoes.

"I like the idea no better than you, but you must do as Mr. Bloom requests. And as they say in English, 'that's final.'"

"I need new shoes."

"If we are beginning a game of non sequiturs, I concede defeat even before further play."

Though at the other edge of town, Prickly Pear Gas and Auto Repair was not far. The garage door was open, but no cars were present. At the back, however, a supine man held aloft a steel bar weighted at either side with metal discs. He lowered the bar to his chest then raised it, repeating this action twelve times, before placing the bar on the forked tops of two vertical steel bars.

Having seen us, he stood and walked over, limping subtly. This was the strong man I'd seen at Rosita's. Double slabs of chest muscle rested under his loose t-shirt and his forearms seemed as large as my calves. A round cloud of curly salt-and-pepper hair surrounded his head. The color of strong dark coffee, his skin tone appeared much healthier in my eyes than the paleness of so many others.

"Well, howdy, Watson. And you must be Cricket?"

He shook my hand.

"I heard all about your little run-in with Barker. I got a lot of respect for a person—for a family—that stands up to that bully. Don't know how you did it, but you must have freaked him out. Man, that is something else. Freaking out Barker. I could break the guy in two but he still spooks me a little. He's unpredictable—might pull a knife or sucker punch you or something. What can I do for you folks?"

"Mr. Jones—" began Father

"Just Hoppy. No mister necessary in this case."

Father nodded and continued.

"Foolish of me, I'm sure," said Father, "but perhaps I was mistaken about the Riggins boy. Perhaps he was not the thief. Perhaps his mother was ill. Perhaps he has returned."

"That's a lot of perhapses, Watson. Look, showing that kid a piece of gold was like dangling a mouse in front of a cat. You know what I'm saying?"

As Hoppy outlined an abbreviated biography of Jerry Riggins for Father, I looked around the empty garage. Mr. Jones explained that he felt an obligation to keep the garage open until late at night as it was the only gas station in town. He'd even filled a tourist bus's near-empty tank one night, that is, Jerry Riggins had. But the wages he paid were poor and it was often night-shift work so the position had not been filled.

Father put his hands in his pockets, perhaps to hide them lest they demonstrate uneasiness.

"May I offer my services?" said Father.

"You mean...Ever worked in a garage?"

"I have not, but I am—how does the saying go—an accelerated apprentice."

After a brief discussion of hours and salary, the arrangement was made final with a handshake.

On the way home, Father said, "The man is highly civilized. No paperwork." A little further, buoyed by the good news, Father turned to me and said, "We will see about new shoes."

We were near the corner of Quintana and Main Street when Mayor Cummings accosted us.

"Just a minute there. I'd like to talk to you."

He seemed stockier even than before, his bald head shinier, his mustache brasher.

"What an unexpected pleasure," said Father, extending his hand. Cummings ignored it.

He pointed a thick finger at me, moving it forward and backward as if pushing a button for a tardy elevator.

"Your daughter there," he blurted, "scared the daylights out of my little girl and I don't like it."

"I am so sorry," said Father. "Her bark is bigger than her chomp. She is actually quite harmless."

"She disgusted a whole group of girls by eating a handful of bugs in front of them."

Father shifted his weight to his right leg, then back and forth several times.

"Again, I am so sorry. She meant no harm, I am sure. She is somewhat slow, if you understand me, and may have been hungry."

"Then maybe she belongs in a different school or maybe not in school at all. There are the other children to consider."

I should have been prudent, but both Cummings and Father made it impossible for me to keep quiet.

"She make fun. From first she make fun. Call me insect. Bad."

"And that's another thing, Sminth," said Cummings ignoring me. The girl here and your wife sound like Russians to me. And not just to me. The whole town thinks so, too. What do you say to that?"

Father's shifting from leg to leg increased in frequency.

"It is but a speech impediment and mental slowness, as I explained."

"Looks like you're building radar antennas on the roof. What's that all about?"

Cummings, it seemed, had begun his own game of non sequiturs and he was better at it than me. He continued asking unrelated questions and making unrelated comments about Father, Mother, and me, though, in his mind of course, they were connected. He talked about citizenship, the need for constant vigilance, the dangers of espionage.

Father had stopped trying to respond other than saying, "Pardon me" or "Could your repeat that please" or adding his own non sequiturs: "The sun is exceptionally bright today" or "How long did it take to grow that attractive mustache?" Cummings' face and head grew red. Would his skull soon violently separate along suture lines? And given his baldness, might one peek into his molten brain when the parietal and frontal bones blew apart?

Neither Father nor I wished to spend a minute longer with this alarming man, but Father, as usual, did not wish to be rude. Exasperated, I grabbed his hand and simply pulled in the right direction.

"You see how simple she is," said Father. And this time I didn't even mind. I even considered babbling. Cankers and warts! This man was as bad as his daughter. I must remember to carry a supply of *Stenopelmatus* with me for just such occasions.

"It was nice speaking with you," lied Father.

Cummings surprised us by answering "likewise." He swiveled away so fast a tiny dust devil formed at his feet.

Mother was mopping the bathroom floor when we returned. Father in reasonably good spirits despite our encounter with

Cummings, stood outside the door, grinning. "I bring you glad tidings," he said in English. He enjoyed practicing new, often archaic phrases.

"The thief has returned?" asked mother dubiously.

"Riggins, it appears, has absconded permanently. Mr. Jones had found no one to replace him because his business is barely profitable and the only salary he can offer is small." He paused for effect. "Wife, you are looking at one of the newly employed."

"What a relief," said Mother, leaning the mop against the wall to embrace him.

That night at dinner, while Father recounted our run-in with the good mayor, I examined the contents of my bowl: chopped onions, kidney and pinto beans in the ratio of two to one, one inch squares of red and green pepper, chili-pepper spiced tomato sauce. To call the food weird—how could it be otherwise—was an enormous understatement. A neighbor had provided the recipe. It was called chili sin carne. Chile without meat.

When they spoke of my behavior at school, I interrupted.

"She was teasing me. Constantly. I did not wish to be mistreated. I have told you this."

"I believe even your father commiserates..."

"I do—"

"...but," said Mother, "you must ignore, not frighten—or nauseate —the teaser. Why had you not mentioned the incident before exacting your revenge?"

"The two of you have been worried enough. I did not wish to add to your worries."

"Yet by not telling us, you have added to our worries," said Mother. "We would have assisted you in maintaining equanimity."

"I am not finished," said Father. "Your insectivorous displays are the least of our worries, Daughter. The least. Cummings has doubts that we are who—or what—we say we are. He says the two of you speak with Russian accents and that the whole town agrees. He says that my showing people my birth certificate is odd. He says that my building an unusual parabolic antenna on the housetop that appears to point at the air force base is suspicious. He says your previous school transcripts have failed to arrive. With less certainty he suggests that your exhibition of geometric prowess at the blackboard indicates you were not schooled in this country and that you are only pretending to be 'retarded'—his word. That, too, is suspicious."

"The man is reprehensible," I said.

Mother asked, "He thinks we are spies?"

"He thinks we are spies."

"That is the most absurd thing I have ever heard in my life."

"It does not seem absurd to him. He says he may have the authorities look into it. I did not ask which authorities. I would request of you both several things. Please master English. And do not answer if someone knocks on the door."

"How will that help?" said Mother.

"I am not certain but until we are better prepared, it is probably best pretending we are not home. I believe some sort of legal maneuver is necessary before they can enter the house without our permission."

"Do not open the door. A sophisticated plan," said Mother.

"There is sufficient irony in the situation without sarcasm. And I would ask you, dear wife, to strive toward the average in all things."

"I do my best to be average," said Mother, "though my role models have been women from greater than half-century old entertainments: *I Love Lucy* or *Leave It to Beaver*—the latter a quirky program as the Beaver, a boy, has no relationship to an actual beaver, except for an extremely remote common ancestor, *Protungulatum donnae*, which scurried through the underbrush of early Paleocene forests. I need a new wardrobe and I need to get out of the house."

"I would rather you did not leave the house."

"My dear husband, I am no longer staying home all day. I have made arrangement to rent that small storefront downtown. Even as we speak Hector is painting the sign: Crick's Medicinal Herbs. And I am accompanying our daughter to meet with Mr. Bloom tomorrow. "

"As long as you do not answer the door at home," he said finally.

"While you were away, our neighbor, Cindy Penny, came back with her decrepit little cocker spaniel, Junior. It's right hind leg was dislocated. I maneuvered it back into place."

"Then you must have scanned it first," said Father, shaken. "Did she see you do it?"

"I could not separate them. She asked if I were a veterinarian. I told her I'd taken a first aid course and steered further questions away from the scanner."

"Treating the dog was unwise."

"You are not the sole repository of wisdom in this house," cautioned Mother, piqued.

As the sky darkened to royal blue, distant swatches of fluffy white clouds turned to pink. How bizarre this room, I thought; the window open to the atmosphere, the walls and ceiling flat, the flooring of wood, freely flowing potable water from a faucet. Indeed, the bizarreness never ended. I immersed myself in it that I would not think of the possibility of our arrest by Cummings or tomorrow's meeting with Mr. Bloom and Martinez.

10

Tom Martinez and his mother arrived a few minutes late. Mrs. Hughes led them directly into the inner office. A tall woman, her dark hair in a long braid, Mary Martinez appeared nervous. Bloom stood and came around his tugboat-sized desk to greet the Martinezes and make introductions. Mother had insisted that we arrive early.

We sat at the conference table. Perhaps it was my imagination, but it seemed that Martinez guided his mother to a seat allowing him to sit as far from me as possible. We avoided eye contact. Bloom briefly clasped his hands tightly together on the tabletop. His knuckles paled as if alarmed.

The purpose of the meeting, Bloom explained, was simultaneously to help a new girl adjust to the school and to help a boy remain in school.

"Let me begin with you, Tom. We've been through this before. We talk, you make promises, keep out of trouble for a while, and then relapse. Another fight. And as I understand it, you are failing math. Frankly I'm thinking of expelling you."

Why did Bloom choose to reveal Martinez's personal problems? Because they were so well known that no secrets were being revealed? Or to impress upon Martinez and his mother how serious he was about the task with which he was about to burden the boy? It was clearly a violation of privacy. I didn't understand it. And for a moment I felt sympathy for the boy, but only for a moment. I saw him glance up at me, his lips tightly sealed.

Bloom sighed. "What was the fight about this time?"

Inclining his head towards me, Martinez asked, "Did she tell you about this?"

"No, she did not."

"Why is she here?"

"Tom," interjected Mrs. Martinez, "answer Mr. Bloom's question, please."

"Sorry. Rick pushed me."

Bloom shook his head, unclasped his hands, and folded his arms across his chest.

"And you punched him."

"In the *chest*."

"Kindly tell me what the fight was about. He didn't push you for no reason."

Tom put his hand in his pocket. His head tilted from side to side like a finely balanced scale approaching equilibrium.

"They were bullying the Driscoll kid, you know, the one that walks like a duck. It made me mad. I told them to stop."

"I know who Eddie Driscoll is. So, you are the defender of the weak. You could have told me about it."

"It was happening right in front of me. What should I have done? 'Hey guys, stop that. I'm going to tell the principal on you.' I'd look pretty stupid, wouldn't I?"

"The problem is that everything seems to make you mad. I'm sorry about your accident, but being expelled from school won't help any."

Mrs. Martinez did not appear surprised at this. She and Mr. Bloom must have already talked about the accident's effects on the boy. That sad, empty shirtsleeve dangled. Since I first saw him, I now admitted to myself, I had wondered what had happened. And why he'd done nothing about it?

"Unfortunately, you are not the only student at risk. There's a new girl here who has some problems I don't quite understand, and she's gotten off to a rocky start."

How ill-mannered of him to speak of me as if I were not present. What was he trying to do?

"She's already made enemies among students. The teachers are as concerned about her as I am. I've been thinking of finding her a companion for the first few weeks of school. Someone to show her around, introduce her to people, get her involved in school activities. Now you used to be well-liked before you became a hothead. You know just about everybody *and* you seem to be the champion of the underdog, so I've decided that you will be the young lady's school guide."

Dismayed, Martinez shook his head.

"Tom," said his mother, "you will do as Mr. Bloom tells you and furthermore if you fail math again, your father is taking his motorcycle back."

"Mom!"

"We've discussed this at length. No more negotiations. This is serious."

So, the motorcycle, probably the thing he cared about most, was his father's, not his. The boy looked pained. He was about to speak but caught himself.

"You're to be her guide," continued Bloom, "and if not her friend, then at least her guardian angel. Walk her home after school. Get to know her. Give her advice. Introduce her to people. Do you understand what I'm telling you?"

The boy nodded.

"I didn't hear you."

"Yes."

"Cricket, do you understand what I'm saying?"

I forced myself to nod, though I felt like bolting from the room like a rabbit flushed from a bush by a fox.

"If I see you're not really trying to help her out, that's it. This is your last chance. And no more funny business from you, young lady. I mean it."

Outside the office Martinez and I turned our backs on each other while our mothers amiably asked each other to forgive their respective child's sullenness. We weren't always like this, they assured each other. To my dismay, Mary Martinez then invited our family over for dinner so that we might all be better acquainted. No!

11
———

By school day number four I was well known around campus, though only Melissa greeted me, walking by my side for a while before wandering off.

As usual, I'd eaten a big breakfast and would not eat lunch. I sat in my spot under the eucalyptus, thumbing through the college calculus textbook that Ms. Hardy insisted I examine, but it was pitifully elementary and held no interest for me. I must admit I was getting bored. At home a long, long time ago—my real home—I'd organized holographically projected get-togethers of my friends, danced and sung with them, played games, and discussed art, music, science, philosophy.

I closed my eyes to picture myself in our module. The high arch. Everything rounded. The overhead window stretching the length of the cylinder. The long rectangle of noonday sun along the floor. No edges, peaks, points, corners. Organic. Comforting. Cylindrical. I missed the cylindricality of it.

My sad recollection was disturbed. Martinez stood before me. His helmet, like a lunch pail holding a brown paper bag, dangled from his hand. He wore jeans, tall black boots, and a white t-shirt. Passing students glanced at us.

"Uh, hi."

I composed an expressionless face as best I could and said nothing. But I felt a faint tingling, well described by the cliché: dragonflies in the bowel or perhaps it is butterflies in the stomach. My old body would never have responded this way to an unwanted encounter.

He sat next to me, placing helmet by his side on the bench. I considered just leaving, but disliked the idea of being driven away and besides, I knew what this was about. I did not initiate voluntary blinking, nor did I look at him, except initially.

He brushed back his hair. He looked at my calculus book.

"You blew them away in geometry."

This was a usage of "blow away" I was unfamiliar with, but I did hope my coldness would blow him away as I understood the meaning of the phase. But instead of being blown away, he removed the paper bag from his helmet and began eating his lunch. Claudia came over, accompanied by Rick, the freckled red-haired boy with the number 14 Jersey. I feared another fight, but Martinez stood, and curtly introduced me, though Claudia and I were already well acquainted. I remained seated, my face motionless as a flagstone. I looked at each of them for a moment before opening the calculus book on my lap and pretending interest in it.

"Bloom asked me to show her around for a few days until she gets the hang of the place."

"Is that so?" said Claudia.

"Yep."

"I don't think you'll find her much of a conversationalist, isn't that right, Cricket?"

I looked up for a second before returning to my book. She laughed and shook her head.

"You still sore?" asked Rick.

"Nah," said Martinez. "But lay off Driscoll."

"Yeah, okay. Kid's got enough problems, I guess."

"Tom," said Claudia. "I'm sorry, but I can't see *Amy Gets Mean* with you. Rick's got his dad's car this weekend and he's taking me."

"Oh," said Martinez.

The boys glanced at each other. A moment later Rick and Claudia had left.

Martinez sat back down. Ferociously he bit into his sandwich. He chewed and swallowed, chewed and swallowed. He finished the sandwich.

"You freaked her out by eating those bugs. Pretty gutsy, I have to admit. Not so bright, though. What were you thinking?"

I turned a page in the book.

He finished the second sandwich and before eating his candy bar, offered me a bite. He asked me where I was from? Did I like sports? What did my parents do?

I turned a page after each question.

By the time he'd started his apple, though, his tone had grown surly. I stood to go, but he grabbed my wrist and pulled me back down. Forcefully I wrenched my arm free. My strength surprised him. I picked up my book and stood. I was furious. I would not be intimidated. Facing him I held the hefty text in both hands like a battle shield. Contraction of my abdominal musculature reinvigorated the dragonflies.

He sprang from the bench, his chest a handbreadth from my shield.

"Look, you stuck-up little jerk," he whispered, "I was trying to be nice. I don't like this any more than you do, but I'm in deep doo-doo if I don't make a good show of this, as you well know. So I'm going to tag along with you whether you like it or not and we're going to pretend that everything's hunky-dory. You don't have to say squat."

I stood my ground until he turned.

Standing there in turmoil, still clutching my book as if an attack were imminent, I simply wished to leave the grounds. Indeed, I got as far as Quintana's statue, but the sight of it stopped me—the bronze solidity of it. I'd admired it from the first, scanned to learn about the man, read commentaries about how Quintana chose to portray himself. Not in a smock as artist, but rather in sombrero and sarape as peasant, the way he'd started off in life.

The statue calmed me. I turned back for the last class of the day—art.

I was tardy, but Mrs. Hess said nothing about it. Nicole looked up at me and indicated a chair next to her. But she belonged to Claudia's entourage. I sat at her table but braced myself for ridicule. Melissa was at another table, but all the chairs were taken.

"I am happy to see so many of you back in my class from last year," said Mrs. Hess with a hint of an accent other than English. "This year we continue with sculpture, but the medium is not clay this time. Also, this time we paint our sculptures like the ancient Greeks. That paint faded, but it was hundreds of years. Your paint will last maybe that long. But before the paper maché, the armature."

Succinctly she showed us where the materials, receptacles, and tools were stored, and spoke about etiquette at the sinks and about the sharing of tools at our tables. Last years' students had been taught not to waste time. As soon as she was finished they were out of their chairs and moving toward the supplies.

Nicole stayed seated. Her face, as usual, was powdered completely white, her lips red. She looked like a life-sized porcelain doll.

"Do you know how to use chicken wire?"

What could I do but shake my head? I didn't even know what chicken wire was. Prepare yourself for an insult, I thought.

"Well, I'll show you. Do you know what you want to make a sculpture of?"

For some unfathomable reason I wished to avoid providing this girl with more evidence of my supposed stupidity. So instead of shaking my head, I nodded.

"Okay, let's get the supplies."

As we stood in line waiting for our turn to shear off a section of chicken wire, I flashed through eidetic images of Earth: Joshua trees, people, sand dunes, street lamps, windows, motorcycles, brooms, coat hangers, potted plants, cash registers, water faucets, bathtubs, shower stalls, carpets, shoe laces, coffee cups, shirt buttons, zippers, sunglasses. No inspiration here. I should make a sculpture of something I miss.

"Always cut more than you think you'll need," instructed Nicole. "There's always leftovers." She pointed to a barrel of chicken wire scraps.

After she had unrolled and cut a section of wire for herself, she handed me the metal shears. The piece I cut was so long that I had to roll it up to carry it.

Three others sat at our table: compact, athletic Hayley; red-headed Rick; and a girl I didn't know. All were busy at work shaping the frameworks of their sculptures.

I visualized the shapes and sizes of the pieces I would need, mentally projecting them onto the wire, and cutting them out. I further cut, bent, rolled, flattened, and shaped the pieces. I entered a meditative state, calm and devoid of thoughts.

"Hey, you're good," said Nicole. "I thought you'd never worked with chicken wire before. And it's going to be one big tamale, too, isn't it?

Melissa came over to see what I was working on, but wisely did not ask.

I liked the analogue clocks used on this planet, the faces framed by numbers, the arms slowly pushing their way into the future. The arms of the clock in this room had impatiently jumped ahead. When it appeared that I wished to stay late to work on my project, Mrs. Hess was content to work on her own. But at four o'clock she said it was time to leave.

I could not deny, and why should I, that I had enjoyed that class, that it had released me from the grip of tension, if only temporarily, like a potent, soothing balm that sank deep into the muscles. And instead of taunting me, even when I appeared doltish, Nicole had been helpful. Why? The peacefulness I had experienced drifted away like a feather in a breeze.

And then, only a few steps out the door, I saw Martinez waiting at the corner of the building for me. I had not expected this and was disconcerted. What a persistent nuisance.

I walked briskly through the quad towards the front of the school. Mr. Bloom was examining the bark of a eucalyptus tree. Martinez's stride was long. He was at my side as we passed the principal.

"Fancy meeting you here. Cripes, did she keep you in after school? What the hell kind of mischief could you do in art class? Splatter paint over everybody?"

I quickened my pace.

"Hi Mr. Bloom," he called in an unnecessarily loud voice.

The principal nodded at us and waved.

We were in front of the school now, passing Pablo Guzman Quintana's sentinel statue.

Walking east on Quintana Street we passed the thirty-foot-tall fan palm that I admired each time I saw it. Dead brown fronds hanging under the green canopy swaddled the trunk like a petticoat. Halfway to the top hovered a tiny bird with an iridescent violet crown and green under parts. A majestic plant. An exquisite animal. Analogous wonders on our planet had become extinct a hundred generations ago. Spell-bound I watched the bird suspended motionless in the air. Inexplicably my face grew hot and I sighed. Why?

Not surprisingly I had more insight into myself as the original me than I had into the human me. I would have examined my emotions but for the presence of Martinez. The violet-headed bird darted away and the spell on me was broken. I'd almost forgotten that Martinez was attached to me like a parasite.

I stopped at the corner of Quintana and Main to look for traffic before crossing, but there was little more traffic than would be expected in a wildlife refuge. Would he continue all the way to the house, I wondered?

We reached Sandstone Street, two blocks east of the school.

"Say something, damn it," he blurted.

I could not outpace him, so I did not try. I turned north. We passed Arroyo.

"Let me tell you something, Miss Stuck-up. You're not as cute as you think. And if you keep up this silent act, you're going to regret it. You'll get yourself into trouble and be friendless as a hermit. And don't think you can stop me from walking with you. But I have learned my lesson and will shut up. That much I'll give you."

Wordlessly he walked me all the way to the house. Then he turned away and walked back.

I hoped my lack of response would discourage him from walking and talking with me, but I knew he was walking and talking for Mr. Bloom, so I was not surprised when he sat beside me again the next day at lunch. Several people came up to say hello and, in a perfectly ordinary manner, they greeted me as well—no smirks or giggles. Melissa came up to say hello, but after looking at Martinez, left.

"What are you, anorexic or something? Why don't you eat?" he chided when we were alone. By now I had read the entire college calculus text, but I examined it as if it held the secrets of the ages. The lunch break ended, my having said not a word to him.

I had learned something of the planet's bizarre fauna and flora, so when Martinez came striding towards me across the quad after school, I saw that he had the grace of a jaguar despite the loss of an arm. I avulsed this thought like a rank weed. I wished to see nothing appealing in him.

"Hi there, Cricket, I'm Tom Martinez, in case you've forgotten, and—surprise!—I'm walking you home."

He looked around the quad, presumably for Mr. Bloom, but he was not there. He adjusted his pace to mine as we walked.

"Why the hell can't you be civil?"

The timbre of his voice deepened. How different from our speech. One might have thought the higher the pitch of a human's speech, the more it would appeal to us, but the opposite was true. Speech in a high pitch disappointed in some indefinable way. Sun spots! I was not speaking of us. I was speaking of me. Where was my objectivity? Was I growing to like his voice?

The afternoon sun cast our shadows on the sidewalk. Everything here was strange, of course, but seeing one's shadow cast on the surface of the planet, on a sidewalk no less, meant that such walks were perfectly ordinary. That sidewalks were maintained.

"Okay, so maybe I haven't been so civil myself. I hereby resolve to become a better person. Well-mannered. Polite. Suave. Sophisticated. An exemplary specimen of American manhood."

He must have taken my second peek at him as encouragement.

"A penny for your thoughts, Miss Mystery."

We walked another block before he spoke again.

"Fine, I'll tell you my thoughts first and then you'll be obliged to tell me yours. That's fair isn't it? Hmm. Where to begin? I wouldn't want to bore you."

He spoke at first about his motorcycle, a 450 cc Ducati, which was too small he thought. It had been modified so he could ride with one hand.

"There's this kid from Alabama, Brett Cole, who was hit by a car and lost his arm. He still races motorcycles, though. Everyone knows Lawrence of Arabia died in a motorcycle accident, but did you know Pete Conrad, did, too—the third man to walk on the moon?"

He spoke of his extra vigilance now while driving and how he had the best helmets available, the pleasure of living in a place where he could ride all year long. How did I like desert living? I assumed he'd heard I was from Hawaii. I looked at him for the third time.

"Oh, you love it here, do you?" he quipped. "Because of all the similarities, right? You've got palm trees; we've got palm trees. You've got sand; we've got sand. You've got sunshine; we've got sunshine."

By the time we'd got to Sandstone and Arroyo, three blocks from the school, he'd run out of things to say, and probably realized he needn't walk all the way home with me because Mr. Bloom would not see him do so. He said goodbye and walked back.

The next day he told me about some of the "kids" at school. Mr. Bloom's daughter Sarah was a party girl, who liked to drink, though her father didn't know it. Rick was the captain of the basketball team, and a bit of a bully at times, but they'd been friends once. Melissa was "new age," believed in the paranormal, but was quite sharp. Nicole was a Goth, dyed her hair black, wore black clothes, powdered her face, but wasn't as weird as she looked. Ms. Hardy was a lesbian, but nobody cared because she was such a good teacher. Her partner Vera Camacho, was a policewoman.

"Oh, and you might be interested in this story. There's this town Leavenworth in Washington. When the railroad got rerouted and the sawmill closed, it started dying so a bunch of people decided to dress it up like a Bavarian village and have German type festivals. Every store downtown put on these facades. And guess what. The tourists started coming and the town did great."

"So Cummings decides that Prickly Pear should do the same thing. 'We've lost our doctor,' says Cummings. 'Your neighbors are leaving. Most of us can't leave. Do you want this to be a ghost town?' That was his spiel."

"I swear to God I don't know how he did it but he talked a lot of people into spending money to hire this consulting firm—bunch of crooks—to see if it can do something like Leavenworth did.

"But we don't have snow-capped mountains like the Alps, so

Bavaria is out. We don't have any lakes, so fishing lodges are out. We don't have canyons. We don't have hot springs. Hell, we don't have anything."

He'd become animated.

"So what does the damn firm have the balls to tell us to do—be another Roswell, New Mexico. Make the buildings look like a bunch of rocket ships, make up some stories about flying saucers landing. Photoshop some pictures. Little green men and all. Everybody's interested in UFO's. People will come in droves, he said. So we spend more money putting up all this aluminum sheeting. We tried. Big flop. We get maybe twenty visitors a year. It pisses me off because we lost all that money and I don't much like the idea of posting fake pictures on the Internet. And anyway, anyone who believes in flying saucers must be a crackpot. Know what I mean?"

Despite myself, I had begun glancing at him more frequently than I should have as he sat beside me on the bench at lunchtime or walked beside me on the way home. I was annoyed with myself as much as with him.

———

Tom

I hadn't talked this much since before the accident. Why was I talking now? I got nervous there for a second when I let slip that tidbit about Brett Cole losing his arm. But she didn't ask about mine. She was listening to me, though. I was sure of it. Wish she'd say something, damn it. I was curious about her, even if she was an oddball.

———

Cricket

Until now, I had disappointed Mother and Father with vague responses to their questions about school, but today, I went into the back yard where Father was constructing a second parabolic mirror, and Mother attending to some genetically modified creosote bushes and cacti.

"The Martinez boy is on me like a sheep dog and I don't like it."

"What is a sheep dog?" asked Mother, still kneeling on the ground. "I have not completed my survey of the animals yet. Frankly they are of considerably less interest than is the botany of this region. Did you realize that it may take the agave ten years to flower? That the creosote ring not far from here has been estimated to be over eleven thousand years old?"

"Please! Please!" said Father, putting down his tools. "Let not discussions of the breeds of *Canis familiaris* or of the growth of desert plants divert us from the topic at hand."

We entered the house and sat at the kitchen table, our default conference area. Mother poured us glasses of orange juice thinned with water, but no one drank. Father periodically stood only to sit again. Mother occasionally reached out to take my hands, which I pulled away each time, eventually placing them on my lap out of her reach.

"So the boy has approached you."

"Yes, Father. Nor did he merely approach me. He has attached himself like a leech. Mother, when you get to the subclass *Hirudinea* in the phylum Annelida, you will understand what I mean."

"Watch how you address your mother, if you please."

"I do not feel in need of defense, husband."

"After what you agreed to in the principal's office, you should. Why did you not simply object? The boy's daily proximity to our unthinking daughter may lead him to suspect the truth. And you," he said, gesturing toward me. "Please stop performing in front of your mathematics class. The less attention we receive, the better."

"Shall I play the dimwit?"

"No. Your father is mistaken in this. It would be more suspicious of hidden secrets if you did not participate at school," said Mother. "You must also have at least a semblance of a social life. You must fit in."

"Under no circumstances are you to confide anything to him," said Father. "What more can I say?"

While Father worked on the rooftop transponder and power projector later that evening, Mother took me aside.

"Are you attracted to the boy?" she asked.

"Mother! How could you possibly—? He is...Martinez is...I don't wish to speak of him."

12

_____

Compared with nuclear fusion drive physics, auto mechanics was as difficult as eating candy, and for Father as pleasant. He enjoyed working, even without pay, astonishing Mr. Jones, by diagnosing a car's problem by listening to the engine for a few seconds, though sometimes he did have to open the hood.

One day after school I decided to see what Father was working on at the time. More than idle curiosity, it was a way to get my mind off school. Mr. Jones had made me feel welcome, so I sometimes went to the garage. I expressed an interest in motorcycles and he allowed me to tinker with an old one he'd thought of junking.

When Clyde Cummings came by to top off his tank, which was already five-sixths full, Father wondered what was behind the visit. Instead of paying at the pump with his credit card, Cummings came into the office to pay in cash. Claudia and Annie remained in the car squabbling. I stayed at Father's side.

"Good afternoon, Sminth."

"Yes. Good afternoon. Is your wife well? Are your girls well?"

"We're separated," said Cummings.

"That must be difficult."

"It is,"

"The girls must have done something wicked for you to separate from them."

"*What?*"

"I am sorry. I am being inappropriately personal, I think. We are very personal in Hawaii. I must adjust to your desert ways."

Cummings sputtered something unintelligible. He began inspecting the two brands of motor oil displayed on a rack, picking up one plastic bottle, then the other, appearing to read the labels.

Trying to be helpful, Father offered his thoughts:

"I am unconvinced that the more expensive oils have more efficacious mixtures of polyalphaolefins and polyinternal olefins than the less expensive oils. They taste and smell the same to me. Are you in need of motor oil?"

Cummings grabbed the closest bottle, holding it awkwardly by the neck.

"I'll take this. Put it in a bag."

Father returned to the cash register.

"So you ask personal questions in Hawaii," said Cummings.

"At times," said Father.

"Then I hope you won't mind me asking what your wife and daughter's first language was."

"Would you repeat your question, please, Mayor."

"What was your wife and daughter's first language? Which language did they first speak? How much clearer can I be?"

"Ah, you are, of course, saddened at their ongoing problems with the language, which shows that you have a kind heart. English is their first and only language but they both have speech impediments and my daughter is additionally burdened by developmental delay. I do believe I have explained these things. My wife is somewhat slow as well. I hope they have not done anything inappropriate."

"Now that you mention it, there is a little something. Your daughter is still annoying Claudia. You need to talk with her about this."

"With your daughter?" asked Father. Even I understood whom Cummings meant. Was Father teasing him?

"That's not funny, Sminth."

"I am so sorry that I misunderstood."

In the most patronizing manner, Father patted me on the head as if I were a dog so I barked.

"Arrf. Arrf."

"You see how simple she is. We have already spoken with her about her inappropriate behavior."

Father turned towards me and with theatrical harshness said, "It is impolite to bark while adults are talking."

Facing Cummings again, he added, "And we have had a meeting with the principal as well. As I said, she is cognitively impaired, but she will cause your daughter no more distress. I assure you."

Cummings harrumphed and left, but he left more suspicious of us than when he had arrived. I felt like leaving, too. Cognitively impaired!

13

When the Martinezes invited us to dinner I did not wish to go. It was not only I who was reluctant. In such an intimate setting, said Father, our eccentricities would be revealed. Consolidated sleep eluded him. He paced the house at night, awakened by nightmares of mobs of frightened vigilante yokels coming for us, pitchforks and torches on high—images from old Frankenstein movies he said. Only after consuming nearly a pint of strawberry ice cream could he get back to sleep.

"Your worry is excessive," said Mother on occasion, "as is your consumption of over-sugared congealed milk."

"Who will maintain vigilance if not I?" was his usual response. The ice cream critique he ignored. "Certainly not our daughter. Certainly not you."

It was Mother who knocked on the Martinez's door precisely at 6:30 PM, Father on her right, I on her left. Her outfit was the same she'd worn when we met with Mr. Bloom, a black polka-dot dress and tire-rubber-soled huaraches. She'd arranged her wig's hair in a long braid. Father's attire, too, was that of the Bloom meeting day, tasseled brown leather jacket, white cowboy shirt, blue jeans, string tie, and faux alligator-leather cowboy boots. He believed it matched the clothing of many a Western movie hero, and that it would subliminally suggest to others that he was a good person. The three shirts he now owned were all the same. He lacked only a large white hat to complete the outfit.

I wore a long, striped blue dress. My artificial hair was in pigtails, which tended to stick out sideways. I looked like Pippi Longstocking someone commented.

Friendly Mary Martinez greeted us. She wore black slacks and a pink blouse, her braided black hair coiled like a snail at the back of her head. I was again struck by how tall she was. She led us into the kitchen. Tom made the introductions. The Martinezes insisted I call them by their first names.

Oscar Martinez, red barbecue apron over his shirt and pants, had prepared the one dish he had complete confidence in—broiled salmon.

"Wild caught," he said. "Get it in Twentynine Palms, when they have it."

To be sure that the food would be acceptable to us, Tom had been instructed to tell us what was planned. Consequently, we'd scanned for salmon and knew what it was.

Now we stood mutely baffled.

"Is something wrong?" asked Mary.

Father looked at Mother, and seeing no suggestion that he remain silent, said, "Do not salmon from the West Coast of North America live in the Pacific Ocean and in waters draining into that ocean?"

Oscar smiled broadly. "You're pulling my leg." But Father's deadpan expression gave him pause and, amused though he was, he added that yes, that was true. There was nothing for Father to do but continue.

"And yet it is caught in the desert?"

"Caught in the desert? What do you mean?"

Five sets of eyes turned to Father.

"You did say, did you not, that they were caught in Twentynine Palms?"

Oscar, Mary, and Tom laughed.

"You are a real joker, Watson. I like that." He looked at his son. "We could use a little levity around here."

The puzzle unresolved for us, Oscar pointed to the other dishes that would be served.

The rice pilaf he admitted, as if it were something to be ashamed of, was from a box. He'd stir-fried the string beans. The lettuce and tomato salad now only required rice vinegar and olive oil. Dessert, the only Mexican dish, was flan.

We were shown to our seats. Mary, Oscar, and Tom bustled about filling water glasses, bringing dishes to the table, checking things in the kitchen. Meanwhile the three of us anxiously scanned for salmon. There could be no doubt about it. Salmon did not live in the desert. What did this mean?

We put the question aside as the Martinezes joined us at the table.

"Would you like some wine?" asked Oscar.

"What would you suggest?" asked Father.

"Give it a try. I think you'll like it."

"Thank you."

"Does Cricket get some?" asked Mary. "We allow Tom to have wine with dinner, but we totally understand if that's not how you do things. Totally."

Before Father could ask what Mary recommended, I held out my glass, which seemed to settle matters as my parents did not object.

A prayer of thanks briefly baffled us, before we, too, bowed our heads. After a toast to friendship that also baffled us—we didn't know what to do with our raised glasses—we began to eat. No sooner had Father taken his first bite of salmon, than he said, "This fish is very good." It *was* good. We had to suppress the premetamorphic inclination of our tongues to dart from our mouths.

"Very good," repeated Mother, after making several high pitched, but melodious sounds, certainly like nothing Mary or Oscar Martinez had ever heard before. Father casually raised his right hand and touched his thumb to his forehead, as if to scratch an itch, but lowered his arm quickly.

"Thank you," said Oscar. "You can't go wrong with salmon. Any fool can do it."

"Don't be so modest, Oscar. He doesn't just broil fish," said Mary. She turned to my parents.

"I hear you folks are from Hawaii. What brings you all the way out here?"

"Air-o-plane," said Mother.

"Oh, that's funny," said Mary. Whether her chuckle was genuine or forced I could not tell.

"Yes, if you don't mind my saying so," said Oscar, "the same question occurred to me. Why would anyone move from a tropical paradise to the desert, not that it isn't beautiful here and all, but still, you know, we don't have the beach, and it gets pretty hot." He sounded like Mr. Bloom.

Mother was about to speak when Father again made the gesture of thumb to forehead, this time with his little finger extended.

"Pineapple allergy," said Father, adding, after a pause, "My wife and daughter developed bad cases of it. I myself can eat pineapple all the livelong day."

"I see," said Oscar.

Tom and I, seated next to each, were mute as mummies. Father did most of the talking for the family. Mother, saying little, finished her wine before the others. Oscar refilled her glass twice.

After commenting about the weather, Mary asked a few questions that had probably occupied her for some time, as might have an engaging crossword puzzle.

"What sort of work did you do in Hawaii, Watson?"

"I repaired boats and dispensed gasoline," he said.

"Oh. And what did you do, Crick?"

Despite Father's attempts at silencing her, Mother, sufficiently fortified with wine to ignore his thumb-to-temple gesture, became almost voluble.

"I am housewife. I am garden. I am...."

"She means gardener," interrupted Father.

"I talk," said Mother, casting Father a look of disapproval that could have cowed a coyote.

"I am gardener. I am mother. I am wife. I am home. I am neighbor," said Mother, before trilling a few times and stopping. I shared Father's concern. Her English was embarrassing even to me. What must the Martinezes be thinking? But I put these unwanted thoughts away and finished the meal. Mrs. Martinez said that the grown-ups' conversation might be boring and asked if, perhaps, Tom and I might wish to study for the big math test on Monday.

Tom said, "Uh, that's not necessary."

Good, I thought. I was already shackled to this minder at school. Away from school I should be free. But it was not to be.

"It's necessary if you want to pass the test," said Oscar in an unusually harsh tone. "And you do want to pass, don't you?" It was an order dressed as a question.

Martinez led the way into a den. I was not about to speak but I accepted paper and pencil and worked through geometry problems, showing every step clearly. Grudgingly, he watched, pointing to a problem he wanted me to solve, or solving one on his own and showing it to me. A consequence of neither of us saying a word was that we solved a lot of problems.

What follows is my retelling of Mother's retelling of events after Tom and I had left the dining room. Her retellings were as detailed and cinematic as Father's. Dialogue is accurate. We all had memories like miraculous baling machines that left not a straw behind.

Father asked the Martinezes to tell them about Mayor Cummings.

"Well, first, mayor is only an honorific title and he's going to lose it next election," said Oscar. "After talking people into investing in his harebrained Roswell make-over scheme, he's the most unpopular man in town. I'm sure you've noticed the aluminum on some of the buildings. They were going to be completely covered so they'd look like spaceships, but the plan went bust when no one came and people got stuck with all that metal."

"On the other hand, he's had his comeuppance. His wife asked for a trial separation because he'd been so consumed with the project that he totally neglected her and the kids and almost ruined them financially. He thinks he's going to redeem himself by identifying undocumented aliens and riding Camacho to do something about the Hoods—Heaven's Hoods, the gang."

"Why don't we play a game?" said Mary after a while.

Oscar cleared the table. Mary brought out a deck of cards

"This game is called Set. I lay out twelve cards, like this."

She made four rows of three cards each.

"There are three symbols: a diamond, a squiggle, and an oval."

She pointed them out. "There are three colors: red, purple and green. There are three shadings: empty, striped, or filled. And each card has either one, two, or three symbols. So each card has four different characteristics."

"You can see she's explained this before," said Oscar.

A set was composed of three cards if the characteristics on the cards were either all different or all the same. You could have three cards that each had one oval on it or three cards with one, two, and three ovals. The color of the ovals could all be the same, all red, for example, or each a different color. So also for the shadings and symbols, all the same, or all different. Mary made several sets to demonstrate, pointing out and again naming the characteristics. My parents had no questions.

"When you see three cards that make a set, you say 'set' and pick them up. There are always at least twelve cards on the table. If no one sees a set, I lay down three more cards. Let me show you."

Mary lay out four rows of three cards each. Before the last card touched the table, Mother said, "Set. Set." She picked up two sets of three cards and showed them to Mary.

"Yes?" asked Mother.

Oscar whistled. Mary examined each set of three cards and then forced a smile.

"You should have told me you'd played before."

"We have never played this game. My wife, despite her speech impediment and mental slowness, recognizes patterns quickly."

"Oh," said Mary, likely wondering how he could call his wife slow with her sitting right there. "Well, there are no more sets so I'll put down three more cards."

When she'd finished, Oscar said "set" and picked up three cards.

"That is not a set," said Father. "Only two of the fillings are the same."

"You're right," said Oscar. He put the cards down on the table.

Mary began to lay out the next three cards but before the third touched the table, Mother said, "Set." Each card had a different symbol, color, and shading, and one, two, or three symbols.

Oscar whistled again.

After two more rounds, in which Mother picked sets before Mary could even focus her eyes on the cards, Oscar said that was enough game playing for the night. Mary sighed.

"Talking about recreation," said Oscar, "you folks ever go jack rabbit hunting? It's a blast. Ha ha. Hey, Watson, I've got two shotguns. Come take a look." The men disappeared into the den.

"That's men for you," said Mary. "But I'm not touching the dishes without him. Let's sit in the living room." Mother followed Mary and sat beside her on the sofa.

Mother stared at Mary, forgetting to blink her green eyes. She answered questions in one or two words, some answers making no sense. Mary, looking uneasy, asked if Mother would like a drink to which Mother said simply, "Yes."

"Black Russian, okay?" asked Mary.

"We am American."

Mary didn't respond to this. She prepared a couple of black Russians large enough to mollify the most habituated alcoholic, whether or not in DTs. Two parts vodka, one part Kahlua, a coffee liqueur.

By the time they started on their second, Mary had become loquacious and animated, and Mother, if not exactly talkative, was amused by everything Mary said so she might chuckle, chirp, whistle, or roar with laugher.

"...so I do aerobics to keep in shape. Let me show you my routine," said Mary, slurring her words.

To Mother's delight, Mary bounced off the sofa and, unaccompanied by music, began to dance. She spread her feet, bent her knees, bounced from leg to leg, or rotated her pelvis like the drum of a washing machine in a drying cycle. She put one leg back, brought it forward, flexed and extended it, raised and lowered her arms, while she sang scat to a Mexican tune. "Deedee da da da...."

Mother stood up laughing. It was her turn. Gently she pushed Mary back to the couch. She removed pictures from the wall, took off her shoes and socks, and then, to Mary's astonishment—in what would later seem in the telling to be irrefutable evidence of a hallucination—Mother began to climb the wall. She was three feet off the floor when Father entered from the den and lost his composure, berating her in our language, which must have sounded to the

Martinezes as if the room had filled with angry birds. Mother sprang from the wall, landing on her feet. She wobbled a little as she picked up her shoes and socks and took her place next to Mary. They were laughing.

Oscar, came out of the den, having missed the excitement.

"So what do you say? Rabbit hunting this weekend?"

But it was as if Father had already spotted a rabbit and couldn't take his eyes off it. Mother stopped laughing, though she giggled as she put on her shoes and socks.

"Well," said Oscar, "if that's not a good time..."

"I am pleased to go with you. We have a date," said Father.

At that point I was called back into the room. We thanked the Martinezes, said our goodbyes. They watched as we walked away.

———

Tom

B ecause I'd felt more pressured than usual, I swallowed my pride and actually studied with Cricket that night in the den. I got an A- on my math test. But instead of making my parents happy, it made them unhappy because it proved I could do well if I tried. I could get good grades if I tried. I could win an academic scholarship if I tried. Stop moping they scolded. Stop reading those paperbacks and motorcycle magazines. Start studying. You can do it if you try. Jeez!

I couldn't promise them anything. All I said was that I heard them. I felt sick.

They started fighting again about Mom's hallucinating that Mrs. Sminth had climbed a wall the night of the dinner.

"For crying out loud, Mary, you were drunk. Why do you keep talking about this?"

"Because you don't believe me."

I blamed myself for the tension in our household. You didn't need two arms to study. But I didn't feel like studying.

14

Cricket

Oscar Martinez and Father indeed had a date to go rabbit hunting and I surprised both—and myself as well—by accepting Mr. Martinez's invitation to go along. But before we entered the car, Father finally expressed his misgivings.

"Please do not think me a fastidious person, nor preoccupied with the suffering of animals, but I cannot shoot a rabbit. I should have spoken sooner. Forgive me."

"Well, of course you can't shoot a rabbit right off the bat," answered Mr. Martinez, misunderstanding the nature of Father's announcement. "Those little critters are quick as—ha ha—I was going to say rabbits. It takes practice. Don't worry. You'll get the hang of it."

Father's long silence made me uneasy and irritated me as well. He should indeed have spoken sooner. I imagined Mr. Martinez thinking Father fickle and indecisive. I imagined him thinking Father unmanly, which of course he was—literally. Had Father and I been alone, I would have scolded him, as he so often scolded me.

"He not want kill mammals," I said. "Not his philosophy."

"Oh," said Mr. Martinez, his previously enthusiastic smile dropping from his lips.

"But I would greatly enjoy learning to shoot." The smile sprang back to our host's lips. Father had saved the day, as the expression goes.

"Great. I love target practice. Wait here."

Mr. Martinez went back into his house. We were now alone, but before I could speak, my perceptive father anticipated my criticism. Softly in our language he spoke.

"After impulsively accepting his invitation, I was planning to make an excuse for not going, but your mother objected. 'Go with him,' she told me. Fit in. Fit in. How often she says it. I am sufficiently chagrined without my child telling me that I am a disappointment to her. Have I read your expression correctly?"

I shrugged.

Mr. Martinez returned with a large cardboard box of empty aluminum soft drink and beer cans, which he put in the trunk along with the shotguns.

"I invited Tom to go with us," said Mr. Martinez.

Oh no, I thought.

"I always invite him to go, but he never does. Not hard to understand, though. You can't shoot a shotgun with one arm. He doesn't want to just stand around. But this time I thought he might go. You know...because you're going."

He smiled weakly at me. I remained expressionless.

"Thought you two could spend some time together."

He thought we wished to spend time together? Absurd. Clearly the Martinez boy did not speak with his father about me.

"Thought it would be good for him," he continued. "Oh, well, let's get going."

Mr. Martinez was downcast, but as he drove and chatted with Father about things inconsequential—small talk—his mood improved.

After arriving at a place less than a mile out of town, our host, now in the role of shooting instructor, removed the shotguns and targets from the trunk and girded himself with a cartridge belt holding fifteen red shotgun shells. There were more in the trunk.

"You hold this one, Watson. First two rules of gun safety. Make sure you always know if your gun is loaded or not. And never point it at anyone. This is a double barrel break-action gun. Watch this."

He pushed a lever on the top of the gun. On a hinge, the double barrel separated from the stock at a one hundred thirty-degree angle. The backs of the barrels were exposed. They were empty. Father pushed the release on his gun. Mr. Martinez lifted the barrel, which clicked back into place. Father did the same.

"Cricket why don't you take some of these cans out there and put them on top of that ledge? Spread them out about six feet apart."

They were ready to load their guns.

"Hold it against your shoulder. Break it. That way when you close that gun it's ready to fire. To take a shell, put a thumb behind it. Put a finger on top and the others on the side. And slip it in."

After the demonstration he handed a shell to Father and then the second. They closed their guns and walked to their firing positions. I stood back.

"Be prepared for a little kick."

He showed Father how to aim and then himself took two shots in rapid succession. Two cans jumped off the rock ledge.

After four practice shots, Father began to hit the targets. I replaced them. He was clearly enjoying himself.

"Daughter, can you throw one high in the air?"

Father hit it with the second shot.

"You're a natural, Watson. I'm impressed."

"This body surprises me at times."

"You mean not like your other body?" joked Martinez.

"The other body held no surprises, I can assure you."

"You're a kick, Watson. Let's give the girl a shot at it."

After handing me his gun, with only a slight hesitation, Father set up more cans on the rock.

With little practice, I too was hitting targets. I was astonished to be enjoying this as much as Father and pleased that Mr. Martinez complimented me.

When Mr. Martinez spotted a slinky yellow lizard fifteen yards away he raised his gun to shoot it. I put my hand on the barrel and pushed it down, awaiting a sharp rebuke. But there was none.

"You're right. You're right," apologized Mr. Martinez. "No need to be trigger happy. I wouldn't have made a stew out of it."

On the way home I began asking myself questions and answering some of them. Were shotguns not killing tools? Was I not becoming a savage for having enjoyed myself? What significant difference was there between shotguns and weapons of war? Stop this. Don't ensnare yourself with questionable equivalents, I told myself. Shotguns were not designed to kill people. Perhaps not, but they were designed to kill rather smaller mammals. And birds. How did I feel about eating birds? How did I feel about eating fish? Fish were acceptable, if humanely put to death. I'd have to think more about birds.

It was the skill involved, I finally realized, and the happy feeling of seeing a beer can jump off its resting place. I even enjoyed the kickback of the stock against my shoulder.

I leaned forward.

"Did you enjoy that, Father?" I whispered in his ear.

He answered in English by speaking with Mr. Martinez.

"I wish to thank you for a pleasurable experience. I may purchase my own shotgun."

"I'm glad you liked it. You'll be shooting rabbits right and left before long."

"I will shoot at targets."

"That's fun, too."

At home after the excursion, we surprised Mother by telling her of the pleasure of shooting shotguns.

"There is an English idiom," she said. "By encouraging you to go, I have 'created a monster.' Two monsters."

"We shot no rabbits," I protested guiltily.

15

Tom

I didn't want to study in chemistry either, but I did ask for a truce. Frankly I was worried.

"Look, if we don't cooperate someone could get hurt." I was thinking of the Bunsen burners, acids, boiling water, and stuff. Cricket agreed right off the bat. Didn't even make a face. She was all business. Kept me on task. Someone did get hurt though.

When it came to setting up the apparatus and doing an experiment, she waited to see if I could do it. If not, she offered a helping hand, but was diplomatic about it. She gestured to see if it was okay. For sure I would have blown off this class if she hadn't been my partner.

Rick Croft and Eddie Driscoll were lab partners on the other side of the bench from us. They'd been among the last to find partners and were stuck with each other. What a pair of unhappy campers. Compared to them me and Cricket were like honeymooners.

We were doing titrations of sulfuric acid. Cricket filled the buret with a known concentration of sodium hydroxide, but I got to add it, drop by drop, into the acid in the beaker, waiting for the indicator to turn pink.

Rick wandered off across the room to talk with Claudia. Driscoll was left to set up the equipment by himself. Cricket stood by me but must have had an eye on him, too.

I was totally focused on the acid in the beaker. I'd turn the stopcock a smidgen. Let a drop or two fall. Wait. Let another drop fall. Wait.

Out of the blue, Cricket bolted, rounded the bench, and headed toward Driscoll. Before she even got there, he started screaming. I overshot the mark. The solution turned bright pink. Jeez!

The crazy girl was struggling with him. She had an arm and was pulling him away from the bench.

I joined her even before Gonzalez got there.

She kept hold of his arm with one hand and pointed to the emergency eye wash sink with the other.

"He got something in his eyes," I told Gonzalez. "Cricket saw it."

I put my arm around Driscoll's waist. Gonzalez and Cricket each took an arm. He struggled but we got him to the eye wash fountain. As two streams of water washed over his eyes, he began to settle down. Gonzalez kept the water running for ten minutes. Driscoll was okay after that. Embarrassed but okay.

Lucky for him the acid was dilute. How he got it in his eyes is a mystery. Driscoll didn't know. Cricket didn't answer any questions, but it was clear she acted even before Driscoll felt the burning.

Gonzalez thanked her for acting so quickly. The class took note.

I wanted to talk with her after school about it, but for some reason Claudia begged me to give her a ride home. Just before we started I saw Cricket watching us. She had a strange look on her face. She was absent the next day. And the next...

16

Cricket

My anger, like a light beam through cloudy glass, had become unfocused. I was angry with my parents, yes. They had lied to me about the true meaning of our "excursion" to the colony ship. It's a once in a lifetime opportunity to see the planet from space, they'd told me. We won't be gone a week they said. Only when we arrived by shuttle at the enormous interstellar spaceship did I learn we'd never return. I'd never see my friends again.

But I was also angry at Mr. Bloom besetting me with Martinez, that ever-present nuisance. And with Martinez himself, though he had no choice in the matter. And at Claudia for her mockery. And with everyone at school.

And I was angry and disappointed with myself, but I was not entirely sure why. I'd have to think more about it, I told myself. But I did the opposite.

Martinez continued walking me home two or three times a week to mollify Mr. Bloom. He'd ask a few questions, get no response, and then start talking, apparently about whatever was on his mind at the time, but he never spoke of his accident.

"You know I'm trying to make this as painless as possible. Why do you have to be such a numbskull? And if you're worried that this is going to go on forever, so am I. If you'd just start talking to people and acting normally, Bloom would call me off and we'd both be happy. Is that too much for you to get through your thick skull?"

Being talked to like this only hardened my obstinacy. Were he to cajole me in the most diplomatic manner, I still would not speak. Yet I found myself listening to his every word. Martinez's chatter had become curiously engaging, even when he was chastising me for my stubbornness. What is wrong with me, I wondered.

In comparison with my original body, this body's emotions were amplified, insistent, domineering at times, but not easy to name. But even unnamed they impeded cognition.

After school the day Eddie Driscoll got acid in his eyes, I was startled to realize that I had dawdled, waiting for Martinez. He emerged from the quadrangle. I half turned to face him when I saw Claudia run up to him. He looked at me and must have seen my perplexity. He half frowned, half smiled. Tilting his head to one side, he shrugged, then walked with her to the motorcycle. She helped put their books in the saddlebag. She put on a helmet. He mounted. She mounted behind him. She put her arms around him. The engine whined, scoffing at me. Confused and churning inside, I looked away and hurried down the street.

I had been largely successful in suppressing recall of the comforting, cylindrical rooms of my home, of my virtual get-togethers with my friends, of my parents relaxed and playful, as they no longer were. But this night I could not stop the vivid, eidetic images from scrolling painfully through my mind. I could not stop cursing my parents for taking me away, for bringing me here, for making me look like this. And now, after the loss of the Colony, for damning me to solitude. Once or twice I saw a snapshot image of Claudia riding behind Martinez.

Claudia and Martinez! Sepsis and stench! Don't you have better images than that? Yes. A meeting with my dance instructor on Sassatha, a male a few years older. We had begun to learn about each other, to share some experiences.

"Does your family ever leave the module," he asked one day.

"My father and mother repair damaged sections of travel tubes." I was not lying. I was ignorant of the truth. They were working on the expedition, the pilgrimage, though Mother often worked from home.

His pupils widened.

"But there are no resources for repair. I was told that all material and talent were dedicated to air, water, and food sectors. Have you ever gone with them?"

"No. They say it is too dangerous. I've never left our module, but I am going to."

I hesitated then. I had said too much. Mother and Father had been explicit. I was not even to hint at our plans, but they were away from the module at the moment and I was so excited at the thought of what was coming that I abandoned discretion. In addition, I liked this male. I wanted to tell him something interesting.

"We are going on an orbital tour of the planet. I will see all of Sassatha from space. I will see the stars."

He laughed. "That is a good story. I am going to the surface to build sand cities."

I remained silent and unamused. I had just shared a big secret, but he had responded sardonically. We were standing face to face, if only via holographic projection. He studied my features as if searching for something small and hidden.

"What you said. Was that to be humorous?" He was earnest now and contrite, which again made him appealing. I forgave him.

"What I said is the truth, but there is irony in it. My first time out of the module will be a trip into space."

He took a step back. "You are serious then."

I wish we'd had more time together, both then and in the future. I told him what I knew. It would be a short trip. Possibly only a few orbits before return. My parents wouldn't tell me how this had been arranged. I would learn later. It was a secret. He was to reveal it to no one.

He may not have believed me. I could not be sure. But he seemed sad.

We spoke for a while longer, curtailed my dancing lesson. His image shimmered and was gone.

This memory was to be distracting. I was mistaken. It led to a more disturbing image—Claudia's arms around Tom.

The next day, Mother shook me awake. "You'll be late for school," she said.

"I'm not going to school."

Crisis.

Father came into the room, directly from his job, still dressed in his overalls, his hands still in his garage work gloves, which he pulled off and threw on my bed. The cacophony of threats, cajoling, needling, pleading, and pointed questioning went on intermittently for a week. I got up from time to time to nibble a bit and drink some water, but that was all.

"It is our lives, dear heart," said Mother, repeatedly. "Do this for us. I beg you."

On the evening of the seventh day, the dreaded knocking came at the door. A loud, insistent, authoritative knocking. A sinister, endless knocking. A knocking that forebode doom.

"Cover the devices," whispered my panic-stricken father. I heard the frantic scrambling to throw sheets and clothing over the telltale technology that would appear, if not otherworldly, then at a minimum, highly suspicious for sophisticated spyware, satellite monitors, or just plain weird stuff, that is, if the authorities wished to look in the master bedroom.

Driven from my bed by fear, I dressed quickly, combed my artificial hair, and wobbled into the living room, where I lowered myself into a chair. I should have stayed in bed, except that I couldn't.

"Everyone act normal," said Father. "We'll just say you've been sick."

I have been sick.

Mother and Father, their backs stiff, took several deep breaths in unison, and then Father stepped forward to open the door after all.

"Sorry to bother you, Mr. Sminth. Good evening, Mrs. Sminth. I just...I just wanted to see Cricket. Is she sick?"

Perhaps I should become an actress, for I surely was acting. Despite quivering, I stood, sauntered nonchalantly to the doorway, nudged myself between my dumbfounded parents, and stepped out into the night air, where the Martinez boy stood on the doorstep, helmet dangling from his hand. As I gently but firmly pulled the front door closed my parents were forced back into the house. I didn't want them listening.

"Are you all right?" he said.

I walked past him out to his motorcycle touching the saddle impulsively. He followed.

"I have small cold," I said, looking back at the door to be sure my parents had not opened it. This was my personal business.

"Small cold? You've been out for a week...Hey! You can talk."

"When I want, I talk." *How much easier it is to understand the language than to speak it.*

"To tell you the truth, I think you've been playing hooky."

"Hooky?"

"Don't they use that word in Hawaii? Hooky, you know, truancy. Skipping school."

I looked away from him, north into the desert. The sky was darkening.

He shook his head.

Why the answer to my next question seemed important, I was not sure, and I hesitated before asking it.

"Mr. Bloom send you?"

"No, Mr. Bloom did not send me. I was worried about you. You're such a numbskull, anything might have happened."

He looked at the front door.

"Want to go for a ride? Would your parents mind?"

"Would Claudia mind?"

"Ha. I knew it. I saw it in your face. Do you want to go or not?"

But he did not wait for an answer. He hung his helmet on the left handlebar. He removed a spare from the back of the machine. I put the helmet on and clicked the straps together. Deftly with his one hand, he guided me through the adjustments, his long fingers touching my cheeks, my neck, and the underside of my chin, evoking a completely foreign, but delicious, sensation, which rose in me like a wave of warmth.

Thin, bright pink clouds nestled on the horizon, the sky turning cerulean. In an hour the stars would be out, but my star was in the southern hemisphere. The rushing wind exhilarated me. I wrapped my arms more tightly around the boy so I would not fall. I suppose I could have grasped the seat, but I did not.

The thrill of speed, the night air rushing past me, washed me clean of messy emotion. Exhilaration is a powerful detergent. Ridiculous as it may sound, I thought again of learning to ride a motorcycle.

We rode for less than ten minutes before turning onto a narrow, packed sand road, and then onto a narrower trail. A lone Joshua tree stood in a small sandy area with few creosote bushes. We dismounted. We removed our helmets and hung them on the handlebars. He took a small cotton blanket from a saddlebag and threw it over his shoulder, so his hand was free.

He took mine in a firm grip. I was confused by the turn of events and by my own feelings. Should I reciprocate and squeeze his hand or leave my hand limp? To squeeze his hand would be to send a message but what message would be sent? To leave a dead hand, limp in his, was also to send a message. I maintained my grip as he led me to the middle of a clearing.

We sat on the blanket.

"School has been pretty rough for you, hasn't it?"

"Rough?"

"Is that another expression they don't use in Hawaii? How can you be a math whizz and not know English? I mean how can you be a math whizz and not know English if you're from Hawaii?"

"Speech impediment."

"That makes no sense at all and your mother can't speak English either. You're Russians, aren't you? That's what half the town thinks."

Denying that we were Russian would lead to other questions about our origins. I looked up at the moon. How its face changes. Tonight it was bemused. Could the stars tease? They winked at me. Worlds colliding! I was enjoying myself.

He waited for me to speak, but I would not. Before he spoke again, three or four minutes passed as if we were moving through a thick, existential syrup.

"Okay. Let's say you're from Hawaii. But tell me why you're always so angry. You've been angry from day one."

"You angry, also."

"Hmm...Are you going back to school? Look, if you'd just smile once in a while and say 'hello' to people the girls wouldn't be so catty."

"You teach me motorcycle?"

His laughter surprised me, like finding something impossibly large in a tiny box.

"I don't know about that. It's tricky, especially with most of the controls on the right."

We sat quietly for a few more minutes before he said he'd better get me home or my parents would worry.

"My parents worry always. You teach me motorcycle?"

"Yeah. Maybe. We'll work something out, but we'd better go."

We returned to my house. I dismounted fumbling to remove my helmet, but with thumb and forefinger Martinez helped me undo the catch.

He put a hand on my shoulder.

"You ought to go back to school, you know."

He sighed and said good night.

"Good night," I said. In the house, I listened to the pitch of his engine drop as he drove away. Doppler effect.

I could not deny that something in me had changed. I would return to school. But what about Claudia?

17

Cricket

Until that first encounter with Claudia, I had never been taunted in my life. Being the object of ridicule galled me. Only now, however, for some inexplicable reason, did I see that eating insects in front of her was, to say the least, unsophisticated.

What use intelligence unless applied? Where was my sense of humor? I searched the Internet for the sound I wanted. I practiced it in the back yard until it was indistinguishable from the original. I was now prepared for the next day at school.

Again at noon Martinez joined me on the bench in the eucalyptus's dappled shadows. He sat on my right, his empty left shirtsleeve dangling beside me. Again I wondered about it.

"Oh, brother," he said, irked. "The silent treatment again?"

Melissa walked over to say hello and asked if she could join us. She had a glittery star-shaped barrette in her hair.

I nodded.

The two of them now flanked me.

"Is that a person you're making in art class?" she asked.

I shrugged.

She chuckled softly.

"Okay, surprise us," she said.

Martinez said nothing, looked at neither of us, and appeared glum.

Claudia, Sarah, and Nicole approached. Sarah was Mr. Bloom's daughter. I did not expect teasing from her. Claudia said, "Let's say hello to the bug lady."

They came up and greeted us. Claudia brushed her hair's black spirals to the side, fluttered her eyelashes, and stood arms akimbo, so her already tight white blouse was stretched across her breasts. Her green and black Douglas plaid skirt barely reached her dimpled knees.

Tom and Melissa returned their greeting. With an effort, as if my face had to break through a plaster mask, I smiled weakly at Claudia. Maintaining this feeble grin, I cleared my throat. The girls looked at me thinking I would speak. I cleared my throat again and then startled everyone with a loud, long, uncannily authentic cricket trill. After a moment of shocked silence, Melissa laughed, then Sarah and Nicole, but neither Claudia nor Tom did.

"That was something," said Sarah, probably under instructions from her father to be nice to the new screwball. "How'd you do that?"

I shrugged.

"Lucky for you there are no frogs about," said Claudia, turning to leave. Nicole and Sarah followed her. Melissa left shortly thereafter.

Martinez looked at me, scowling. "Isn't enough, enough? Why the chip on your shoulder? What's with this me-against-the world attitude? Give us a break, would you?"

I did not understand some of his allusions, but the general idea I did understand. I rose from the bench, and walked away. His disdain I could do without. Him I could do without. I saw him catch up with Claudia and her entourage. Now I felt even worse.

———

In a chance encounter with the gym teacher, Mrs. Tonya Jones, Hoppy Jones' wife, Mother learned that I was not participating in Physical Education. She scolded me.

"You may no more avoid participating in that class than in any other. You must fit in."

Like a truancy officer, she now accompanied me to Vintage Duds, the second-hand clothing store on Main Street, where I bought a pair of faded orange shorts, a pink t-shirt, a canvas bag, and a pair of shoes variously called tennis shoes, athletic shoes, trainers, or sneakers.

In P.E., with a knowing smile, Mrs. Jones gave me a towel and a piece of paper on which she'd written the numbers 45, 16, and 2.

"Glad you're joining us, Cricket." She sounded sincere. Why did I not then ask what the numbers were for? Fear of mockery?

"Your locker is number 17," she said, pointing me towards a door marked Girls. Perhaps she thought I could not read.

Wooden benches ran alongside bright red lockers. As I entered the room, the buzz and the chatter quieted. Every girl in the room turned towards me. To stare at me in an ordinary classroom, students had to turn in their desks. No teacher would allow that for long, but here I was exposed, like a ripe red apple ready to be picked.

This time I did not disdainfully meet their stares. I averted my gaze, and quickly found my locker. Seeing the lock, I understood what the numbers were for, but not how to use them. I sat on the bench pretending to look through my bag. Why did they need locks in the first place? Because of thieves? How uncivilized they were.

My neighbor, a compact red-headed girl, quickly turned her lock's dial clockwise, counterclockwise, and clockwise. This was of no help at all.

I would not be forced into speaking. I would not! But if I sat for an hour and did not change into gym cloths, I would appear foolish. Did I care? Yes, decay and degradation, I did care!

I stood up, touched the girl's shoulder, showed her the piece of paper, touched the dial, and shrugged.

"What's wrong?"

I shrugged again and looked at the floor, trying to appear doltish. Well, croon to a tragaloon! How I bobbled back and forth between caring and not caring what humans thought of me.

"You want me to open it?"

I nodded.

When the locker door swung open, I smiled weakly at the girl.

In the proper attire, my clothes locked securely away from the hoards of clothing hungry girls who might snatch them up at the slightest opportunity, I followed the girls into a very large room. The shoes I'd bought in my haste to leave the clothing store were too tight and pinched.

At one end of the room a metal hoop mounted on a backboard was held ten feet aloft by a metal pole.

At the other end of the room, a sixteen-foot-long beam raised four feet from the floor, dominated the space. Around it, on the polished, straw-colored wood floor, lay thick blue mattresses. A wedge-shaped board with six-inch springs under one end had been placed before the beam, another by its side.

Without prompting, the class split itself in two. Twelve girls began bouncing a ball and throwing it back and forth among themselves or at the hoop.

The remaining six girls sat along the wall near the beam, removing the shoes they'd just put on a few moments ago in the locker room. Even though Claudia was among them, here I'd be able to remove my own shoes, so I joined them rather that the girls playing with the ball.

"Have you done gymnastics before?" asked Mrs. Jones.

I had no idea what this sport was, but inexperience of sports should be nothing to be ashamed of. I shook my head. She glanced at my bare feet.

"But by the looks of it you want to learn." I nodded. "That's fine. You can stand by the wall and watch."

Hayley, the compact girl who'd opened my locker, stood seventeen or eighteen feet from one end of the beam, her legs perfectly straight, feet touching each other, her back stretched into a slight arc. She held arms up and out in a V-shape, palms down, parallel to the ground, as if she were about to fly. Was I about to learn that humans could fly? I hoped not.

She lowered her arms and ran towards the beam, jumped onto the spring board, flew into the air, and landed on the beam with one foot, the other leg stretched behind her, arms out like wings. A graceful arc ran along the back of her legs and up her spine. She took a long straight-legged step and then jumped off the beam.

I was astonished, never even having imagined such...such an action. In the module I had danced quite acrobatically at times. I had jumped off the floor, but this...This was something special.

A small, almost delicate girl, blond hair in a pony tail, stood alongside the beam, legs together, arms at her side. She raised and lowered her arms, took three running steps and flew off the spring board onto the beam, landing on both feet, legs bent. She stood, spread out her arms, and jumped to the floor.

"This is called mounting the beam," said Mrs. Jones. "Maybe we'll get around to walking the beam later." She had remained standing next to me, but I was oblivious of everything except the gymnastics.

Next, came a tall, perky girl, who, I was relieved to see, would not use the intimidating spring board. She stood beside the beam on a stack of mats. I paid particular attention to her technique. She put both hands on the beam, bent her knees, jumped, and swung both straight legs sideways over the beam, by raising one arm to let them pass. Her final position was on the other side of the beam, rear end resting against it, body straight, supported by her arms on the beam behind her. Amazing.

How well formed these girls were, the elongated ovoids of their calves and thighs, the fullness, power, and roundness of their gluteal muscles. We Sassathans were a slender race, having lost muscle mass over the centuries from indoor living. I squeezed my thighs with both hands. Solid.

Claudia now stood alongside the beam. I recognized the standard stance of arched back and outspread arms reaching up in a V. Each gymnast announced herself with this maneuver.

She took a long straight-legged step onto the springboard, and, supported by a straight arm on the beam, swung both legs over it, to end sitting gracefully, one arm on the beam, the other reaching out.

Though I tried to conceal from myself this feeling of awe, I could not. What grace these beings were capable of, even chilly Claudia. On the one hand, they were capable of cruelty, violence, and ugliness. On the other, they could be...

Mrs. Jones interrupted my thoughts. She said I should try a mount. I froze.

"A couple of the girls will help," she added.

To my surprise, Claudia came over.

"Oh, come on. Give it a try. Hayley and I will be there." Was it a challenge or encouragement?

I didn't like Claudia and she didn't like me, but I doubted she wished to see me physically hurt. I pointed at the girl who'd used the mats and then I pointed at the beam. As the girl demonstrated her routine, Hayley narrated.

"Okay, standing tall, hands on the beam. Now she bends her knees and arms. Remember all your weight will be on your arms."

Claudia squeezed my triceps.

"They'll do."

Hayley gave her a look and continued.

"As soon as you jump you swing your legs to the side. Keep them straight. Your arms carry all your weight and for a moment only one arm will, because you have to raise the other to let your legs pass. Okay, let's try it."

Behind me stood Claudia, on the other side of the beam, Hayley. Claudia put her hands lightly on my hips.

I turned to her and shook my head.

"Have it your own way," she said indifferently, removing her hands.

I put my hands on the beam.

"Remember to keep your legs straight and point your toes."

I bent knees and elbows and jumped, straightening my arms. My head and torso leaned to the right, my legs to the left, but they were neither straight nor high enough to clear the beam. They landed on top of it.

"You concentrate on keeping the legs straight," said Hayley. "Give them a lift, Claudia."

"She won't let me."

Chagrined, I turn to Claudia and nodded seven times in rapid succession as if my neck were a spring.

"Should I wash my hands first?" said Claudia.

"Okay, you guys, stop," demanded Hayley.

This time, with Claudia deftly giving my legs the slightest boost, my legs cleared the beam. The third time I cleared it without help.

"You're a natural," said Hayley.

"A natural what?" whispered Claudia so softly only I could hear.

Next came beam-walking practice. I had much less trouble with this, though I engaged the setae of my feet a few times.

Towards the end of the class the advanced students did routines I could only wonder at. Mounts, handstands, cartwheels, dance steps. The dismounts in themselves were amazing. Mean as Claudia was, I could not deny her grace.

I wondered whether gymnastics had induced muscle development in ordinary girls or if well-muscled girls became gymnasts. I would do a little study in the shower room, comparing the hoop ball players' bodies with the gymnasts'.

Naked in the shower room, unaware that nudity was uncomfortable for some, I walked around looking at people's arms, legs, breasts, backs, and buttocks.

As I stepped out of the luxurious shower, Claudia, draped in a towel, came up to me.

"You're looking at everyone's butt. You must really like them."

I was flummoxed. Even were I speaking, I would have been unable to respond. Without thinking what it might mean to a non-Sassathan, I slapped my buttocks with both hands and walked away. I had read about this gesture in a book of ancient cultures and for a while my friends and I had used it to indicate that we had to end the current holographic get-together. There was an element of humor in it, of course.

"Oh, you want to play," said Claudia behind my back. She snapped her wet towel at me, stinging my buttocks, but this left her naked.

"Hey," said Melissa and snapped her towel, hitting Claudia's buttocks.

Then Nicole did the same to Melissa.

In a true chain reaction, the room was quickly filled with screaming, laughing, and shouting girls, half of them snapping their towels at bare behinds, the other half rushing to get away from the melee. Some were so eager to escape that they left the room before they were fully dressed.

Mrs. Jones burst into the room, bellowing.

"Stop it! This instant!"

Everyone wrapped themselves in towels, but Claudia had dropped hers and it had been kicked a few feet away. She caught Mrs. Jones's, eye as she picked it up.

"Claudia, who started this?"

Here it comes, another trip to Mr. Bloom's office for slapping my own buttocks. But Claudia just shrugged.

Mrs. Jones came over to me. "Who started this?"

In this instant I rethought the situation. I had not "started this." Claudia had, but I shrugged as well.

"This is the sort of behavior I expect of immature boys, not young women. You should be ashamed of yourselves." Mrs. Jones's tone was not as harsh as I suspected it would be, given her initial bellowed order that buttock-whacking be halted.

———

That people—human people—are complex is what is called a platitude, but that platitudes are often true, if unimaginatively stated, was demonstrated that same day.

Claudia came up to me. Expecting the worst, I stiffened.

"I shouldn't have hit you. I'm sorry." She said it quickly, then slapped her own buttocks and walked away. She must have hit me with that towel to revenge herself for my embarrassing her with my cricket song. And then had second thoughts.

Hayley, passing at this moment, saw what Claudia had done. As she walked by me she slapped her buttocks. This time I responded by slapping my own buttocks. We laughed.

This greeting or gesture or joke or whatever it was, appeared contagious. Soon most of the girls were slapping their own buttocks and laughing when passing their friends.

Mr. Bloom was not psychic—a ridiculous notion in any case—but he had discovered, by his own means, that Claudia and I were the first ones to start the buttock-slapping, indeed that we'd started with towel-snapping in the shower and locker rooms. He called us both in.

"There is a certain vulgarity in that gesture," he said. "It demeans the school. Whether you see it this way or not, it is a form of violence. Several parents have spoken to me about this. Your father twice, Claudia. Did you start this?"

She shook her head.

"Did Cricket?"

She shook her head again.

When he asked me, I did the same. Frustrated he dismissed us.

As we left the office, I slapped my behind. Claudia did the same. We were fleetingly sisters in rebellion, but as Claudia was a trendsetter, the fad quickly extinguished itself when she no longer slapped her rear end.

Along with art, I now had a second class I enjoyed. I devoured YouTube videos about mounting, walking upon, and doing routines on the balancing beam. For a while, though, I was pestered by the thought that I was betraying myself, because how could I like things like this in a place I despised. On a planet where slapping one's rear end was seen as the height of hilarity. I caught myself in my hypocrisy.

18

Cricket

Above the door of her little store on Main Street hung a sign in neatly painted green letters: Crick's Medicinal Herbs. A more accurate sign might have read: Advanced Medical Evaluation & Potent Pharmacological Compounds. Or simply: Sassathan Doctor.

Mother had not had a single client—she must not call them patients—and felt the outlook for her practice was bleak. We were, after all, the Russian oddballs with the hostile daughter. Why should anyone wish to take the risk of inadvertent poisoning with some strange foreign potion? On the other hand, the town had no real pharmacy, only a grocery store with a limited choice of drugs.

I thought I might stand in front of the shop, urging people to enter, like a barker at a circus, yelling, "Dr. Sminth's Magic Potions! For catarrh, rheumatism, dropsy, weak nerves..." But Mother would have none of it.

"You can help me make some pills."

She used a 3D printer to make pills with alternating layers of medication and liquid binder. Since the pill was not pressed it was porous. It dissolved in the mouth with just a sip of water. A child need not swallow a bulky tablet.

When we'd finished that task, I was to straighten up the blue, orange, yellow and clear bottles on the shelves in the front room: Ointments for insect bites, syrups for cough suppression, poultices for corns, moisturizing creams, salves for sore muscles, rinses for hair loss, and such. Energizers, sleep potions, pain killers, vision enhancers, and various other less benign preparations were locked up tight in the back room. The antineoplastic agents were in a special locked cabinet of their own.

Mother put her hands on hips and looked around the small room, slowly shaking her head.

"You might consider spreading the news of my business among your friends because—"

"I have no friends. I want no friends. I need no friends."

"Ordinarily I would not mention this, but your father taught me a useful phrase, 'drama queen'. Scan for it when you have time. As I was saying, I would appreciate it if you would tell your acquaintances that I am open for business."

I turned away to examine the labels on some of the bottles and jars. Otherwise scrupulous, Mother had "fudged," as they say. Heeding Father's advice, vagueness in all things, she'd described ingredients as "tested and safe proprietary medicinal and herbal compounds." In some instances, she had given Latin names to herbs, fungi, or bacteria that came from Sassatha.

Father was sour that she was increasing her vocabulary in a dead language to mimic scientific nomenclature, but working little on her English.

The first customers, Nicole and her mother, arrived at 9:34.

"Oh, hi Cricket," said Nicole.

I raised my hand in greeting.

"This is my mother, Kimberly Bennett. This is Cricket Sminth. I told you about her. She's making a huge statue in art class."

I was relieved to see Mother emerge from the back room, now wearing her white smock.

"Good morning," she said, as I should have.

"Good morning," said Mrs. Bennett.

"How I help you?" asked Mother hopefully.

Mrs. Bennett glanced quizzically at Nicole, as if to say, "Why did you bring me *here*?" The owner couldn't speak proper English, the shelves were rough boards, the bottles looked handmade.

"Oh, just browsing," hastily replied Mrs. Bennett. "Come on, Nicole, let's get going."

Mother moved quickly to door. Oh, no. Was she actually going to block the exit.

"I treat sleep. I treat backache. I treat headache. You have headache?"

The last question was a lucky guess. Who on earth didn't have headaches from time to time?

"Well, tell her, Mom," urged Nicole.

"Oh, I have headaches and the doctors can't seem to find the problem and the things they give me for them, well... Probably just tension. Uh, but I can live with it."

"Mom!" protested Nicole.

"I prepare test," said mother. "You sit down a minute please."

Then she actually took Mrs. Bennett by the arm and led her to a comfortable, but worn chair that housed sophisticated scanning and monitoring devices. Imbedded in the ceiling above the chair was the second half of the device.

"I... I don't know about this," complained Mrs. Bennett.

No sooner had she sat down than Mother took her hand, pulled her to a stand, and led her into the examining room cum laboratory cum office. Mother sat next to her, both on ordinary wooden chairs. Nicole and I stood.

Mrs. Bennett looked as if a kidnapper had just abducted her.

"Nicole, I don't know about this. I..."

"Fear natural in strange setting. I help headache."

With Nicole's encouragement, Mrs. Bennett answered an abbreviated series of discrete questions about her health and medications, and about the quality, location, frequency, intensity, and duration of the pain, Mother withdrew from a drawer a device that looked like a tambourine, but without the drum skin.

"I put on your head."

Mrs. Bennett tried to rise, but Nicole's simply saying, "Mom!" halted her ascent.

Mother explained that she would change the settings on a smartphone-sized console to find the cause of the headaches.

"When you feel tingle in head or see light or feel dizzy you say."

"Is this going to hurt?"

"Maybe little. Little."

Nicole took her mother's hand.

After thirty seconds, Mrs. Bennett grimaced and raised her hand for Mother to stop whatever she was doing.

"That's it. That's it exactly."

Mother removed the metal crown and tried to explain that the problem was a feedback loop between two of the cranial nerves that provided sensation to the face.

"Maybe stress begin cycle."

"I don't want a tranquilizer," said Mrs. Bennett.

"No. No. We stop loop."

Mother provide her with 12 pills and told her to take one pill once a week, whether or not she had pain.

"Once a week?"

"Yes. Like religion," said mother.

"You mean religiously?"

"Yes."

"In three months you back. Early if need."

"What do I owe you?" asked Mrs. Bennett, eager to escape.

"No money. Tell your friends."

Baffled, dubious, and agitated, Mrs. Bennett departed.

The second and last customer of the day arrived two hours later.

"Good morning, Mrs. Sminth," said Clyde Cummings, amiably enough, which in itself was suspicious, but his patronizing a store he believed was owned by secret agents dispatched by a foreign power was more suspicious.

"Do you have anything for muscle tension?"

"Of course. This for you?"

"I'm afraid so."

"What your problem?"

Cummings looked around the room.

"We can talk private in back," said Mother.

"No need. No need. Just ordinary muscle tension. I'll take anything you recommend." He refused to answer any questions.

She asked him to sit in the chair while she searched in back. When he demurred, she insisted. Mother had a good idea of Cummings' health when she returned.

"Your blood pressure high," said Mother.

"How'd you know that?"

"Oh... Guess. Only guess. I am right?"

"Look, this isn't funny."

"Forgive me. Here. Something for tense muscle."

"One teaspoon when tense muscle. Only one a day." She tried to hand him the bottle, but he wouldn't take it.

"That's all right," he said. "Just put it in a bag if you have one or wrap it with some paper."

"What was that all about?" we wondered after he'd left.

19

Cricket

Melissa had not been put off by my mute haughtiness, even from the first day. When she invited me for an ice cream, I accepted.

Each day after school, Rosita's transformed itself into a popular ice cream parlor. It was half full when we arrived. Ensconced in a booth, I spoke with Melissa for the first time. It pleased me that she made no comment about my abrupt use of language.

"What to order?" I said.

"Well, I always get a chocolate shake. Why don't you try that?"

And so I discovered this delectable comestible.

Melissa touched the yellow butterfly clip in her hair. Then, as the expression goes, got right down to business.

"You and Tom go everywhere together. You like him?"

In broken English, I told her no, that I did not like him at all, that he annoyed me, that Mr. Bloom insisted he look out for me, but that I could look out for myself.

"I'll say you can. That was really something with the cricket sound. Claudia's probably going to think twice about calling you a bug from now on. But, really, she's not that bad. She raises money for the homeless. She tutors some kids. And she's got her own problems. Her mother ran off to...I think San Diego. So now her father's stressed and she's stuck taking care of her little hyperactive sister a lot of the time. Anyway, I guess your not talking rubbed Claudia the wrong way."

"And she's jealous, of course, because you're always with him. They used to go together."

"Where they go?"

She laughed. "That's funny."

I shook my head.

It was a few seconds before she realized that I didn't understand the phrase.

"Really? Boyfriend and girlfriend. They broke up after the accident."

"What make the accident?"

Melissa shook her head. Nobody at school knew exactly what had happened, only that his arm was severely damaged and was lost.

We sipped our shakes while I pondered what she'd told me. Attuned to my pensiveness, Melissa stopped talking. On the walls, Aztec maidens painted on black velvet beseeched us to save them from sacrifice. Implacable priests stood poised to strike. But perhaps they were not beseeching us at all. Perhaps they accepted the need to propitiate the gods, perhaps they felt honored, if frightened, by the role they played. I ran my fingers over the lizards carved into the wood of the backrest.

"I hope you don't mind my saying so," said Melissa after a time, "but you're different in a special way. And it's not just the language thing. What is your native language, by the way?"

"English first language. I have speech impediment."

"Speech impediment?" She paused before continuing. "Well, that's not the only reason you're different, but I can't put my finger on it. There's a mystery in you, isn't there? You've got a secret. You know, Claudia's father doesn't believe you come from Hawaii. He thinks you and your family are Russian spies. With Edwards Air Force Base so close, testing experimental planes all the time, and with those antennae things, or whatever they are, on your roof."

"On the other hand, I hear that people are starting to go to your mom's little shop. Nicole's mom is telling a funny story about your mom twisting her arm to take something for her headaches. She thought your mom was bonkers. She was even a little frightened."

"But it was a wonder drug and she's glad she had her arm twisted. It snuffed out the headaches. People are even talking about bringing their pets to her. She fixed some neighbor's dog's leg. I heard she put a cast on some kid's broken arm. Someone even saw Clyde Cummings go in. And word is out that your father can fix anything that can go wrong with a car. Hoppy Jones's business has picked up. So most people here don't care if you're Russian or not."

She chuckled. "That's rich. Russian spies! It's just as likely you're from Mars."

"No. We not from Mars."

Notwithstanding Father's continual warnings to be mindful of everything we did or said, I believed nothing would convince these people that we were extraterrestrials. I would later discover that I was mistaken, but sitting here in the wooden booth, sipping a chocolate shake with a pleasant companion, I saw no harm in testing my theory, so certain was I of disbelief. Or was I just feeling playful? Impish?

"We from planet Sassatha. *Very* far away. Come in spaceship. I alien creature."

"Well, you're pretty cute for an alien creature. Is that what that big lizard thing is you're making in art class, an alien creature?"

"You very smart," I said. "That me." There was no point in telling her any more. Besides I couldn't express myself. I'd really better learn the language.

"Don't worry. Your secret is safe with me," she said so seriously that I wondered if she believed me.

The restaurant was filling up with students, everyone, like us, having walked the short distance from school. I was comfortable that, with the din of chatter, we had not been overheard.

Sarah Bloom came over to our table.

"Hi, Melissa. Hi, Cricket. Listen girls, I'm going to have a slumber party and I'd like you to come."

"Oh, how fun," said Melissa. And then turning to me. "Sarah has the best sleepovers."

"Will you come, Cricket?" asked Sarah.

Without thinking, without knowing what a "sleepover" or a "slumber party" was, I nodded.

"Great!" said Sarah. And gave us the details.

————

Melissa became my English teacher. I asked her to correct a homework assignment, an essay entitled One of My Favorite Childhood Memories. This was the work before she edited it.

When I am a child my parents play with me. For years they play with me. Mother is my zebra. I ride on her back. Father is a lion. He chase us around the room. "When I catch you, I eat you," he roar. It is funny and scary a little. I have delight. I squeal. Around and around my mother runs, my zebra. The lion always catch me. It pulls me off my zebra. It puts me on my back on the floor. It tickle me so I do not escape. I laugh too much. He put his face on my belly. He say, "I eat you up now." And play like he eat me. I laugh so hard, my zebra say stop. Then the lion bite my zebra. My zebra laugh so much. Years we play this game. I love this game. But my parents change. They do not play this game. They be serious. They work all day and all night on a secret. They do not tell me the secret. They do not tell the secret to their friends. One day they take me to a big boat. They say only to make a vacation. But the boat never go home again. That is the secret. I see not my friends again. I play not with my zebra and lion again. That is my memory.

Both the tronz and the tragaloon were unearthly creatures, of course, not to mention having been extinct on Sassatha for millions of years so I had replaced them with a zebra and a lion.

20

Cricket

A local merchant had called the police, in the person of Officer Camacho, to report that the Heaven's Hoods had just invaded their stores, causing a ruckus. They only bought some beef jerky. After they left, two bottles of wine were missing, as well as candy bars, packages of hot dogs, and marshmallows.

I had just stepped out of Mother's medicinal herb shop after a visit when, two stores away, I saw twelve men in black on the sidewalk and street in front of Danny's Market, "horsing around," almost literally.

No sooner was I outside, than Martinez approached me from out of nowhere.

"Come with me. You need to get out of here."

I likely would have left on my own, but his imperious tone rankled me. Nor did I imagine any harm could come to me out here on the sidewalk in daylight.

"I want to watch."

"I'm telling you it's not safe. They're unpredictable and if they see you watching...Well, you never know. Come on, don't be a fathead."

"Call me names. I stay anyway. You go if you want."

He tried several more times, but I was stubborn as usual.

"Fine," he said. "Fine." He stood silently beside me, a grim look on his face, as if seeing a car crash in the making. He seemed frightened, looking behind him and to the right and left as if seeking an escape route. But he did not move from my side.

Three of the men in the role of horses, carried on their backs three other men, the riders, each pair trying to pull a rider from his mount, or knock the pair to the ground. The others, hooting, had made a ring around the fighters. When a rider was dislodged another horse and rider entered the ring. Levi Barker was a horse, his rider Billy Bob, the baby-faced young man with the incongruous scar on his cheek. Barker's approach was to knock his opponents over by ramming into them. From a distance or from their hiding places behind storefront windows, townspeople watched but not because they appreciated a good rodeo.

Officer Camacho crossed the street at the corner, walking down the sidewalk towards the circle. I heard grumbling among the bystanders.

"Here she comes," said Martinez. "But she won't do anything."

Among the riders were the shoplifters, but she would be unable to identify them and even if she could she'd be unable to safely make arrests without help.

Her right hand rested on the butt of her gun. Her left arm hung loosely at her side, in a charade of nonchalance. She looked anxious.

A few gang members saw her. Whether out of respect or amusement, they made a space so she could see the spectacle from down the block.

Two horses and their riders fought with horse Barker and rider Billy Bob, ramming them or grabbing and pulling them. Camacho joined the ring of onlookers.

"That's enough," she called out. "You're disturbing the peace."

When one rider, heeding her call dismounted, Billy Bob grabbed the arm of the remaining opponent, and pulled him off his horse. Now, Barker, victorious, his rider still mounted on his back, approached Camacho.

"Good afternoon, Officer," said Barker.

"I'm asking you to disperse," she said.

"Right after my victory round."

Billy Bob began waving one hand over head, yelling "Yahoo!" as Barker high stepped slowly around the inside of the circle of cheering men. He had begun to circle for the second time when Camacho spoke again.

"I told you to disperse."

Only after Barker and rider had completed two more rounds, did they approach her.

"We're just having a little fun, Officer," said Barker. "You're a real spoil sport. But if you insist we'll stop playing."

He turned to the group. "Okay, boys, you heard the officer, we're heading out. After one more victory round."

"No. No more victory rounds," said Camacho.

"What are you going to do, arrest me?"

"If I have to."

Barker held out his wrists, but in doing so his arms encircled Billy Bob's legs even more tightly. Had handcuffs been applied both would be restrained. Some of the others were amused by Camacho's conundrum and laughed.

Camacho bit her lower lip. Barker turned and walked away, delivering Billy Bob to his motorcycle before returning to his own at the head of the line. He raised his hand and bellowed, "Forward ho!"

I thought she'd used good judgment in refraining from handcuffing Barker because of the possible injury to him and to the man on his back if they fell, but she was mortified and angry.

Clyde Cummings came out of hiding to face her.

"That bunch is getting away with murder and you don't seem to be doing anything about it. For crying out loud! Those hoodlums just left with a booty of stolen goods. How many times has this happened? I'm calling the County about this. We need a real policeman."

Several others complained to her as well, though more politely. They were as little afraid of her as were the riders.

"They're out there camping," added Cummings, "so they'll be back for this and that."

She turned and walked away. She did indeed appear ineffectual in this instance. I felt sorry for her.

As in an old Western, the townspeople slowly emerged from their hiding places after the bad men had ridden out of town, their dust settling behind them.

Fuming at my stubbornness, Martinez stomped off.

21

Cricket

Dented, second-hand, copper-bottomed pots dangled from a steel loop on the ceiling of our faded yellow kitchen. The sun was setting over the creosote-dotted landscape. Newly planted prickly pear cacti lined the gravel path to the slightly askew front door of our dilapidated rental house. No coyote calls yet, but they were due in an hour or two.

Mother had prepared hamburgers—though she used a concoction of tofu, black beans, blenderized insects, eggs, and peanut butter rather than beef. She boiled the string beans so long that they had not only given up the ghost—an odd expression I'd learned recently—but also any vitamins they may have hoarded away in their acquisitive little cells. The lemonade, though, had ample sugar and the angel food cake was as fluffy as the box said it would be. Three places were set on an embroidered white Mexican tablecloth, a knife on the right side and a fork on the left of each plastic plate. A small, flowering, prickly pear cactus in a clay pot graced the table.

When I told my parents that Leopold Bloom's daughter Sarah had invited me to a sleepover, Father, continually worried that we would be found out, forbade me from accepting, though I'd told him I already had. We sat at our rickety kitchen table, Father periodically standing, only to sit again.

"You will be exposed to questions you cannot answer—or should not answer," he said. "And your inability to answer these questions will expose us. Do you want the authorities knocking on our door, asking where we came from—where we *really* came from—checking our birth records, going through our belongings, even taking blood samples? Tell the girl your parents said 'no.'"

"Fine! I'll tell her I have a contagious disease that's turning me into a puddle of protoplasm. That I'll soon be oozing along the ground."

Why should I react so angrily when I was, in any case, ambivalent about going? On the other hand, my parents had abducted me and were continually telling me what I must do and what I must not do in this new place. I disliked it.

"Tell her anything you like. You are not going."

"Have you forgotten that I am one of those parents you mentioned?" scolded Mother. "When will you finally accept that the longer we stay isolated, the longer we do not mingle, fit in, the more it will appear that we have something to hide? I say she goes. You know how to answer their questions, Daughter."

"We're from Hawaii," I said. "We moved here because of my pineapple allergy. Do you think they're going to ask for identification at a slumber party?"

The winning argument was that the principal of Prickly Pear High School had probably asked his daughter to invite that odd, new girl to her overnight get-together. My imagination is robust. I could almost hear him say, "Have a heart, Sarah. Give the poor kid a break. She's having a rough time." And I could hear her objection, "She's stuck up. Never talks to anybody."

After being subjected to Mother's logical, hermetically sealed thinking, argued as if her self-esteem depended on her winning the argument, Father, outmaneuvered, finally said, "I yield. Do not allow them to examine your hands and feet."

Two days later, when Mother gave me the pajamas she'd sewn for the occasion, Father again lost his composure. "Is this supposed to be humorous?" he asked irritably. They were red, decorated with little yellow geckos. The sight of these lizards, though they walked on all fours, inevitably elicited in us a wistfulness we preferred not to experience.

"This was the only material available," apologized Mother.

The day of the party, I started off a little late because of Father's last minute nagging. Speak as little as possible. Be vague. Don't do anything strange. Don't talk about us. Eat what they eat. Laugh at what they laugh at, even if you don't understand it—especially if you don't understand it. Agree with them in all things. And then Mother said it was getting late. She would walk with me.

"Yes," said Father. "I will walk with you as well."

"No," I said. "No!"

"But dear one—" began Mother, before I cut her off.

"No! And again no!"

Walking, just ordinary walking, had become one of my few pleasures. Gone was my fear of the open sky. The tingling freshness of cool night air no longer seemed like a warning. I enjoyed the rhythm of my striding body, the thrust of my legs against the ground, the swinging of my arms. How much more aware I was of the senses than I had been in the old body. I had become a sensuous being. That I was also a sensual being I had yet to fully realize.

The town was so small that I could walk everywhere. How particularly sweet a pleasure walking was this evening. I felt like a prisoner released from a cage. Jauntily, I swung my night bag of pajamas and toothbrush. I recalled what Mother had said that first day outside Rosita's restaurant. "We have survived centuries in deep space and a crash landing on a new world. We will survive breakfast."

Yes, and I would survive a brisk evening walk and a slumber party. I was no longer ambivalent. I wanted to go. My heightened alertness was natural, nothing to be alarmed about. I would be in a small room in intimate proximity to humans, but no harm would come to me.

Two blocks from my destination, a residential neighborhood near Sandstone and Rosebush, the ominous rumbling of a motorcycle paralyzed me for a second. It was not Tom's whose engine tone I knew by heart. After a second I strode away.

Levi Barker, turned a corner and zoomed up to me. He came to a halt, dismounted, parked his machine and fell in stride beside me.

"Well, if it isn't Little Red Riding Hood on her way to Grandma's. Brave little girl. But what if the Big Bad Wolf comes to gobble you up?"

He was clearly alluding to some story, probably for children, his tone ironically gentle given that he must see himself as the villain in the story, the wolf.

I took a few steps more when he grabbed my upper arms and swung me around to face him. He was very strong. I held my bag tightly and looked at my bracelet. I was afraid.

"My, but we're impolite. Look at me when I'm talking to you."

There was no one else on the street. I looked at him and considered yelling, but I didn't want to make a commotion. Were my parents to learn of this encounter, even Mother would forever forbid me from walking alone.

I even considered striking him down with a bolt of electromagnetic radiation from my bracelet. The blow would be swift, silent, and certain, but if even one person standing at a window saw him fall someone would come out to help. Maybe two or three. I would be questioned. I was already late for the party. And, stupidly perhaps, my pride entered into the decision not to scream or to strike. Prudence, I thought. I must be prudent.

I looked at him and said, "I'm sorry."

"That's better. You folks are a strange bunch, but I'm a friendly and forgiving guy. Why don't you get on?" he said, nodding towards his motorcycle. "I'll give you a ride. A pretty girl like you shouldn't be out all alone. There really are wolves, you know."

"Please. You are hurting my arms."

He released his grip. "Yeah, well, you were being unfriendly. No reason for that, is there?"

"No, I'm sorry."

"Come on. I'll give you a lift."

What was I to do? I fully understood that he could drive off with me to his desert camp. But after striking him unconscious and escaping, I would have to walk back. Word of my incredible escape would pass from person to person like the common cold. And what if I had to incapacitate the entire gang? What a fascinating idea.

But no. How would I explain these things? Again I considered yelling. Again I heard my parents speak in absolute agreement. I would be under house arrest unless at school or being escorted to and from there. That would be intolerable.

"You promise take me to my destination?"

"Well, of course, sweetheart. What do you think I would do?" He snickered. "Come on. Let's go."

I took the risk.

He put my night bag in the saddlebag, and mounted his steed. I climbed on behind, avoiding contact with him as best I could. Instead of putting my arms around him I held onto the seat with both hands. He followed my directions, but when I told him we'd arrived he ignored me.

"Stop. Please. You promised."

Turning back towards me he said, "Relax. Enjoy yourself. I'm just showing you a good time."

In less than two minutes we were out of town heading into the desert. When he turned up the throttle, the machine jumped forward like an eager beast. Each time I asked him to stop, he accelerated. My bracelet was useless unless I wanted to die, but the thought of using it crossed my mind. The accident though would be horrendous.

So great did our speed become, so powerful the rush of air, that I was forced to put my arms around him for fear my grip on the seat was too feeble and I might fall. As soon as I did, he slowed noticeably and if I held him more tightly he slowed more. He used my fear to make me embrace him. As soon as he stopped I would fell him with the highest intensity shock wave the device could deliver.

Shortly, he made a U-turn, drove back to town, and parked directly in front of the Bloom house. I dismounted promptly but had to wait for him to get my duffle. His grin revolted me. If Claudia merited a stinging revenge for an inconsequential slight, what caliber revenge did this ogre merit? But in front of the house I was harmless.

"Here you are, safe and sound at Grandma's house. Give her my regards."

I no more wanted to make a scene here than I wanted to kiss this monster on the cheek. I almost choked on it, but forced myself to say, "Yes, thank you." Death and decay! His time would come.

The girls, already in pajamas, had been sitting at the kitchen table gawking out the front window. Levi Barker waved a jolly goodbye as I ran up to the house.

Mrs. Bloom opened the front door. I think Barker remained on the street long enough to be sure everyone saw him.

"Good evening, Mrs. Bloom. I am sorry I am late."

"Hello, Cricket. Uh...is he a friend of yours?"

"No!"

"I see."

But she did not see. Nor did the others.

Safely inside I allowed, or tried to allow, my face to relax. I loosened my grip on my night bag and unclenched my free hand. I took deep breaths, exhaling slowly. I would not cry, quashing the inclination with adrenaline animated visions of revenge. He would be knocked down repeatedly, but that would not be enough. He would grovel through town dressed in diapers. But that would not be enough...

How much more powerfully this new body responded to threat than the original. What a capacious vessel for emotions it was. Losing my original body, I lost that cool disposition, especially toward threats.

I entered the kitchen. My smile must have appeared as if I'd just heard a tasteless joke. Indeed, I'd just been subjected to one.

Here was officious Sarah, in brown pigtails, who was well behaved at school but had a reputation for being "wild" behind the scene. Smiling Melissa, black bangs almost covering her eyebrows, genuinely happy to see me. Earnest Hayley, the gymnast, brushing her fingers through hair freed from its confining bun. Facetious Nicole, in striped pajamas that could not be called Gothic, her dark hair cut short, thrumming the table with two fingers, her face unpowdered, lips without lipstick. And—wouldn't you know it—my adversary, Claudia, her curly, black hair, cascading well over her shoulders, framing her pretty—or so thought the boys—face. Why did I pay such attention to their hair? Because mine was a wig and I'd become self-conscious about it. Tonight, Father had made certain that it was firmly affixed to my scalp, which later would prove prescient.

Their expectant faces calmed me more than my own attempts.

They warmed me up like heat lamps. I was suffused with gratitude. My harrowing encounter was over with. I must exist in the present.

They greeted me and made a place for me at the table, which was part of a breakfast nook. Rolling her eyes, Claudia looked around the table, then at me.

"You should have invited your boyfriend in."

"He is not my boyfriend. He made me ride. I don't like him."

"You don't like him?" said Claudia. "We all just adore him, don't we?"

"Oh, yes," said Nicole. "He's Prince Charming all right, once you get over the body odor and the chewing tobacco."

"He made you ride with him? How'd he do that?" asked Hayley.

"By force."

"Why didn't you run?"

Father's words of advice came to me, though he had another subject in mind. Be vague.

"It is hard to explain," I said.

They pummeled me with questions. Where did the ride start? Did I hold on to him? How fast did he go? Were the others with him? Here vagueness would not do. Thankfully, Melissa spoke up.

"Let's leave her be. She looks like she's in shock."

So, they could see it. I said, "Thank you."

"Do you know what he does to girls if he gets his hands on them?" asked Claudia. "I won't use the word but it's very ugly. He did that to a girl last year, but she was afraid to tell the police. It was foolish of you to trust him, if I do say so. Any girl who rides with that creep should have her head examined."

I touched my temples with my fingertips. I walked my fingers to the top of my head and down again, pushing, palpating, probing. I felt my forehead and my ears, then I placed my palms on my crown before ending the examination of my head.

The girls laughed. Claudia tried to suppress a smile.

"It's not a laughing matter," she said.

"Oh, come on now," said Nicole. "Let it ride."

"Okay." She sighed to no one in particular.

Before dinner, Sarah took me upstairs so I could change into pajamas. Dinner was served when I returned to the table. We devoured two and a half pizzas, two quarts of soda, and a homemade apple pie with vanilla ice cream. I said little while the girls chattered about school and family vacations.

I was experiencing a pleasant emotion I don't remember having experienced before. Affection for them? But I could only count Melissa as a friend, though Nicole did talk with me from time to time. I would have to ask myself later what sort of relationship I'd had before with my friends on Sassatha.

They asked me about Hawaii. Did I surf? It sounded like "serve." Did I serve what I asked. The girls laughed, taking this as a modest "yes." Had I learned the hula? Again I had no idea what they were referring to. Were I to scan for it, my eyes would twitch back and forth. An epileptic seizure would appear imminent. But if I continued being vague or nonsensical they might doubt I was from Hawaii.

"Yes, I learned the hula."

"Will you show us?" asked Melissa.

"Another time."

Sarah's parents had offered up the master bedroom for the night so there would be ample room for all of us to sleep on mattresses spread out on the floor. We sat cross-legged in a circle facing each other. A motionless gecko clung to a wall two inches from the ceiling.

Claudia wanted someone to chase it away, but the other girls said it wasn't hurting anyone and we should leave it alone. Melissa said they ate insects.

I expected Claudia to say, "crickets" but she didn't.

Sarah said, "My dad will catch it later. We'll keep it for a pet. They're good pets."

"I think that's cruel," said Melissa.

I thought so too but said nothing. The girls began talking about the upcoming Halloween dance, who their dates were, if they had dates. What costumes they might wear and what they might do after the dance.

"You're new in town and already have a boyfriend," said Nicole, winking at me. "I mean Tom, not Barker. Fast worker."

"Tom's a cutie, too," said Melissa softly.

"He's not her boyfriend," said Claudia. "Sarah's dad asked him to show her around because she's new here. Isn't that right, Cricket?"

She spoke the word "Cricket" as if it were a curse, and, in a way it was.

From time to time this new body of mine seemed a separate entity, unwilling to submit to my wishes. I sensed the heat of my blossoming blush and I didn't like it. My old body had no such reactions.

"That is right."

After a moment of silence Sarah said, "Let's play a game. How about quack diddly oh so?"

"That's like from middle school," said Hayley. "I have a better idea. Volleyball. All we need is a balloon, which I brought, and some rope, which I also brought."

Hayley, self-appointed captain of her team, chose Sarah and Claudia to play against Melissa, Nicole and me. The rope was strung across the room about four feet from the floor. We lay on our backs on either side of the "net" and kicked the balloon over it with our bare feet. Hayley, the gymnast, was well coordinated and Claudia was too. My teammates were not.

"To me! To me!" yelled Hayley to her teammates.

The most common refrain from Nicole and Melissa was, "Oops. Sorry."

The score was four to zero when my competitive nature took charge. I stopped using the tips of my toes. Allowing my setae into play, I held the balloon with the sole of my right foot, and tapped in over the net with the toes of my left foot. We quickly evened the score and moved on to victory. After the rematch, which we also won, Claudia and Sarah had had enough.

Hayley said, "How the heck do you do that?"

"I play much in Hawaii," I said, absurdly.

"I know a kissing game we can play," said Melissa.

"I'm not kissing anybody," said Claudia.

"How about Tom?" said Nicole.

"Oh, is he under the bed?"

"I hid him in the closet," said Nicole. "I hope that's all right."

"Now listen," said Melissa. "It's not like that. We each put lipstick on and then we kiss a piece of paper. Then we mix up the papers and we have to guess whose kiss is whose."

Sarah got a couple of bright red lipsticks, two hand mirrors, and six three-by-five inch index cards. We turned around, backs towards each other, while the lipstick and mirrors were passed around. After my lips were covered, my tongue flicked out, as of old, and touched the lipstick. Inexperienced as I was with kissing, indeed essentially ignorant of the mechanics of it, I made a wide-open oval of my mouth, pressing it against the card. My tongue made a pink spot in the middle. Sarah collected the cards in a straw hat.

She laid them out on the floor and immediately the girls began to laugh.

"Someone's big into French kissing," said Sarah pointing at my card.

"It's you, isn't it, Claudia?" said Nicole.

"Wrong. I think it's Sarah. She's trying to put us off."

"Not me," said Sarah.

I was the last person they guessed. All the other cards looked more or less the same, with tightly puckered lip prints, so the rest of the guessing took some time. I'd learned what French kissing was.

Hayley showed us some yoga positions. We stood on our heads, or tried to. My wig stayed put. We did play quack diddly oh so, which I learned after two rounds. We played truth or dare in which we learned that Nicole liked Rick; that Ms. Hardy was the teacher Claudia hated most; that Hayley wouldn't tell us if she'd petted with Dave, so had to get dressed and then do a strip tease; that Sarah had a bottle of coffee liqueur in the room; that Melissa had once had her period in church; that I didn't want to say whether I was a virgin or not, so had to sing a song. (I didn't know what "virgin" meant and couldn't scan for it in front of them.)

I said I'd wait until Sarah returned from the kitchen with a bottle of milk and some glasses before singing. I went to the bathroom, locked the door, and scanned for a song. My eyes jiggled from side to side as I accessed the implanted neurotransponder network. I found what I needed in seconds.

They applauded me, even Claudia, after I sang "Goodnight Irene." And then, as Sarah put it, we got down to some serious drinking. Before pouring the coffee liqueur and milk into our glasses, she asked us to put our hands over our hearts and swear that we would never tell.

"The heart's on the left side, Cricket," said Claudia.

I said, "Thank you." And repositioned my hand.

The drink was tasty and very sweet. Sarah had made it strong. After two large drinks we were all giggling. Melissa told a joke about two whales at a bar, which I didn't understand but it was funny anyway. Nicole made noises like the passing of gas and we joined in until we were all doubled up with belly laughter. Sarah told a gruesome ghost story, but that, too, seemed hilarious. Nicole described how her father had caught her in the back seat of the family car, smooching with a boy. The car was in the garage. Eventually we began to tire. One by one we lay down, pulling light blankets over us. Sarah turned the lights off.

In the morning when the girls went downstairs for a late breakfast, I said I was going to the bathroom first. The gecko had not moved all night. I suspected it was ill, though that may have been projection since I had a slight headache myself. I placed my left hand on the wall, then the toes and ball of my right foot. I climbed, right hand, left foot, left hand, right foot, up to the gecko, but as I reached out, it moved onto the ceiling. I had my left hand on the ceiling, when Claudia, returning for something or other, appeared in the doorway.

Her mouth dropped open. She gasped. I sprang to the floor, landing in a crouch. I stood up and said, "Good morning." She scampered down the stairs to the breakfast table. The gecko was in the middle of the ceiling as I went down to the kitchen.

Claudia had not yet taken a seat. She stood before the table addressing the girls like a prosecutor in front of a jury, though the jury was about to eat.

"You won't believe what I just saw. Cricket climbed the wall up to the ceiling."

I joined the group at the table as if nothing had happened. On my plate were two pancakes and two strips of bacon. Sarah poured me a cup of coffee. I put the bacon aside, hoping I would not appear unappreciative, but I would not eat the flesh of higher animals, particularly not mammalian flesh.

"I swear. All the way to the ceiling! It was completely... completely...demonic. Hey, listen to me everybody." A trace of the hysterical tinged her speech.

Sarah whispered, "Not so loud. Mom and Dad will hear. Did you drink more Kahlua this morning while we were sleeping? They'll skin me alive if they find out we had alcohol."

"You don't believe me," said Claudia.

Hayley, in her capacity as gymnast, turned to me.

"Did you climb up the wall?"

"Yes," I said.

"Okay," said Hayley. "We believe you, Claudia."

"You're not lying, are you?" said Nicole with a mischievous smile. "It's not right to lie."

"I am not lying," I said. "I climb to the ceiling."

"How did you do it?" asked Hayley. "My parents make me want to climb the wall sometimes."

They were having fun at Claudia's expense. Confused and angry, she sat as far from me as possible, asking Hayley to scoot over to make a place for her. She said not another word for the rest of the meal.

Seeing how upset Claudia was, Melissa said, "Maybe that's enough." They now spoke of their favorite breakfasts and asked how much bacon was left. Melissa passed me a dish stacked with sweet, juicy yellow rings with holes in the middle. I put a couple on top of my pancakes. They were delicious. Sarah and Claudia took note, puzzled. But they said nothing, and I was unaware of my error as I had never seen a pineapple entire or in slices.

When Sarah was sure everything necessary was on the table, she sat next to me.

"You know, Cricket, you're a lot of fun. Who would have guessed? You didn't exactly make a good impression when you started school."

I thanked her and told her she was a lot of fun, too, and thanked her again for inviting me.

"I'll be honest. It was my father's idea, but I'm really glad I did."

"Me, too," said Melissa. Hayley and Nicole nodded, their mouths full of pancake. Claudia glowered at me, but I no longer felt hostility toward her. In fact, I was sorry for her. No one would ever believe what she saw, I thought, but I was wrong.

22

_____

Cricket

S aturday morning, Tom came over for my first motorcycle lesson, but he was in a foul mood. I'd seen him coming and had stepped out of the house into the front yard, Mother's Japanese rock garden, whose raked sand and artfully placed stones, suggested a tranquility none of us possessed.

Instead of coming up the walkway, he remained standing by his motorcycle. Curtly, he crooked his finger at me to come over.

"I'm only here because I promised. Frankly, I'd like to call the whole thing off. Don't you have any sense or does everyone from Hawaii have a screw loose? What were you doing riding around town with that thug? Will you explain that to me?"

I was taken aback by the sharpness of his voice. Of course, I knew that Barker had taken girls for joyrides that held no joy for them, as everyone was fond of saying.

"He made me," was all I could say at the moment.

"It didn't seem that way. You looked perfectly comfortable with him. He dropped you off at Bloom's and waved goodbye, didn't he?"

I had taken a risk, I admitted. A cry for help might have freed me from his grasp, but only by calling people out into the street to witness the danger I was in. My parents would hear of it and would forbid me from ever again walking the streets alone, day or night. That I was certain I could have struck him down with one electromagnetic blow, I did not mention.

He turned away from me, looking north into the desert. Released from his binding gaze, I had a moment to think. His back was still towards me when I asked, "Who told you this?" I knew the answer before he spoke.

Facing me again, he said, "What does it matter?"

"Tell me."

"Claudia."

I sighed.

He glared at me, but I was not deterred.

"Teach me to ride."

Grudgingly he handed me the spare helmet. From his saddlebag he removed a leather jacket fitted with plastic armor for elbows, shoulders, and back.

He wanted to help me with the helmet, but I took it in hand.

"I must do myself."

Without prelude, I pointed to and named the parts of the machine.

"Here, the clutch. Brake lever. Rear brake pedal. Shifter. Pegs. Light control. Throttle. Here, lights. Low beam. High beam. Hazard light. Turn signals."

"You've been studying," he said, his voice less hostile.

"Yes. YouTube."

I straddled the machine.

He watched as I moved the shifter down one click and then up five clicks. To confirm the motorcycle was in neutral, I pushed it forward several feet.

"You say you've never been on a motorcycle before?"

"I have never."

He straddled the bike, sat in front of me, and drove out of town to a suitable cross roads in the desert with very little traffic. We dismounted.

"Okay. Go slow," he said gruffly.

Over the next two hours I tirelessly practiced shifting gears, accelerating, braking, turning. Tom's tone remained gruff.

Back at the house, I noticed Mother and Father peeking at us through the window. Tom noticed, too.

"Spies," I said, trying to lighten the mood with humor.

"What are they spying on?"

"Me."

He looked thoughtful, but he wasn't thinking about this silliness.

"The next time you see that bum, you disappear. Do you understand?"

"I understand."

Later, alone in my room, I was forced to admit to myself what I'd felt since I first saw him. Curses! I was attracted to him. I looked at him longer than I should. I wanted to be near him, to touch him or have him touch me. What was worse, I was fond of him, and worse still, I had made the acquaintance of what is referred to in English as "the green-eyed monster."

I also wondered if his concern over my riding with Barker was more than the ordinary concern he would have had for any girl in that situation. Was he particularly worried about me? Ooo. That was a nice thought.

————

Tom

I had to admit she'd gotten under my skin. But she didn't like me too much. And who could blame her? What girl would ever be attracted to me again. Claudia had drifted away. That was for sure. Yeah, we still did things together from time to time, but she was more interested in Rick now.

Another depressing idea. For a while I thought Cricket got her interest in motorcycles from me, but now I wondered if it wasn't after seeing that gang on their Harleys. Seeing that asshole on his. Did she want to ride to impress Barker? Oh God. The thought made me sick.

23

Cricket

Father had been more unsettled by Cummings' confrontation at Hoppy's gas station than was evident even in his constant entreaties, pleadings, solicitations that we act "normal." He'd begun to think of taking us elsewhere. In Southern California the only feasible way of going elsewhere was to drive.

When he announced he was going to get a driver's license, I asked to go with him, already thinking of getting a motorcycle license myself. I wished to see what might be involved. And, to be forthright, I wanted to see what lay outside confining, little, run-down Prickly Pear.

The irony of breaking the law by driving without a license to obtain a license so that he could drive without breaking the law, escaped neither of us. Hoppy Jones lent him a car and told him not to worry. There would be little traffic on the road and Watson was as likely to be stopped by the police as he was to be abducted by aliens. Why did people keep making stupid jokes about aliens?

Yet so apprehensive was Father that, as we drove off, he appeared to rapidly swivel his head back and forth through a physiologically impossible 360 degree angle. He was in search of "the law." I worried he might twist his head off or detach a cervical ligament. Only after we were a few miles out of town did the head twisting became less frequent as he allowed me to become his lookout, though what he might do if I saw a police car was uncertain since he always drove below the speed limit.

I now dared to speak. "Where are we going?"

"We have the great good fortune to be traveling to the Twentynine Palms Department of Motor Vehicles at the corner of Adobe Road and Indian Trail. I say good fortune because most of this trip is through sparsely inhabited territory."

"So we will not be seen."

"Exactly that, Daughter. You are astute when you wish to be. Our good fortune extends beyond the sparsity of habitation on our trip. You may be pleased to know that the building housing the motor vehicle office also houses a pizza restaurant, sandwich shop, and tattoo parlor."

"What sort of tattoo would you suggest for me, Father?"

"Naturally an ordinary tattoo as might be displayed by an ordinary person on an ordinary part of their anatomy."

"A butterfly on my posterior?"

"Let me consider it. In the meanwhile, see if you can identify someone for us to abduct, preferably a pleasant person with access to strawberry ice cream."

So we passed the time indulging ourselves in whimsy, which had been so lacking in our day-to-day lives. When had I last enjoyed Father's company? I couldn't remember for certain.

After approximately two hours we arrived at a long, low-slung building, roofed with overlapping red tiles. A covered walkway flanking it was entered through one of the sixty or seventy archways around the building. The excessively large parking lot was surrounded by desert. The town itself was further south.

The pizza restaurant and the tattoo parlor were indeed in the same building as the DMV, but the sandwich shop was across the parking lot in a small separate building.

"This Department of Motor Vehicles is, as they say, in the middle of nowhere, conceivably reducing the risk to pedestrians of new drivers, I suppose."

I read a brochure on motorcycle safety while Father took the written examination.

Larry Lopez, the examiner, a portly, older man with round perspiration patches on his shirt around the axillae, almost forbade me from riding along for the driving test.

"I could get in trouble for this, but your papa got a perfect score on the written test. Get in."

I climbed into the back seat.

Father adjusted the rearview mirrors and the seat. He tested the blinkers. He touched the safety brake to demonstrate he knew where it was and he turned around to check that I had my seatbelt on, even after I assured him I did. He pulled on Lopez's belt to be sure it was fastened. Would he get out and take the engine apart?

"Watson Sminth, is it? That's an unusual name," said Mr. Lopez. "Bet people call you Smith all the time."

"Indeed, they do."

Lopez glanced at his clipboard.

"All right. You can pull out here and make a right turn. I'll give you directions as we go."

Father put on the turn signal while also signaling out the open window with his arm, and looking to see if it was safe to go. He pulled out onto Adobe Road."

"We're going downtown where there are a few stop lights and a bit more traffic."

Father drove to Del Valle Drive, turned left, then turned right on First Street, did a couple of parking maneuvers, a Y-turn, a U-turn and we were finished.

"You know the way back to the office?"

"It is merely a few miles south of here on Adobe Road," said Father.

"That's the ticket."

We'd been out on the open road for less than a minute, when I, still in scout mode, saw in the distance a line of black-clad motorcyclists. They were approaching rapidly.

"Father—" I began.

"I see them," he said.

Mr. Lopez turned around to look through the rear window. "Just hope it's not the Hoods."

A moment later I told him it was. Yes, this was the collection of reprobates our family had so grown to admire. And the chief reprobate was in the lead.

"Should I perhaps pull off to the side of the road?" asked Father.

"I don't think so. They'll just pass, maybe give us the finger if they're in a good mood."

Quietly I undid my seat beat and knelt on the floor. I did not wish to see those criminals. Less so did I wish them to see me. But curiosity overcame caution, and I peeked out the window.

Barker began to pass, coming very close to the car. I resumed my hidden position.

"You know him?" Lopez asked Father. "He waved."

I took another quick look. He and the gang had dropped back and were following us.

Father had been watching him through the rearview mirror. Lopez, his body contorted, had been watching him, too.

"He just pumped his fist up and down. Christ! Excuse me miss. The signal—whatever the hell it means—is going down the line. He's reaching back for something. I think it's...It looks like a crowbar. Why the hell would he have a...."

Barker did not display an upright middle finger as he accelerated and passed by. Instead, with both daring and skill, he came close enough to the car to scrape the crowbar along its entire length, producing the prolonged cry of a screech owl.

"That son of a bitch," cursed Lopez.

With Barker past, I was slightly more audacious in my spying, but as the next rider began to pass, I again crouched as low as I could. Billy Bob struck the passenger window with a long chain, a spider web of small cracks forming instantly.

Father, remaining silent. Rather than allowing further damage to the car, he directed it onto the soft shoulder, slowed further, and then drove several yards into the desert, out of reach of the marauders. The three of us watched as the troop grew smaller in the distance and disappeared.

Back at the office Lopez asked if Father knew the hoodlum.

"We are acquainted. I believe his dislikes me."

"Dislikes you? Hell, he must hate your guts."

"His dislike is not limited to my gastrointestinal tract."

"You're a cool cucumber if you can joke about this. When are you going to report it?"

Father, I knew, would not report the incident because, even were Barker arrested and go to jail, a trial would threaten us from another direction. I could hear the defense attorney.

"You told Mr. Lopez that this was your first driver's license. Mr. Sminth, is it not conceivable that as a new driver you came out of your lane, threatening to sideswipe the members of the motorcycle club? Or, if you knew how to drive, why at your age was this your first driver's license? Didn't you have one in Hawaii? What did you do there? What was your address? Can you give us any character references?" etc.

"When are *you* going to report it?" asked Father

Clearly embarrassed, Lopez admitted that he was afraid of retaliation, a fear widespread in the Mohave Desert area. Everyone knew Barker. Everyone feared him. And he was too smart to be caught in flagrante delicto by the police.

———

"Vicious," said Mother on hearing the story.

Father said, "I would add evil, villainous, reckless, destructive, daring, foolhardy, immature, criminal, and vulgar."

"How are you feeling, husband?"

"I have never been so angry in my life."

———

When his permanent driver's license arrived, he made an announcement towards the end of dinner.

"Tomorrow I purchase a shotgun. You may object. You may think me a romantic, a thinker of shapeless thoughts, but I am adamant in my decision. I request that you do not try to dissuade me."

Though I had not kept a tally, I believed that Mother prevailed in most disagreements with Father. But here she was too wise to let even a puff of doubt escape into the air. She simply touched his hand.

"I would like to go with you," I said.

"Did you know that the passenger next to the driver is said to be 'riding shotgun'? Your presence could only be a good omen, though I do not believe in omens, of course."

There was no levity or whimsical wordplay on this drive. Instead Father, preoccupied with the subject, talked to me about shotguns. After our outing with Mr. Martinez, he had learned more about them.

"It is a gun for the short-range shooting of small spherical pellets called shot through a smooth bore barrel. Each pellet receives a fraction of the power of the explosion making the energy of a single pellet low."

"Among the types are break-action, pump-action, lever-action, semi automatic, and bolt-action."

"Thank you, Father. The school I attend has completely failed to provide this information."

"I asked you to indulge me."

"You are right. I apologize."

———

Peering through the window of Johnny's Gun and Ammo Shop, Father asked me whether I thought a shotgun would make our family more secure. Before I could respond, he said, "Why should it not?"

A bell rang as we entered.

At least thirty assorted rifles, shotguns, and semiautomatic assault weapons stood at attention on a rack along one wall. Another thirty or so hand guns lay cozily on blue velvet in a long, glass topped display case.

A lean man, with a nose that had been broken more than once, came striding toward him. He shirt was military style with epaulets.

"I'm Johnny," he'd said. "Have anything special in mind?"

"I would like to purchase the least expensive break-action shotgun you have and ten shotgun shells."

"I've got a 12-gauge, break-action gun for $225. Used. Only ten shells? What are you going to do with it?"

"I am going to shoot ten jackrabbits."

"You must be a damn good shot."

"Fair."

On the counter now lay a 12-gauge, pump-action Marcus and Cooper shotgun, and ten red shotgun shells. Johnny gave a form to Father and handed him a pen.

"Just fill that out, please."

The form asked for his name, address, height, weight, sex, and birthdate, and a long series of other questions. Was he buying the gun for someone else? Had he been convicted of a felony? Was he a fugitive from justice? Was he addicted to drugs? Was he mentally defective? He answered all honestly except for two, hesitating before checking off his race, not because he was not even human, but because one of the choices was "Native Hawaiian or other Pacific Islander." He chose it. He also lied when asked, "Are you an alien illegally in the United States." The word "illegally" was printed in bold letters.

Johnny read the completed form and asked for Father's I.D. He looked at it, at Father, at the I. D. again, and frowned.

"Your hair's a different color than in the photo," he said.

"Yes. It is a different wig," said Father.

"Oh."

A few minutes after entering some data from the form into the National Instant Criminal Background Check System, Johnny received some data in return.

"Hmm," said Johnny, looking at the screen. "You ever go by Winton Smith, or Winston Smith, or Wesley, or Weston, or Whitson?"

"Go by them? I do not know your meaning. I've never even heard of them?"

"Just trying to be careful."

After we left, the owner had become suspicious and called the officer assigned to Prickly Pear. This was understandable given that the purchaser's name was Sminth. He wore a blond wig. Marked Polynesian as his race. And purchased only ten shells. We did know this at the time, of course.

24

Cricket

Astute Melissa had discerned my developing feelings for Tom. How embarrassing that other people, too, might be as discerning. At our next English lesson, she asked why I wasn't ordering a chocolate shake. When I shrugged, she gently probed.

"Lost your appetite for sweets, huh? That's a bad sign. Unless you're on a diet, and believe me, if there's anyone who doesn't need to diet, it's you."

Her eyes fixed on me, she took a delicate sip, then pulled the straw out of the glass and plunged it back in as if spearing a fish.

"You won't get anywhere with him if you don't go."

My English was getting better by the day, but idioms had to be learned by rote. I was puzzled.

"I mean to the dance," she added.

"Get anywhere with him? What is that?"

She explained what it meant. She told me that he'd asked Claudia to the Halloween dance at the beginning of the school year. She warned me against allowing jealousy to cloud my judgment. I must go to the dance. I must show an interest in one of the boys. Rick would be a good choice. She'd help me with my makeup. I'd look gorgeous. Oh, and I should go as a hula dancer to show off my figure. Her interest in me was moving, her animation captivating.

"Why I should show interest in Rick?"

"Are you really this naïve? Now don't tell me girls from your planet don't scheme." She chuckled, amused by her little joke.

"I'll give you the benefit of the doubt. Now listen carefully."

She leaned over the table and in a whisper said, "You want to make him as jealous of Rick as you are of Claudia. Show him you're having a wonderful time. Show him you couldn't care less that he's with Claudia. Make him want you."

Another sip of milkshake and she continued. "I don't believe I have to be this graphic. Are you for real?"

It is tautological to say that only humans have human nature. Even our most advanced computers did not understand what this girl understood, could not teach me what this girl was teaching me. And she would help me with my make-up. I ordered a chocolate shake.

Father, relieved that I would be riding in Melissa's car rather than walking, relented, allowing the witch, as she now appeared, into the house the night of the dance. Anything whose provenance was not of the Earth, was hidden from sight.

"I look wicked I know, but I have my good side. Tonight I'm your fairy godmother. Let the magic begin."

The artist and her canvas—me—sat at the kitchen table. Melissa had a basket filled with a dazzling array of eyeliners, eye shadow, eyelash enhancers, lipsticks, rouge, glitter, powders, perfumes, brushes, applicators, tweezers, and sprays. She'd also brought a large hand mirror, but kept it out of my reach until she was finished. Mother, fascinated, hovered about us, but sagely made no comments.

Blue eye shadow seemed to enlarge and deepen my blue eyes. Deep pink lipstick made my lips even more kissable said Melissa. My cheeks took on a rouge blush. My hair was off limits, though. I'd chosen my formal wig, the hair braided and pinned on the top of my head.

My midriff was bare, framed by a synthetic grass skirt below and a multi-flowered top above. My lei matched my lipstick. I wore sandals.

Days before she'd told me of the secret arrangement she'd made with the D.J., Daryl Jones, her brother. When I objected, she'd scolded me, "I know what I'm doing. Just do as I tell you, okay?" Yielding, I had done the required research and practiced what I'd learned.

"All right. Let me see how you look."

She whistled as I walked around the kitchen, swaying my hips.

"You have a figure to die for. Did you know that?"

Father came in to look at me.

"Very good. You look Hawaiian." Father had said something positive for once. This must be propitious.

"Thank you, Father."

As Melissa and I walked to her car my parents stood in the front yard, waving as if I were going away on a long trip, though "long" is a relative term, as I well knew.

The application of my makeup had taken longer than expected because Melissa was satisfied only with perfection. Deciding on the right amount of glitter around my eyes had taken time. We arrived a little late.

The gymnasium's overhead lights were dimmed. Its floor of polished blond hardwood was as dear to Mr. Bloom as were the eucalyptus trees. Dancers were required to take off their shoes. Most wore socks, some were barefoot.

Everyone was in costume, including the chaperones. Twenty or so couples were already dancing. Others stood at the periphery or at the refreshment table, which had been covered with blue crepe paper, with punch bowls at either end. A small stage had been built for the disc jockey. Disco dance music blared from two powerful speakers.

The style of dance, for lack of a better word, was freestyle, with much extension and flexing of limbs, thrusting of pelvises, and stepping to a beat that even a deaf person could hear.

We went to the refreshment table for a drink and to observe. Nicole, in a skintight blue suit was a comic book super hero—heroine —of one type or another. She was sipping from a plastic cup.

"You look good," said Melissa.

"You too," said Nicole. "You too Cricket."

I looked around the dance floor. Claudia was unmistakable as—no surprise—a princess in a long, blue, off-the-shoulder dress, which flared when she spun. Martinez wore boots, dark brown tights, a long-sleeved white shirt covered by a close-fitting, green, sleeveless vest, and a little canoe-shaped green hat with a feather in it.

Claudia had her back towards him, periodically nudging him in the area of the groin with her rear end. How grateful I was for my rouge camouflage, though the lights were dim enough to hide the flush in my face.

"What is he?" I asked.

"What is who?" said Melissa.

I pointed.

"Tom?"

"Yes."

"I'm not sure. Robin Hood maybe? Peter Pan?"

Three boys, having worked up the courage to approach us, asked us to dance. Melissa and Nicole accepted. I demurred, saying I'd like a drink first. Taking the dipper in hand, I filled a glass to the brim. The boy, Gary, introduced himself, tried to engage me in conversation and then wandered off in search of a partner. I felt bad, but Melissa's instructions were explicit. In ones and twos, boys approached me, boys I recognized but who'd never spoken a word to me before. I smiled at them and made a big show of sipping my drink.

When Rick finally approached me, I was ready, though my drink was untouched. He wore a long cape, black on the outside, red on the inside, over a double-breasted black suit. Most striking were his long, pointed fangs.

"Hi, Cricket. I'm Dracula. Would you like to dance?"

I extended my hand. He led me to the middle of the dance floor. Freestyle dancing was not that difficult. The pulsating beat practically did the dancing for me. I simply had to trust my body to move to the music. My head and chest bobbed forward to the beat as I stepped and touched to the side, crossing and uncrossing my arms. As I became more comfortable I began tensing and relaxing my muscles. I turned one way, then another, then around in a circle.

He attempted to talk with me, but I just smiled and kept dancing. When we took a break at the refreshment table I had little excuse not to respond, though I did not understand his allusions.

"I like your costume," said Rick. And then, with what I learned was supposed to be a Romanian accent, he said, "And I like your neck."

"Thank you."

"May I take a bite?"

"Later."

He dropped his accent and said, "Really?"

Tom came over to talk.

"Hi, Cricket. Rick."

"I was telling her I'd like a bite of her neck."

Rick talking like this was, Melissa told me later, "Just what the doctor ordered."

Slipping back into his accent, he said, "And she said I could, too. I've always wanted to taste the blood of a hula girl."

Tom had never lacked for words before. He was clearly unhappy with this talk. When he asked me to dance, I hesitated.

"She's with me," said Rick.

"Are you?" he asked.

"We can dance," I said.

He took my hand.

The current record ended. A so-called oldie came on, as if Daryl knew what to do, a slow piece called Earth Angel, which I found ironic. It was over half a century old. This was a style of dance I was unfamiliar with as I'd never had a flesh and blood partner on Sassatha. Tom put his hand in the small of my back up against my bare skin and pulled me to him. I put both hands on his shoulders, giving us a frame so he could lead.

When he'd first put that helmet on my head, touching my face with his long fingers in the process, I had experienced a delicious sensation like a rising wave of warmth. Successfully I had put it out of my mind. I have a strong will, but the feeling now returned. And the lyrics heightened the feeling.

Earth Angel,
Earth Angel,
Will you be mine?

My darling dear,
Love you all the time.
I'm just a fool,
A fool in love with you.

I was hoping these were his thoughts. Fire and Ice! I liked this boy too much. Claudia stood with a group of girls staring at us. Could her glare have done what it bespoke, I would have turned to stone.

"Watch out for him," said Tom. "He'll paw you if he can."

"You dance with me to warn me? That is considerate of you," I said, as sardonically as I could, though I wasn't very good at these intonations.

When the music ended, and another song came on, he looked at Claudia and then back at me.

"Do you want another motorcycle lesson?"

I shrugged. Rick appeared. Claudia took Tom by the hand and pulled him away.

For the next hour or so, Rick and I danced. Fortunately, the music was too loud for us to do much more than exchange a few words.

Perhaps forty-five minutes before the dance was to end, Daryl made an announcement.

"We have a little surprise. A treat as it were. All the way from Hawaii. Would Ms. Sminth come up here please?"

As I ascended the six wood steps to the platform, my heart beat as if I were about to run a gauntlet of Heaven's Hoods. Did the teachers and students see my trembling, I wondered. I cursed Melissa for doing this. People moved forward, their curiosity piqued. I looked over the crowd.

Daryl asked if I were ready. I whispered yes. Ukulele music filled the gymnasium. I began the hula, swaying my hips, moving my arms and hands to tell the story as I sang. I had not expected the wolf whistles and bursts of spontaneous applause, but I was essentially in a trance. They did not bother me.

Pearly shells from the ocean
Shining in the sun, covering the shore;
When I see them

My heart tells me that I love you
More than all those little pearly shells.
For every grain of sand upon the beach,
I've got a kiss for you.
And I've got more left over for each star
That twinkles in the blue.

I looked at my audience. Tom was at the very front. He was smiling so broadly I could see most of his teeth. Near the back stood Claudia, a blank expression on her face. She was looking at Tom, not at me.

As soon as I finished I left the platform. No bow. No acknowledgment of the loud applause.

People crowded around me. Someone said, "So you really are from Hawaii." "That was beautiful," said someone else. Several times I heard the word "sexy."

Daryl put on another disco tune. I made my way to the refreshment stand through a throng of people who wished to speak with me, so that my progress was slow.

Sarah, Nicole, and Hayley pushed their way through to me.

"You're a kick," said Nicole.

I was happy to see them. We chattered about the fun we'd had at the sleepover, laughed again about the vulgar noises we'd made, and games we'd played. Ms. Hardy, dressed as a dragon, came up to tell me how much she'd liked my dance. Mr. Gonzalez, a pirate, asked if I'd taken lessons. I told him I had.

The lights flickered signaling the end of the dance. The crowd began to thin. Melissa appeared. She'd extended the thumb and little finger of her right hand, the three middle fingers curled, and rotated the hand back and forth. It meant something, but I had no idea what.

She whispered in my ear. "Claudia's gone home with Rick. Just hang loose, okay?"

"Hang loose?"

"A fine Hawaiian you are. Never mind. You were great. Absolutely great. I'll see you on Monday."

"But aren't you driving me home?"

"I don't think so."

Only ten to fifteen students remained, and teachers were shooing them out. Melissa walked with me to the exit. Tom was waiting for me at the door.

"Hey, Cricket, would it be okay if I walked you home?"

"Good night," said Melissa to the two of us.

25

Cricket

Until we passed Arroyo and Sandstone, three blocks from the school, we had walked wordlessly, the waxing crescent moon accompanying us. Street lights were more abundant in the small town center. It was darker here; few lights shone in the windows of the houses in the rundown part of town where I lived. The streets were empty.

I surprised and disappointed myself by speaking first.

"Why you are not with Claudia?"

"Uh, we had a little argument."

I wished to know the subject of the argument, but I did not wish to ask about it. Indeed, I was not yet prepared to speak with him despite my pleasure with his unexpected company.

"Are you cold?" he asked.

"No." I had a jacket with me.

By and by we arrived at my house, having said nothing further. Here the lights *were* on. My parents, perpetually worrying, were visible peeking out from behind the curtains. How long had they been there? What had they been worrying about?

Tom saw them too.

"Could we walk a little longer?" he asked.

"I wave at them. I wish you also to wave at them also." I had added another "also" for emphasis.

We waved and walked on.

"She said some nasty things about you and I said they weren't true, but the straw that broke the camel's back was my going up to the stage to get a better look at you like every other boy in the place. She didn't want me to take her home after that."

The outskirts of Prickly Pear ended abruptly. The expansive desert appeared, stretching for miles to the low mountains. We left the town behind.

"You are sad?" I asked.

"I'm sad she was hurt but I'm glad to be here."

He took my hand as we walked.

"I really like you, Cricket."

We stopped, and turned toward each other.

"May I kiss you?"

I didn't answer, and he didn't wait. He put his hand on the small of my back and pulled me in. I knew enough to pucker, though the only thing I'd ever kissed before was that index card at Sarah's sleepover. His lips brushed against mine and then pushed against them softly. Before I was ready to be released, he released me.

"Cricket—" he began.

Doubtless Melissa would have instructed me otherwise. I now knew what "playing hard to get" meant, but this revved-up, hormone-drenched, adolescent body—so unlike my previous one—was not up to playing games. And it was more than that. There was literally no one else on Earth I would even think of kissing.

"Again," I whispered. Was I totally insane!

Of their own accord my arms floated upward until my hands rested on his shoulders. I felt the muscles beneath his shirt. He raised his hand higher along my back. Parted slightly, our lips fused. The tip of his tongue touched mine, triggering a premetamorphic tendency of my tongue to dart in and out. He responded with ardency. I grew giddy. My chest thrummed. I felt warm and light and happy. But I pulled away to catch my breath and come to my senses.

We separated. He held my left hand.

"I think I go home now."

"Of course."

We turned and walked back. I remained in a heightened state of excitement, making it hard to think. I wanted to say something but didn't know what it was. He may have been in a similar state as he said nothing either.

Eventually I was able to tell him not to kiss me in front of the house. I don't want their retinal blood vessels to burst, I thought to myself. He asked if he could take me to dinner and the movies the next day. We made a date and I went inside.

My parents invited me to sit at the kitchen table with them— where else? Though they had not seen the kissing, they had seen the hand-holding. Father was plainly perplexed and irritated. Had I not perpetually complained about the boy? What had transpired to so abruptly change my mind? Had I confided in him? Confided anything? What was our relationship?

Telling him that we were just friends mollified him not at all.

"Just friends! How does he so quickly make the transition from leech to friend? You hardly know the boy. Has it escaped your attention that he is human and that humans cannot be trusted? And why did you not return with Melissa?"

Father had always insisted that I answer vaguely when questioned by humans. Vagueness appeared to be the safest tactic at this moment as well. But he was not satisfied when I told him we'd been friends for a while and that his walking me home was just serendipity.

Though she, too, had invited me to sit at the table with them, Mother put her hand on Father's arm from time to time when he became overheated, though she never took her eyes off me. Her unwavering gaze, discomfited me more than Father's accustomed haranguing. She was not puzzled. She was curious. She gave the impression of searching for something she expected to find.

I had the uncanny feeling that she had deduced the truth. But if so, how? Did I radiate elation? Did I shimmer with infatuation? Was I vibrating like a struck tuning fork?

Father sighed, ending his inquisition.

Mother took my hand in both of hers.

"Your father is concerned for your safety as well as ours," she said softly. "Is there anything else you think we should know about your relationship with the boy?"

In a measured voice I had managed to answer questions calmly, my acting talent again demonstrating itself. But after this question I feared my renegade cheeks, glowing more brightly, would give me away.

Lying, I told them I was very tired. I would be happy to answer all their questions in the morning. I mimed a yawn. When Father, having gotten a second wind, began to question me again, Mother suggested there would be time enough and that I should go to bed. I yawned again for good measure.

Falling asleep proved difficult. The integration of human cerebral pathways into the originals, the mesh of microprocessors and neurotransponders laid over the cerebral cortex, the ontogeny of chimeric organs, the psychological preparation for our transformation, the journey itself—all these things seemed less miraculous to me than my feelings for this boy. The word for the state I was in existed in both languages. I tried to suppress it but then I heard the lyrics to that song.

I'm just a fool,
A fool in love with you.

26

Cricket

The next day Tom arrived in the late afternoon in his father's tired, gray Toyota pickup truck. A bright green spinning knob attached to the steering wheel was the only modification the truck needed for him to drive.

Prickly Pear was too small to have its own movie theater. We would drive to the next town to see the movie and then have dinner. For the first time, my parents invited him into the house. After all, nothing catastrophic occurred when Melissa had entered to work her cosmetic magic.

He took a seat in the living room, Father and Mother sitting across from him.

"You are taking my daughter to see a motion picture?" asked Father.

"Yes, sir. *Moby Dick*. A remake."

Father already knew the answer to this question as I had told him. He'd even read a synopsis of the story. Nevertheless, this made the beginning of his questioning easier.

"And is this an appropriate motion picture for two young people to see?"

"I'll be ready in a minute," I called from the bathroom, where I was applying make-up. I could hear them talking and hoped Father would not seem unwelcoming. I almost yelled, "Be nice, Father."

"Well, yes. It's a classic, you know."

"Tell us about you," suggested Mother.

"Yes, Tom," said Father. "Tell us about yourself."

I finished quickly before they could do any damage.

"Here I am," I announced. "Let us leave."

Tom stood. My parents stood.

"You look nice," said Tom.

I wore a yellow polka-dot skirt and a gray sweater over a long-sleeved white blouse. Mother had braided my hair into the shape of a pony's tail. Tom wore pressed blue pants and a red and blue plaid shirt. His freshly washed, unruly hair was still damp, the part showing clearly.

"You look nice also," I said.

I interrupted Father's incipient disquisition on guidelines for safe driving. We said goodbye and left.

When we were on the main road, I said, "My parents too much worry about me."

He nodded but did not respond. After a while he asked about the hula dance. Had I studied it? And what about the singing? Following my father's guidelines, I answered with vague generalities as best as I could, lying when necessary. Getting nowhere with this line of questioning, he asked if I had read *Moby Dick*.

"No."

"I did as a freshman. It was required in English. There are pages and pages about whales, but there's plenty of action, too. They've made this into a movie umpteen times. The first time was in 1926. What kind of movies do you like?" He seemed nervous. I was nervous also.

"All of the kinds."

"War movies?"

"I don't like violence."

"Most girls don't. But you're not most girls, are you?"

This seemed liked a silly question, but I agreed with him that I was not like most girls.

The Rialto Theater ticket counter was inside in the lobby, a small carpeted room in which candy and drinks were sold. Faded movie posters hung on the walls. Tom purchased tickets and then asked if I'd like something to eat or drink. He was going to get some popcorn. I declined.

We sat in the back. Only half the seats were filled. Previews of four different films were shown. In three of the four, loud, large, red and yellow explosions were prominent. Of these, one was a science fiction film in which the extraterrestrials were tall semi-translucent creatures that looked like upright hammer-headed sharks. The fourth film was a love story. It was the only one that appealed to me.

The main feature began. Ishmael joined the crew of the whaling ship, and met Queequeg, his wild looking, tattooed cannibal roommate. I was awed at the sight of so much presumably unpolluted water. We were in a darkened room. Tom would not see the telltale twitching of my eyes as I scanned the web for more about oceans.

Much killing and butchering of magnificent creatures began. I closed my eyes. The white whale destroyed their boats so that many men died, but it was a wild animal. Ahab, though disturbed, had a wife and child so I had some sympathy for him when the uncoiling harpoon line wrapped around his neck to pull him under the water to his death. Nevertheless, his end was just. His obsession had led to the death of so many.

Giovanni's restaurant was a short distance from the theater. We sat at a table covered with a red and white checked cloth. A stubby, battery-powered, candle facsimile flickered in its glass receptacle. Feeling adventurous, I ordered spaghetti. Tom ordered a small pizza.

"What did you think of the movie?"

"To kill those fish is too cruel," I said, exposing a profound ignorance.

"Fish? What...oh, you mean the whales. You're joking, right?"

"Yes," I lied. "My humor is strange sometimes." Later in the evening I would scan for whales. They were not fish, though Herman Melville himself thought they were. That people not only killed but also ate these magnificent mammals was abhorrent to me.

He agreed with me that it was cruel and reassured me that whale hunting had been banned, though there were exceptions.

He took a bite of pizza. The waiter, an earnest man with a thin black mustache came to our table several times to refill our water glasses—though they did not need refilling—and asked if everything was in order.

At a table nearby sat a young couple with a well-behaved little boy in a high chair. He too had spaghetti but his mother had cut it into little pieces so he could eat it with a spoon.

Tom was taciturn. This was an Italian restaurant, but I wished for a fortune cookie to tell me if now was a "propitious" time to ask my biting question. Moby Dick had taken Ahab's leg. What had taken Tom's arm? He'd never once alluded to the event. Without the encouragement of a slip of paper, I asked the question anyway.

"Tom...how you lose your arm?"

He put down the piece of pizza and dabbed a napkin to his lips. The young couple's child had begun to cry. His mother took him on her lap to comfort him. Tom looked at their table and back at me.

"It's something I'd rather not talk about, but I have been wondering when you might ask. I'll tell you some other time, okay?"

I suppose I could simply have accepted this, but I suspected he only avoided the subject that would evoke sadness, or anger, or fear or some other uncomfortable emotion. And as I myself had experienced, the human body—though mine was a hybrid—could be a geyser of painful emotion. But my wish to know was greater than any concern that he might suffer too much. Indeed, expression of emotion might be therapeutic.

"You tell me, please."

He took another bite of pizza, chewed slowly, and stared at the artificial candle. His lips were drawn, his eyebrows lowered. He looked so sad I reconsidered my request. As he stared at the candle his face relaxed and an impish smile replaced his doleful expression. Our eyes met.

"All right, then. I'll tell you about my arm if you'll tell me where you're from. Everything. The whole story. Your top secret information for mine. Would you do that?"

Of course, I'd already considered doing this very thing, but now that the opportunity had arisen I was no less hesitant than before.

What would he do with the information? How would it affect our relationship? And most worrisome, would he even believe me?

"If I say, you not believe me."

"That's my decision, just promise me you will tell the truth."

"I tell you the truth. Now you tell me about your arm."

He reached across the table for my hand.

"It's a deal. Shake on it."

He pulled his chair in towards the table. We shook hands. His voice lowered even further, he told me how he'd angered Barker one day last April, by telling Claudia to go home when Barker wanted to flirt with her. Barker had grabbed his shirt, and waved his fist in front of him, and told him to shut up. Tom pushed him away. And then Barker said, "I hope you're not this reckless on your motorcycle."

"It's funny, but that's what I dream about. That day on the sidewalk, not the day this happened." He tilted his chin towards his left shoulder.

"Not long after that, I was on the road north of town cruising along at a conservative 55 miles per hour. Just out for a fun ride. I used to do that all the time."

"I heard motorcycles behind me, a long way off. Sound travels pretty far in the desert. I knew it must be that gang. So what should I do? Pull over and park? But the road didn't belong to them and there was plenty of room to pass. I just kept riding, though I had a bad feeling in my chest."

"They were gaining on me fast. Must have been going full throttle. Again I told myself the road was wide enough for them to pass. I should have known better. Yeah, the road was wide enough physically, but not psychologically."

"There's a story about Barker, which someone had heard at one of his trials. It was supposed to mitigate his sentence. His father had beaten him regularly since he was ten or eleven years old. Sometimes his father beat him when he tried to protect his little sister who was five or six at the time. Other times he just beat him. Child protective services looked into this once or twice, but they were understaffed and overworked. Barker always said his bruises were due to falls or fights at school. And there were plenty of those."

"One day in the garage his father started yelling at him for not putting the tools back in the right place. Barker cold-cocked him and—"

"What is cold-cocked?"

"Knocked him out. Punched him in the face so hard he lost consciousness. He suffered a concussion when his head hit the concrete floor. He wasn't found until a day later. By that time, Barker had run off. He was sixteen."

"You are telling me about Barker or your arm?" I asked.

"Just a little background. Okay, back to the main storyline."

Tom's face darkened. He looked around the restaurant as if afraid the gang might emerge from a hiding place. I had become better at reading expressions. Tom's were telling me this was painful. But I was determined to hear it.

"Barker and this skinny kid, Billy Bob, had fought over the gang's leadership. You'd think this would be like a lumberjack against a sapling but in a street fight that kid is meaner than hell. I think they had it out more than once. Anyway, Barker won and is always in the lead when the gang goes riding."

"They're a quarter mile away, gaining on me fast. I see them in my rearview mirror. A little closer and I see Billy Bob in the lead, not Barker. Strange, but a good sign, I think stupidly."

"Billy Bob passes with hardly a glance at me. Then one at a time, the others. Barker is the last one. Had Billy Bob beaten him out? I figured out later that Barker had dropped back on purpose."

"He pulled up and rode alongside me for maybe an eighth of a mile. His black visor was down so I couldn't see his face. I tried slowing down, but he did the same. I sped up and so did he. And then, out of the blue, he landed a high kick on my bike, just behind my left leg."

Tom stopped for a sip of water. He'd been eating slowly before beginning the story and now, of course, was not eating at all. The server came by and asked if there were a problem with the pizza. Could he reheat it? Tom thanked him. As the server walked off with Tom's plate, he resumed the telling.

"You know for every action there is a reaction. Barker was prepared for this, but I wasn't. His bike swung to the left, but he kept control. My bike veered off the road, hit a bush, and flipped a hundred and eighty degrees so I landed on my left side. The roll bar protected my leg, but my shoulder was dislocated and my arm crushed."

He stopped talking. The server returned with his warmed-up pizza, but Tom ignored it.

"I blacked out for a few seconds. When I woke up I was in shock, but I remember wondering why I wasn't in any pain. That came soon enough, gradually getting worse until it felt like a carpenter had just gone over every bone in my arm with a hammer."

"I tried reaching into my right pants pocket for my cell phone, but movement was excruciating, like the carpenter wanted to go over things again to get it right. I went in and out of consciousness. I thought I was going to die."

"I woke up in the hospital. Someone—someone in the gang—had called an ambulance. It must have been Barker. He didn't want to kill me, just take revenge on me for publicly opposing him. They had to amputate the arm. That's it. The whole story."

It was of course, not the whole story. He was in the hospital for about two months. When he got back he was depressed. He didn't study. He snapped at everybody. He was going to be expelled from school, but his mood improved when his father had his beloved bike repaired and modified so he could drive it with one hand. This was a real act of love. His parents made him swear to ride only around town.

"Why Barker not arrest?"

"First, I couldn't have handled the stress of a trial and I worried about my parents, too. Second, I had no witnesses and Barker had eleven. That's how he gets away with murder—figuratively if not literally. He always has a pack of witnesses and the person—girl—he takes on a joyride doesn't. Even if there's evidence of rape, his witnesses will swear the act was consensual. And as for what happened to me, there was no physical evidence of anything other than a motorcycle accident."

While telling his story, Tom looked as if he had a bad backache he was trying, but failing, to suppress. More pain emerged now.

"The accident kind of cooled things off between Claudia and me. She never said this, but I have a feeling she worried I couldn't defend her if need be. Barker still had his eye on her. Or maybe she just didn't like the way I looked with one arm. But she kept her promise to go to the dance with me."

I shook my head and touched his hand. "You good-looking boy."

"A lopsided boy."

Again I shook my head.

"I took some martial arts classes and looked at YouTube videos, but I didn't talk about it."

When the conscientious waiter returned, Tom asked that his dish be reheated again.

"Other than my parents and you, no one knows the whole story. It's an embarrassment because I haven't done anything about it but avoid him. I told you this in confidence."

"I tell no one."

Questions bobbed up and down in my head like buoys on a windy sea. What was his relationship to Claudia now? How did he feel about her? Did he worry when Barker came to town? What were his plans for the future? But I saw in his eyes and heard in his voice a reluctance to go further.

"Now it's your turn," he said. "Where are you from, Cricket?"

I twirled spaghetti on my fork without lifting it off the plate. I'd made an agreement and I would fulfill it. My heart began to thud. This would be a test of some sort. A test of whom about what? I abandoned the fork.

"If I tell you, it is a secret?"

"Yes, of course."

My cheeks displayed their telltale flush. Seeing this, he moved our plates and glasses aside, reached across the table, and took my left hand in his. "I swear to you I will keep the secret."

The little boy at the next table began to cry. His father leaned over to pick up a dropped spoon. Immediately his crying stopped. The man wiped the spoon off with a napkin and handed it back.

I took a deep breath and just said it.

"I come from another planet. I—"

He looked as if he'd just been slapped.

"Cricket—"

"You let me tell whole story, please."

"You promised."

"I keep my promise. Listen!" I snapped. A few heads turned.

I lowered my voice.

"Later tonight when I finish story I show to you it is true. I show it!"

As if to hold himself back from doing something he'd regret, he put his arm across his chest, resting his hand on his left shoulder.

"My planet is dying. Atmosphere is going bad over hundreds of years. Water is going bad. There are sandstorms so strong. The air is poison. So my parents agree to a dangerous journey. We come in spaceship called The Colony with hundred of others."

I couldn't bear to talk about how my parents lied to me, telling me we were just going on a vacation, a once-in-a-lifetime adventure, a trip around the planet in an orbiting satellite.

I picked up the electric candle, turned it over, took the battery out, and held the candle and battery next to each, two feet over the table. I indicated the candle by moving it.

"This is The Colony." I moved the battery. "This is scout or landing plane."

A server came to our table.

"Battery burned out? I'll get you a new one."

"No, thank you," I said. "The battery is good."

"Are you sure?"

"Yes."

"What can I get for you?"

"Nothing, thank you."

The waiter glanced quizzically at the candle and battery I held in the air and left.

My voice faltered but I continued. "When The Colony is close to your planet, my mother, my father, and I leave the spaceship. We come in the landing plane."

Keeping the candle in the air with one hand, I lowered the battery with the other, flying it in for a crash landing on the table. Softly, I made appropriate sounds. I put the battery back in place and set the candle on the table.

"So you're not here to take over the Earth?"

"I do not understand the question."

Tom took a sip of water giving him time to think.

"Never mind. I don't like this, but I'll play along for now. How long did it take you to get here?"

"Sassatha is very far away. It took millennia to get here."

"Funny, you don't look that old."

"We are in suspended animation."

He expelled a frustrated puff of breath.

"You could go on forever like this, couldn't you? So where are all the other aliens?"

"This hard to explain. You be patient."

Haltingly and laboriously I began. Over the long, long course of the journey three unforeseen supernovae had overwhelmed the shielding. When accumulated cosmic radiation cell damage became too great, the pilgrims died.

Father, however, had been awakened every hundred years or so to check on certain of the ship's functions. Mother had insisted he also wake us each time. During these active periods our cells repaired the damage that had occurred since the last awakening. Taken a little at a time there was never too much to repair. We survived.

———

"Okay, you got out of that one. There aren't any other aliens around because they all died. But there's still an interstellar spaceship floating around up there full of dead bodies, right? We ought to be able to see it."

"Eons of cosmic radiation make engine brittle. It explodes. It was in the news. In September."

He shook his head and took another sip of water. He'd stopped eating his pizza.

When we were a year away from the Earth, Mother refused to go back into the canister. Father was easily persuaded. Entering it was always eerie, like climbing into a sarcophagus. So that last year he studied the language and culture of this area. Mother spent her time trying to mollify me, which was impossible. They had tricked me into going with them. Had they told me the truth, they knew, I might have refused to leave my home and friends. It took a while for me to express all this with my improved, but still poor, English.

"Our trip here from the Colony take fourteen days."

I had spoken like an abductee pleading for release by a kidnapper. Tom's stare had been unbroken, even when sipping water, though he squinted at times, searching my face for some hidden meaning or purpose. By the time I stopped talking his stare had become a glare.

"I am at a complete loss," he rasped. "I don't know whether to laugh or cry, bang on the table or what. You promised to tell me the truth. Damn it!"

"I tell...told you the truth. I will show you the truth."

27

Cricket

The sun had long since set. It was cooler than I'd expected.
Neither of us had spoken a word since leaving the
restaurant. Just before he would have turned onto the road for Prickly
Pear, I pointed out into the desert.

"Go straight here. I show you rocket plane."

"I've had enough of this for one night," he sputtered.

"You go straight here. I ask you pretty please. You go straight
now." I put my hand on the steering wheel.

"Hey, stop that!"

I kept my hand on the wheel.

"I ask you please you go straight. How many times do you want I
say you go straight?"

I prevailed. He passed the turnoff to town. We were on our way
into the heart of the desert. Less than half the moon shone but it was
enough.

"This better be good," he said.

I gave directions until we were north of Prickly Pear and showed
him where to park. He took a flashlight from the glove compartment
and we got out.

"We walk now. I go first. You follow me."

He gave me the flashlight.

"Thank you."

I swept the light back and forth over the path I chose, easily skirting the creosote bushes and a few cactuses. In less than ten minutes I came to a stop beside a sand dune. He came up beside me.

I aimed the light at a patch of pearlescent white, then moved it along the fuselage to the vertical stabilizer, then over a wing, then back to the open door in the side, now partially filled by sand. The desert's occasional winds had done a better job of camouflaging the plane with sand than had Father's hurried labors. I struggled for equanimity against a potent mixture of anger, sadness, confusion, and relief.

Tom blurted, "Holy shit!" An odd, contradictory exclamation.

I handed him the flashlight. He remained fixed on the spot so long I feared for his health. I was about to question him when he began to move around the craft, muttering to himself. Its nose was deeply buried in the dune. He circled the plane four times before returning to its side and climbing through the open door. His muttering was muted. He emerged, took another look inside, and then joined me. We faced the ship. He continued to run the light along its length.

In his excitement he must have temporarily forgotten the reason I brought him here.

"How did you find it?"

"I not find it. It is from Sassatha. We came to your planet in it."

"Just because you're smart doesn't mean everybody else is stupid, understand? You don't want to keep your side of the bargain so you bring me out here. To distract me. Get my mind off your little secret. You really gall me."

It was chilly. When I began to shiver he removed his jacket and handed to me. I hesitated because then he'd be cold.

"Just take it," he demanded. I put it on.

"This thing must be an experimental plane from the air force base. Or maybe a space shuttle. You should have reported it to the authorities. Damn! How could anyone lose something like this? Maybe it's foreign. Chinese. Maybe Russian."

"It is more foreign than that."

"Stop it, will you? Just knock it off."

"You ask me again and again where I am from. I show you where I am from, but you do not believe me. I ask you only one thing. Please say nothing. Please tell no one. They will arrest us. Tell me now you will tell no one."

28

Cricket

He parked in front of my house and took his jacket back.

"Tom, please listen to me. That was our plane. It is not Russian. It is not Chinese. It is not American. If they find it, they search for us. They arrest us. They take us away. Please say nothing. You promised. Do you not care for me? Do you want they take me away?"

"I promised I'd keep your secret but you're mocking me with this—"

Abruptly he stopped. He rolled down the driver's side window and turned toward it, away from me. I was crying now. My nose began to run. I dabbed it on my sleeve. Father had been right. This boy was not worthy of trust. Inside me deep feelings for him were being uprooted. I had never experienced such pain. My crying became sobbing.

He turned back to me, his breathing slowed. He reached out to take my hand, which rested on my lap, but it remained limp.

He moved towards me, putting his arm around my shoulder. "Do you really believe you're an alien and that your parents are aliens, that you're from another planet?"

What had I been saying all along? I did not answer.

"Do you take some sort of medication for...for your nerves?"

He was wondering, I was to learn, if I had schizophrenia.

"Have you told your parents you found this thing?"

"What are you going to do?" I said with difficulty, still crying.

"Someone needs to know about this. The Air Force. The National Transportation Safety Administration. Who knows, maybe Homeland Security or the FBI if it's from another country. Someone must be looking for it. And what about its passengers? What happened to them? Their families must be looking for them, too. It wouldn't be right not to report this. Can't you see that?"

I was not crying for effect. I felt I was being whipped back and forth between grief and terror—grief at losing him and terror of discovery.

My crying ebbed, though I still sniffled. I reached back, firmly grasped his arm, and removed it from my shoulders. Wordlessly, I opened the door and stepped out.

"Cricket," he called out. "Wait a second."

What would I tell my parents? What would they do?

We were ten paces from the front door when I turned toward him and stopped. He must not speak loudly. This was my only concern at the moment. I would need time to find the right way to explain this to my parents. If they heard us quarreling they would hold me captive until I told a coherent story. I needed sanctuary in my room.

I put a finger to my lips.

He spoke quietly. "Try to understand. You had nothing to do with that thing being there. There's no way you or your parents can get in trouble over it. I don't know what's...what's going on in your head, but you won't—"

"Go away," I whimpered.

"Just let me finish. I—"

"Go away."

He might raise his voice and call me if I turned my back on him. I had to be sure he'd left before going into the house.

Twice more he began to talk and twice more I said, "Go away."

When he finally left, I dried my eyes and nose as best I could and entered the house.

———

Tom

Before I'd left the house to go on my first real date in months, Mom and Dad had been debating which video to watch later in the evening. When I got home, an ancient movie called *Intolerable Cruelty* was on the screen. Cricket had been mocking me all night with that extraterrestrial crap. The title summed it up.

"Have fun, son?" asked Dad.

"It was okay." I just didn't have it in me to put on an act.

"Just okay?" said Mom.

"It was good," I lied. "I think I'll hit the sack."

I fumbled getting my clothes off, tossing them onto a chair. This one-armed business sucked. I had to be patient. I'd popped buttons off shirts, and ripped pants when I got frustrated. Getting into pajamas wasn't too bad.

My unsympathetic electric toothbrush buzzed away. I didn't look at my empty pajama sleeve. As I turned the faucet on to rinse the toothbrush, the expression "down the drain" came to mind.

I lay on my back, massaging the back of my neck between fingers and thumb. Naturally I couldn't sleep. I saw that Cricket wasn't being cruel. She had a reason to say what she'd said, and it wasn't to hurt me. And the story was too detailed to have been made up on the spot. But did that mean she believed what she said? If so, she had a mental illness. If not, she was lying to protect herself and her family. But why make up a totally ridiculous cover story. Jeez!

The other thing that bothered me, she'd found that airplane, shuttle, or whatever the hell it was, but she didn't tell anyone. Now why was that?

Maybe they really did land in that thing. So they must be spies after all. I don't know. That's crazy, but if they're spies....

29

Cricket

Too frightened of Father's response, I could not bear to tell him
what I'd done. But alone with Mother, I confessed.

"I need to speak with you." I announced and promptly began
to cry.

She sat next me on the sofa, put her arm over my shoulder, and
said nothing. Eventually the stream of mucous from my nose and
flood of tears from my eyes subsided, until I was taking rapid,
shallow breaths.

"I... I wanted him to know who I am. I wanted to tell him all that
we have been through. I wanted to share myself. I wanted the freedom
of speaking my mind, instead of censoring every treacherous thought.
I made a terrible mistake by telling him who I was. Mother, forgive
me I..."

I began to cry again but gained control more quickly this time.

"...he did not believe me, so I took him to the plane."

Subtly her expression changed from serious to somber. The last
time I'd seen her like this was when I refused to leave the plane after
our crash landing. Her expression frightened me further, but she kept
her comforting arm over my shoulder. Her voice was earnest but not

panicked. How well-balanced and self-possessed was my mother, I thought fleetingly.

"You took him to the plane?"

I could only nod.

"What did he do?"

"He didn't believe me even then. He would not listen to me. He said the crash had to be reported. I hate him. I hate him."

Again it welled up in me, this bitterness I could taste, mingling with the fear, to make a most unpalatable concoction. Mother pulled me a little closer releasing a new bout of sobbing.

"And now...and now we will be arrested just as Father has always warned and we will be alone again. Oh, Mother, I am desolate."

Again I was crying, but more softly. It had been good to confess.

"Dear heart, your mistake was thinking he would believe you were from Sassatha. Had he believed it, he might have kept your secret."

"But why should he not believe it?"

"These people only recently developed telephones without wires, freeze-dried food, yo-yos, satellite telescopes, acrylic paint. The briefest sojourn to their moon—which is so close one could hit it with a stone—awed all of humanity. Robot explorers of the closest planet, they consider the height of engineering. They talk of space exploration but could not maintain a sealed so-called biosphere on earth for even a year. How could the boy believe that we have travelled for centuries?"

"Will they come for us? Will they take us away?"

"I do not know, but if we flee, they would suspect us of some crime. We could not hide for long. We have no one to hide us."

"Will you speak with Father?"

"We will speak with him together."

The talk with Father was anticlimactic. A muffled explosion with expletives and then, ashamed, he hugged me and said, "The deed is done." He questioned me with forced composure, now entirely focused on the dangers that lay ahead.

We sat in the living room, Mother and I on the same sofa, he in the wing chair across from us. Father did not sit long. Hands held behind his back as if he'd already been shackled, he paced.

"When they examine the plane, they will conclude that it was not made in this country. And in the best case, they will assume it was made in another country as opposed to another planet. Where might the pilot be they will ask themselves. And they will return here asking questions. It is not only Rosita who believes we are from Russia."

He stopped his pacing.

"One thing is certain. We must all learn idiomatic American English on, as they say, a crash program. It is of more importance than eating, drinking, and sleeping. I include myself. I speak well enough, it is true, but too often misunderstand certain sayings, aphorisms, figures of speech. Who would have thought that to pull someone's leg means to playfully tease someone with an untruth? In brief, we must not speak like Russians learning English."

Mother said, "Consider it done."

"And it occurs to me," continued Father, "that if the Martinez boy tells them that you showed him the site, we will be among the first persons they question. We must leave before that happens. I will obtain an automobile from Hoppy Jones, if I can. We must begin packing now."

His tone spoke of his conviction.

"We may have a few weeks. Until we leave we must act normally," said Father. "That means you must continue to go to school, but we must start packing now."

"We must learn English and embroider our story, yes," said Mother. "If we are questioned separately, our answers must be concordant. But we will be no safer if we flee. Perhaps even less so."

"I disagree," said Father. "We must go."

30

Cricket

R otund Clyde Cummings, a telling sheen on his high forehead, stood behind the officers at the front door. As usual Claudia had been assigned the task of babysitting her little sister. They tossed a Frisbee back and forth in the front yard trampling the waves of sand that Mother had meticulously raked in her Zen garden.

Officer Mark Toomey's long black, hooded nylon jacket might have been a monk's cassock. He stood legs splayed, hands clasped behind his back. Not an aggressive posture. Nevertheless, I imagined the neighbors thinking the worst when they read the large white letters on his back. The acronym ICE could be chilling. His partner, Wendell Warren, small facial features pulled too closely together, was already looking over Mother's shoulder into the house searching for something suspicious to gnaw on.

Mother invited them in. We sat in a circle. The agents on the sofa, Father on the wing chair, Cummings, Mother, and I on three yellow wooden chairs brought in from the kitchen. From where I sat I could see Claudia and Annie playing outside. I wondered when Annie would dash off.

Cummings began to speak but was interrupted by Officer Warren.

"Clyde, if you don't mind, I'd like to ask a few questions of the Sminths first. We've come a long way and would like to wrap up this business as quickly as possible."

Cummings crossed his legs, pressed his lips together, and nodded.

Scanning our faces for telltale signs of espionage, I suppose, Warren told us that Mayor Cummings had called them out of concern that we might be Russians.

"That is a common misperception," said Father.

"If you'll allow me to finish, Mr. Sminth."

"Yes, of course, excuse me."

Warren leaned forward, hands on knees.

"We're staying at the Still Waters Motel. Ms. Gaylord, the very first person we asked, told us that Mrs. Smith and the young lady here can barely speak English. She also thought you were Russians. In fact, that seems to be the consensus. But you have told just about everybody that you're from Hawaii and came here because of a pineapple allergy. Is that correct?"

"Yes," said Father.

"Mrs. Sminth?"

"Yes."

Officer Warren sighed, made as if to stand, but then sank back on to the sofa.

"So no one here denies the story so far. Yet we have six eye witnesses that young Ms. Sminth here ate a fairly large helping of pineapple at breakfast in the home of the high school principal. Credible witnesses, don't you agree? Ms. Sminth, did you eat pineapple at the principal's house."

"Yes, sir."

"Do you have a pineapple allergy?"

"No, sir."

"And you, Mrs. Sminth? Do you have a pineapple allergy?"

"No, I don't."

"Mr. Smith?"

"Well, we have been caught in our lie, but I would like to explain," said Father.

"Why don't you ask Mrs. Sminth to explain," said Cummings

grinning, eager that Mother's dreadful English clank in the officers' ears. She had a surprise for him.

"Well, it seems the jig is up," said Mother. Cummings eyes widened, and he uncrossed his legs.

"You see the real reason we left Hawaii was fear of mosquitos. We wanted to move to a place with no mosquitos whatsoever. And thank God, we did."

Officer Warren turned to Cummings.

"You said she spoke broken English."

"Well, she...she does. This is new. Have her keep talking."

"I see this may take some time," said Mother. "Coffee, anyone?"

"No thank you, Ma'am," said Warren and Toomey simultaneously.

"Now why did you lie about the pineapple allergy?" asked Toomey, taking charge of the questioning.

"Frankly we were afraid of frightening people," continued Mother. "You see my daughter, husband, and I were recovering from a severe bout of encephalitis and we thought if we mentioned it, people would be afraid we were still harboring the virus. If they thought that, they'd avoid us like the plague—if I may use the expression—so we lied. We're no risk to anyone. The illness has passed. Praise the Lord."

"Something's not right. I don't understand," objected Cummings, squirming. "She didn't used to talk like this, I swear."

"You see," continued Mother, "our speech had been affected by the infection. My husband's speech returned first, probably because his infection was less severe, but my daughter and I have seen a rapid improvement recently. My, how we've waited for this! You have no idea how hard it is to get by when you can barely get the words out. But really everyone has been so kind."

I stifled the urge to add "With a few exceptions."

"And you, young lady," said Officer Toomey. "Tell us a little about yourself, about the illness."

"Like, Mom said, it was so hard. People at school thought I was retard—I mean developmentally delayed. They made fun of me."

I shouldn't have done it, I know, but I pointed to Cummings.

"His daughter especially. The girl out in front of the house. Maybe I scared her. I did seem a little strange. But if you think about it, us supposed to be Russian, it's pretty funny really. *Da. Da.* That means Yes. Yes."

Toomey turned to Cummings.

"Mr. Sminth's employer has nothing but praise for him, the hardest working, smartest employee he's ever had, he says. People are bringing their cars to his garage from all over because Mr. Sminth repairs them so quickly. And apparently Mrs. Sminth has an open door policy. People drop over any old time. Nobody has observed anything suspicious."

"Wait. Wait," said Cummings. "I think they're in disguises. They're all wearing wigs."

Father tilted his head at me.

When Tom had surprised us that night after my week of truancy, I toyed with the silly idea of becoming an actress. I'd feigned nonchalance, sangfroid, unflappability. Here was my cue to feign the opposite.

To help myself along, I thought of the real possibility that we would be arrested and of my break-up with Tom.

Tears flowed freely. I pushed my crying but remained far from hysteria. I left the room, but listened from my bedroom doorway.

"The infection. We all lost our hair," said Mother. "It has been hardest on her. You would have to be a teenage girl to know just how awful such a thing would be."

"I hear you," said Officer Toomey.

I think this was the turning point in the questioning. Officer Toomey himself had a bald spot as large as a saucer and may have been irked at Cummings for bringing up the subject of wigs. Officer Warren, too, I suspected, may have had what might be called "hair issues."

They asked Cummings if he wished to ask us any more questions, but he was overwhelmed, shaking his head back and forth, muttering "I don't believe it." The agents told us they might wish to speak with us again and thanked us for our cooperation.

Just out the door, Officer Warren chided Cummings. We have good ears.

"Well, that was embarrassing. Good thing we knocked instead of breaking the door down as you suggested. You're too suspicious for your own good. They may be a little odd, but we'd have to increase the force a hundred fold to investigate every bizarro living in the desert."

We heard a car drive away. Then came the knocking on the door. Cummings, smoldering, addressed Mother.

"You're not going to get away with this. You're all weirder than any Russians. I didn't tell the police about this because they wouldn't believe me. That girl of yours climbed up a wall and so did you. Mary Martinez told me. I don't know what's going on, but you don't fool me." He stamped down the gravel foot path and down the street.

I emerged dry-eyed from my room.

"That was good," said Father. "These people are suckers, I think the expression is, for a little boohooing." And turning to Mother, said. "You, too, were excellent." After a pause, he added, "But we still must leave. The danger has not passed."

31

Cricket

One Sunday afternoon, not long afterwards, Cummings, his girls in tow, appeared again at our front door. My parents were occupied in other parts of the house, so I answered, putting a stop to his aggressive knocking.

"Good afternoon, Cricket."

Inexplicably he extended his hand. Unthinkingly I took it, but instead of shaking it he grasped my wrist with his other hand, and inspected my palm and fingers, brushing his fingertips over them. All this he quickly accomplished as if he'd practiced the moves.

"Sorry about that," he said, releasing my wrist. "I couldn't think of any other way to do it."

I was flummoxed.

"I'd like to speak with your parents."

I opened the door wider. Claudia looked at her father.

"Dad, you take Annie. I want to go home."

"You will do as you're told. I don't want to be here any more than you do."

"There's nothing to do," said Annie.

"You two can play in the sand. I'm sure the Sminths won't mind."

Mother had carefully raked the rock garden again that morning, restoring to perfection the uniform waves of sand that swirled and eddied in the front yard. But what could I say. In any case, I preferred that Claudia remain outside.

"It's not fair, Dad. I was going to go to Sarah's."

He mimed biting his fist, a gesture of angry frustration I'd never seen before and which was uniquely his. He was keyed up. Claudia took Annie by the hand and led her to the middle of the yard where they sat and began to play with the sand.

I gestured him in and left the room.

He was examining the furniture when Mother invited him to sit. He chose Father's wing chair. My parents sat on the sofa. I leaned against a wall as far from him as I could get without leaving the room.

"Before I start," he said, though he'd just started, "I want to warn you against any funny business. Claudia knows why I'm here and I left a detailed letter at home in case anything happens to me. Oh, and I told Camacho too."

He crossed his arms over his chest and sat up even straighter.

"What is this funny business of which you speak?" asked Mother.

"So your English isn't all that good after all. Just don't try anything on me, understand?"

"You mean harm you?" asked Father.

"That's what I mean."

"Why would we wish to do that?" asked Mother.

"Okay, enough with the games. I don't know why I'm telling you this face to face. I don't owe you anything. Maybe I should have let you find out about it when the police arrived. Maybe I want to make sure you don't make a fool of me again by giving you a chance to explain yourselves."

The proper response to this—if there was a proper response—was elusive. Silently we waited.

"Okay. Here's the evidence that you're foreign agents or maybe just gangsters on the run. There is no record of your births at Kapiolani Hospital. You've forged those certificates. Anything you want to say about that?"

Father looked as if he wanted to pull Cummings out of the chair and toss him out. Mother looked thoughtful. Neither spoke.

"The most damning thing of all is that you have no fingerprints— not even the girl. Incredible!"

"He looked at my hands," I confessed.

He addressed Mother. "I checked for fingerprints on that bottle of syrup you sold me. Nada." He addressed Father. "There were no fingerprints on the bottle of motor oil I bought from you, either." He addressed me, "And your entire palm is blank."

My parents glanced at each other and then turned back to Cummings.

"So what's the explanation this time?" he asked.

"What will you do now?" said Mother. "Go to the police?"

"I already have, if you can call Camacho police, but at least she's already checked the hospital. She'll see about your fingerprints today, I think. Oh, and she got a call from a gun shop. Native Hawaiian! Brother!"

He paused for a moment before asking, "Aren't you people going to make up some story about this?"

When we said nothing, he rose. Mother opened the door for him.

"I don't like being made to look like a fool."

He'd stepped outside when Claudia screamed so loudly that we all came to the door.

———

To turn around in the narrow street Cindy Penny had backed into our driveway using only her rearview mirror, which left a blind spot. She struck Annie who had been playing on the side of the driveway. Claudia had been on her cell phone with a friend.

Mother was kneeling beside the girl even before Cindy got out of the car. Annie was lying on her back, howling. The hem of her dress was bloody. A hint of bone protruded from the middle of her left shin.

A small circle of kneeling figures formed around her: Mother, Father, Cummings, Penny, and me. Claudia, aghast and crying, still had the presence of mind to call 911.

Cindy Penny kept saying, "Oh God. I'm so sorry."

Cummings, white-faced and trembling, repeated, "You're going to be all right, darling. I love you. You're going to be all right."

Mother palpated the girl's neck and head. Discretion forgotten, she whistle/clicked instructions to Father and me. He raised the garage door and brought out a sheet of plywood as a stretcher. I removed from their hiding places a shiny metallic pad, a 3D printer, a projection box, and other instruments, arranging everything on a countertop where the patient would lie. I hurried back with a moldable brace. Mother placed it behind the girl's neck.

Mother, Father, and I began to transfer the girl to the stretcher.

"Maybe we should wait for the ambulance," said Cummings, now in tears.

"Dad," said Claudia, "that could take an hour."

"Do you know what you're doing?" asked Cummings.

"They know," I said.

———

W e left the garage door open because the light was much better that way. Father sent Cindy Penny home. Mother, flanked by Father and me, stood by the shrieking girl, Cummings and Claudia behind us. Mother cut away her clothing using a scissors. When her abdomen was exposed, Mother touched it with what must have appeared to the others as a miniature hair dryer.

"What are you doing?" yelled Cummings.

"Making the girl comfortable," said Mother.

Less than a minute and a half later, Annie appeared to be sleeping.

"What did you do?" asked Cummings. "Is she all right?"

"Please," said Father, in the firm but even tone of a father who understands what it would be like were his daughter critically injured. "My wife must concentrate. Ask your questions later."

Until now, Cummings and Claudia had only seen the effect of one unusual instrument. They gasped as Annie's translucent holographic image appeared above her recumbent body, hovering like a multicolored ghost. The colors changed, organs were magnified and returned to normal size, blood vessel and nerve bundle were displayed, tissue planes defined, and most pertinent at the moment— the image of the tibial fracture was highlighted, magnified, rotated, and explored.

Claudia and her father, wide-eyed, had their arms around each other's waists, occasionally making muffled sounds of astonishment.

The printer produced a small, pale blue, barrette-like bone clamp.

Mother and Father worked wonderfully as a team. They sterilized their hands, then the wound. They exposed the glistening, pearlescent bone and sterilized the broken ends. With the teeth of ingenious forceps just gripping the fragment ends, they repositioned the bone, Father first pulling on the leg and when the alignment in the hologram was perfect, pressing. They fastened the ends together with the bone clamp. Mother closed the wound with a microstapler.

They wound the leg in gauze and then in a clear tape. With the touch of another instrument the layers of tape coalesced into a perfectly clear cast.

Procedures completed, they put away the instruments and stepped away to allow Cummings to be by his daughter. He'd removed his shirt to cover her.

"Oh, darling Annie, please be all right. Please."

Claudia, whose shock had silenced her for a while, began to cry again.

"When will she wake up?" asked Cummings.

"Soon," said Mother. But Annie didn't wake up.

———

B locks away, the siren wailed. Father stepped out and waved to the medics. A young man and woman in short white coats speedily removed the stretcher from the ambulance, unfolded its wheeled legs, and entered the garage. The woman placed her black bag on the counter. She took the girl's pulse, blood pressure, and temperature. She observed, palpated, percussed, and listened.

"Is she going to be all right?" asked Cummings.

"I think so," was all she said as she continued her examination.

As Claudia and Cummings described the events, the man's features, static and unexpressive at first, became mobile. His eyebrows rose and fell, his puckered lips moved from side to side as if searching for something.

"What?" he interrupted. "You're describing major surgery for a compound fracture. What really happened?"

"Tell them," entreated Cummings, addressing Mother.

Mother laconically confirmed the story.

"You put her to sleep?"

"A mild analgesic," said Mother.

"Are you a doctor?" asked the man, his expression changing ceaselessly.

Mother shook her head.

"I know a little first aid, that's all."

"What did you give her?"

"Oh, something I picked up at a pharmacy. I don't remember what it's called. It's for emergencies. I gave it transcutaneously. She should be awake soon, but she will then be in pain."

"It's all true," said Claudia.

"Let's go, Josh," said the woman.

Despairing of getting a believable history, the medics transferred Annie to the ambulance. Cummings was allowed to ride along.

Claudia hugged Mother but was too stunned by events and burdened by guilt to ask questions. Mother invited Claudia to stay, but she wanted to go home.

"The walk will do me good," she said.

32

Cricket

"The girl might have died from shock had we not intervened," stated Mother. "We had no choice." Our family conference was held around the kitchen table. In this custom we were fully assimilated.

"Perhaps we should have simply stabilized her until the ambulance arrived, my dear eager healer. Bone repair could have waited."

"The sooner this was taken care of, the better the prognosis. You know that. She was going into shock."

Father went to the window to survey our street's modest ranch-style houses and yards. Before our arrival, the citizens of Prickly Pear, and of Sandstone Street in particular, had already begun replacing water-guzzling front lawns with rock gardens. But Mother accelerated the trend by showing just how beautiful raked sand and aesthetically placed rock could be, not that she was the only one with good taste. Still neighbors came to her to discuss their landscaping ideas. She was a good listener and always had suggestions. And always invited them in for coffee and freshly baked cookies, which she made every day. Indeed, an informal neighborhood organization had crystallized around her with get-togethers to discuss topics of general interest.

"I have grown fond of this place," murmured Father.

Mother sighed. "You mean to stay?"

"Performing our little surgical spectacular before Cummings was merely more wood for his bonfire. He will return with the police. We can either attempt to flee or prepare for the worst. Perhaps I can activate our telebionic implants that we can communicate with each other at a distance. I mean from separate cells."

Despite these words, he spoke kindly, which concerned me. What did that mean? I did not wish to hear resignation.

I was still at the window when Tom Martinez arrived, parked his bike, and ran into the house. Claudia had called Sarah about Annie's accident. Sarah had called Melissa. Melissa had called Tom.

Mother led him into the kitchen. He greeted Father and me. Rising from the table to stand with my back against the wall, I said nothing. My parents were more gracious. Father showed him a seat. Mother offered him coffee. He declined.

In the retelling of events Mother portrayed the orthopedic surgery as a simple splinting to stabilize the leg. This made the telling easier and reduced the need for clarification. No mention of a compound fracture. None of us were in the mood for heightened emotion, either our own or someone else's.

"Her father was allowed to ride in the ambulance," she continued. "Claudia walked home."

"So she's going to be all right."

"Certainly," said Mother. Only then did he remove his helmet.

As Father began a preamble to what I surmised would be a question about the rocket plane, Tom's phone rang. It was Melissa. On the way home Claudia had been abducted by the gang.

Supercharged by this news, my mind raced along various tracks simultaneously. Barker would abuse her and "abuse" was a euphemism. Someone had to stop him. Only I could. I had the passion. I had the means. I had the access. Even against the ensemble of bad actors I was adequately armed.

But in a moment Tom might go for his bike thinking he could do the same thing—though the thought of a boy with one arm fighting a motorcycle gang was both sad and absurd. He certainly wouldn't take a girl with him.

Flushed with adrenaline I left the house and rushed to the motorcycle. But Tom was right behind me.

"Hey! What are you doing?"

I mounted, started the engine, and began to roll. Seeing a struggle would be dangerous, Tom deftly mounted behind me.

"This is crazy. What are you doing? Stop!"

He tried reaching around me to the throttle, but I gripped it firmly, and pushed back against him so he could not reach it. I accelerated. If he tried pulling my arm away, we would go scuttling on to the shoulder and into the sand, maybe to hit a cactus or two, something he surely realized.

"All right. All right," he relented. "I know where you're going, you idiot. What are we going to do against twelve thugs? Melissa's already called the police."

On a motorcycle again, I was exhilarated. The wind rushing past, howled its approval. I would lay them all low. I would have revenge. Father would disapprove. It might expose us even further, but I could not stop myself.

As we approached, Tom pointed out the turn off. Another five minutes on this dirt road and we saw their campsite. They'd parked their motorcycles haphazardly here and there on the outskirts of camp. I parked by the first one, a silver Harley. The key was still in the lock. They must have been so excited at the prospect of a sex show, that they couldn't wait to get started. The excreta!

We dismounted. I started towards the scattering of small tents, Tom nimbly at my side.

"Do you have a plan? A way to stall things until the police arrive? I'm worried. Really worried. Damn, I'm scared as hell."

"I will remove their conscious."

"Their conscience? That's the last thing you want to remove. What the hell are you talking about?"

"Not conscience. Conscious. Conscious-ness."

I explained as simply as I could that I would render the gang unconscious by using an electromagnetic pulse generator tailored to disrupt human brain function, the reticular activating system to be specific. I pointed to the bracelet.

Tom stopped abruptly, uncomprehending.

"My God, Cricket, these guys are dangerous. Don't do anything stupid. Talk nicely. They're not going to like it much our barging in here. I mean it. Be as sweet as you can."

I resumed walking. Tom had no choice but to walk with me. In a few steps I was flooded with doubts about my plan. Yes, the gang would pass out, but so would Tom and Claudia. That might be acceptable if help arrived before everyone awoke, though the police would pose unanswerable questions. But if the police did not arrive in time, how would I escape with Tom and Claudia? Now I, too, was worried.

Barker, Billy Bob, and terrified Claudia, her arms covering her bare breasts, stood in the center of a tight circle, an arena. But it was not gladiators who would be fed to the lions.

Barker held her by the rim of her skirt while arguing vehemently with Billy Bob, the others goading them on. These men could not long tolerate a lack of drama. Tranquility was boredom. As the group turned toward us, all fell silent for a moment, before some began guffawing.

Claudia screamed. "No! Go away!"

The circle opened for us. The laughter continued.

"Well, well, what have we here?" gloated Barker. "The rescue party, I presume. Hmm. I sense some funny business. Hold him." Two men grabbed Tom.

"The police will be here soon. Just let us go and we won't press charges." I heard the tremor in Tom's voice.

"The police? Camacho? Don't make me laugh."

"Be reasonable, Barker," pleaded Tom.

"I'll deal with you later. First some fun. We already have one topless girl. Let's make it two."

Tom struggled, but one of the men pulled his arm behind his back and threatened to dislocate it.

"This solves the problem, doesn't it," said Billy Bob. "One for you and one for me." He grabbed me by the upper arm and pulled me toward him. For Billy Bob getting a girl for himself was a proxy for shared gang leadership.

"Uh uh, boy," said Barker, punching Billy Bob in the abdomen. "Oooff," went the thin young man before buckling over and falling to his knees. Share and share alike did not appear to be one of Barker's mottos. The mob quieted down, but someone said, "Hey, Barker, that ain't right."

Barker sneered. "Want to make something of it?"

Someone else said, "Let's get on with the show."

Barker began to pull off my t-shirt.

"Wait!" I hollered.

"Wait for what?" said Barker.

"If you don't let us go I will hurt you."

"You scratch or bite me and you'll wished you'd never been born."

There was no point in talking further. I would put a stop to this now. My arms still held over my head, I touched the bracelet. But nothing happened. The effect should have been immediate. I touched it again.

"Oh, no!" I yelped.

"Something wrong?" teased Barker as he yanked off my shirt, spun me around and undid my bra. He put his hands on my breasts and pulled me to him so my rear end pressed against his groin.

Claudia was crying. Tom was cursing. The men were laughing.

As best I could I fiddled with the bracelet. What was wrong? The bracelet wasn't working. Why hadn't I paid more attention to Father's instructions? But then I knew. I was out of range of the power source. Muck and decay! Emotion had interfered with my thinking.

Barker lowered his hands from my breasts to my hips and pulled me more tightly against him. I tried to strike him with my elbows.

"You bitch!" A blow to the side of my head and I saw purple and pink stars.

"Hey, Barker," yelled Tom in a pained voice, his arm held high against his back. "You're pretty tough fighting girls. You chicken shit. Why don't you fight me for them? You win...then...you win."

"Yeah, Barker," said an enthusiastic man from the circle. "A fight for the spoils."

Others joined in.

"Come on, Barker. Beat the crap out of him."

"Not afraid are you, pig snout?" yelled Tom. "I could beat you with one arm tied behind me."

The mob was amused.

I continued tapping my bracelet, frantically, though it was futile. Barker released me. When I tried to strike him, someone grabbed and restrained me. Forgetting about me, Barker turned to face Tom.

"You just ride in here like we're a bunch of pansies. What the hell do you think you're going to do, frighten us? Jesus H. Christ. I am pissed. I don't give a shit if you have only one arm. This is going to be something you'll never forget. Nobody messes with Levi Barker."

Billy Bob by now had been helped to his feet. "And I want at you next, Barker, you slime ball."

Ignoring Billy Bob, Barker boomed, "Let Martinez go."

———

Tom

We did this all wrong. We should have stayed near the road and yelled that we were taking pictures. Harassed them just out of reach. Distracted them until the police came. Crazy did not seem too strong a word to describe Cricket's behavior.

I'd read in a book about the Spanish Civil War how a soldier's tension becomes unbearable before a battle. How his mouth dries up. How his stomach clenches. How his chest aches. Barker would probably kill me, but I didn't care. All I wanted was to stall things. I couldn't stand the thought of what he might do to them.

———

Cricket

As soon as they released Tom from the hammer lock, he began dancing from foot to foot, jabbing his fist into the air before him, pitifully imitating a professional boxer.

What had I done? How could I ever face Tom again? Face

anybody, assuming I was still alive when they were through with me? I wished to sink into the sand and disappear but instead I screamed. Tom would be annihilated.

Tom whooped, "Come and get me, you big slob."

Barker charged. Steam roller against scarecrow.

Tom had lost his arm because of Barker. Might he now lose his life? And afterwards, Tom lying motionless in the sand, would not Barker be even more inflamed. And what of the rest of them? Would they not also want a piece of "the action?" I struggled to get loose, but in a second my captor pulled my arm into that excruciating hammer lock. Helpless, bawling, I wept acid tears.

As soon as Barker was within striking range, Tom delivered a powerful, well-aimed kick to Barker's left knee, throwing him off balance. Barker bellowed like the wounded animal he was. Tom whirled away from Barker in a half circle, kicking backward with his left leg. In a roundhouse blow, his foot sunk low into Barker's abdomen. He completed the turn and hit Barker with an uppercut to the jaw and a knee to the genitals. Barker crumpled to the ground like a rumpled piece of paper and lay motionless.

The fight had lasted less than six seconds. One of the gang knelt beside Barker.

"He's out cold. Jesus!"

For whatever reason, perhaps shocked disorientation, they released Claudia and me. We rushed to Tom, heedless of our toplessness. Coming to their senses, a few of the men moved toward us when Billy Bob spoke.

"Let them go."

"What do you mean?" asked someone.

"I said let them go."

To show that he was serious, he pulled a pistol from a shoulder holster under his vest. I presume neither Barker nor the others had known about it.

The circle widened. We grabbed our clothes and walked out of the camp towards our motorcycle.

"You two go," I said.

"What about you?" asked Claudia.

I pointed to the silver Harley, which still had the key in it.

33

Cricket

Claudia had been traumatized though being fully clothed again helped a great deal. Mother washed her up in the bathroom, then took her to the kitchen to make her a cup of coffee. Claudia called her father who was still in the hospital with Annie.

Tom and I sat with Father in the living room.

"What the hell were you planning to do when you got there?" asked Tom.

Father guessed my plan as soon as he saw me fingering the bracelet. I could not tell Tom the truth, nor could I think of anything else to say without sounding stupid. Furthermore, I was confused. Had he not broken my confidence, reported the plane to someone? On the other hand, I was deeply moved by his courage. I hung my head until he stopped asking questions.

"So you've been taking kickboxing lessons," said Father. "Admirable. I am very grateful to you for protecting my impetuous daughter. I hope to repay you in some way. How badly did you hurt him?"

"I don't know."

Slyly Father turned the conversation towards the very question on my mind. Father surprises me sometimes. Both my parents do.

"My daughter took you to see an object in the desert. Do you know to what I refer?"

"The shuttle or whatever it is?"

Fleetingly Father looked towards the kitchen. Claudia and Mother were occupied.

"To whom have you reported it?"

Puzzled, Tom paused before answering. "You knew about the plane? Didn't you think you should...I mean, why didn't you... She said that that you... Cricket, can I tell them what you said?"

Despite my discomposure a spark of anger flared.

"You didn't answer my father's question. Who did you tell?"

"I—"

The grumbling of motorcycle engines ended our conversation.

Claudia chose to stay in the house. With uncanny foresight, Mother insisted she lie in bed until we came back in.

"Oh, I'm better now," she said.

"Please do as I ask," insisted Mother. Claudia went into my room and lay on the bed.

Father, Mother, Tom, and I went out to meet them. Father cradled his shotgun in his arms.

Billy Bob now led the pack. Towards the end of the line, Barker sat grimly behind another rider, clearly in pain. We boldly looked him over, but he averted our eyes.

Billy Bob dismounted. The others remained straddling their motorcycles.

"We've come for the Harley. Hey, girl, that wasn't too nice. Especially after I let you go. That's grand theft."

"Take your motorcycle and go," said Father, holding the shotgun across his chest more tightly. His face was red and he was shaking. Here were the hoodlums who had terrorized the town, humiliated Camacho, vandalized Hoppy Jones's car, and threatened two girls with rape, one of whom was his daughter. I'd never seen him like this before. I could sense the pressure. One of the first safety rules of chemistry is to never heat a closed system. With little more provocation Father would explode.

"We'll go when we feel like it," snarled Billy Bob, pulling out his pistol. He aimed it at Father. "Let's see who's the quickest shot. If I killed you it would be self-defense and I have witnesses."

Father now spoke in our language.

"I will dial down the range, but the boy and girl will be affected."

"She is recumbent," said Mother. "I will catch the boy." She stepped behind Tom. "Are you certain you wish to do this?"

"As certain as I have ever been about anything."

In turn Father looked each gang member in the eye. "I have memorized your faces." His voice was loud. His words distinctly pronounced. "I forbid you from entering this town ever again. Ignore my warning and you will rue your decision for a lifetime."

Billy Bob chuckled. "You turn that rabbit gun on me and I'll put a bullet through your head. Like I said, it will be self defense."

"Listen carefully, gentlemen. Listen!" boomed Father. "I am going to invoke a supernatural curse. Return to this town and much worse will befall you."

"Supernatural curse, huh? Why, you asshole, do you think..."

Before Billy Bob finished his sentence, Father activated the bracelet. In concentric waves the impulse traveled at the speed of light. The riders' faces slackened. Their hands slipped from handlebars. Quietly they slumped forward, or tumbled from their motorcycles, taking some of the machines down with them. The astonishing jumble of bodies lured the neighbors from their homes.

I heard someone say, "I don't know what happened to them, but it was about time."

Mother caught Tom. We carried him into the house, placing him on the sofa. She stayed inside with Tom and Claudia as they revived. Father and I walked among the fallen, collecting chains, lead pipes, knives, and Billy Bob's pistol. As we were completing the pile of weapons at our feet, who should arrive but Officer Vera Camacho. She parked in a neighbor's driveway.

"My God! What happened to them?"

They littered the street like large black garbage bags full to overflowing.

"Where's Claudia?"

"She is inside and will be out shortly. As to them," said Father gesturing towards the gang, "it is a mystery, but offering an excellent opportunity for you to arrest Barker and his friend."

"For abduction and attempted rape," I added.

"I suggest you act before they awaken," urged Father.

After I completed a hurried retelling of events, Camacho handcuffed Billy Bob. Father, Camacho, and I then pulled Barker from under the motorcycle that had fallen on him. She handcuffed him.

By this time a crowd had gathered. Had they been at their windows watching the inexplicable event? We would know the answer soon enough.

Bewildered and disoriented, the Hoods began to regain consciousness. Several neighbors applauded as Father and I assisted Camacho in locking Barker and Billy Bob in the back seat of the patrol car before they fully realized what was happening to them. A metal grate separated front from back. The wild criminals were caged at last.

Tom and Claudia emerged from the house, Mother behind them. Mystified, Claudia thought she'd fallen asleep. Equally mystified, Tom assumed he must have been more stressed than he'd thought and that he'd passed out.

In a few minutes the gang members were alert enough to understand what they were told. Leaderless, but more relevant, frightened, they did not even grumble when Camacho told them to leave. In less than two minutes the street was free of them.

Camacho took statements from Tom, Claudia, and me.

When she was finished, she asked again what had happened to the gang. Mother, Father, and I shrugged. Perplexed, she shook her head, and then walked to her car and drove off.

34

Cricket

The irony of it! Father had repeatedly upbraided us for careless speech and action, yet neither Mother nor I had exposed our foreignness. But there on the street, under the bright sun, the neighbors watching, Father had sent a tsunami of electromagnetic waves to swamp the synapses of the Hoods' reticular activating systems. And down they went like so many bean bags dropped by an unskilled juggler. This was otherworldly technology flaunted as brazen as a neon sign flashing, "We are alien."

By the time I returned to school on Monday, everyone in Prickly Pear over the age of six had heard the preposterous but true story that Watson Sminth had confronted a gang of twelve men with a shotgun and all twelve men had fainted.

Yet again, had we really been exposed? Would people think *we* caused the en masse passing out? Or would they invent another cause? But what did this matter? Cummings had proof that we had forged documents and that our fingers lacked friction ridges.

Claudia came running across the quad towards me. At the last moment she dropped her books to hug me. She was primly dressed in dark slacks and a modest navy blue blouse, her hair up in a bun. It was almost as if, having garnered unwanted attention from twelve wheeled satyrs, she wanted no more.

"Tom told me it was your idea to come after me. I never thanked you properly. I was in a daze. And that absolutely amazing thing your mother did with Annie. God! I don't know what I would have done if she'd lost a leg or something. Let me buy you an ice cream after school. Please. I need to tell you something important."

What Claudia had to tell me was clearly urgent, because she led the way to Rosita's like a speed walker. We sat in the booth farthest from the door and windows, but before Claudia could tell me anything, four girls swarmed into our booth: Melissa and Sarah next to me, Hayley and Nicole next to Claudia.

"Amazing what happened," said Sarah. "How do you explain it?"

Melissa, Hayley, and Nicole each asked the same question, differently phrased. I went into actress mode.

"Gee," I said. "I don't know. They all just fell down. Maybe it was heat stroke...uh, or dehydration." The deliberate pause emphasized my feigned bafflement.

No one spoke of aliens, alien technology, or divine intervention. But Melissa asked if my father were a sorcerer à la Harry Potter.

"Gee," I said. "Not that I know of. Or if he is, he practices when I'm asleep."

"Was he holding a wand?"

"No, it was definitely a shotgun."

"Your father should get a medal," said Hayley.

"And your mother, too," added Nicole. "Claudia told us what she did. But she's not a doctor, is she? I mean she actually operated on Annie. That's just as amazing as all those guys fainting."

Although I expected questions about my mother's surgical skill, I hadn't thought of any satisfying answers. She'd taken an advanced first aid course, I told them. They bandied this about for a while before ever-sensitive Melissa noted that Claudia and I probably had some things we wanted to discuss privately. This made sense. The girls said goodbye and left.

Claudia spoke. "My father's going to have you arrested. I mean your family. He may call a town meeting. He didn't make any friends when he arranged to have Rosita's kitchen helper arrested so he wants to explain himself this time. He's going to tell them you don't have the proper papers and that you don't have...That you don't have—this is ridiculous—that you don't have fingerprints."

I took a sip of my chocolate shake and kept my left hand in my lap. In a black velvet painting on the wall opposite me, an Aztec maiden lay unconscious in the outstretched arms of a beplumed priest, her shapely ankles decorated with orchids. He had not yet cut out her beating heart.

Earnestly, Claudia examined me. I tried to relax my face.

"I don't know where he got that idea. May I look at your hand?"

I put the glass down, and placed both hands, palms up, on the table.

She took my left hand in hers and brought it closer to her eyes.

"A severe viral illness that almost killed us," I said unprompted. "Our hands and feet shed skin like...molting lizards." Oh, no. Couldn't I think of a better analogy than that? Like discarding old clothes? An old house losing shingles? A beach goer's skin flaking off? It was too late.

"Oh," said Claudia looking even more closely, before releasing my hand.

"I wanted to tell you what my father is planning because I don't want you to be arrested. But I also wanted to tell you something else."

She sighed. Leaning forward, elbows on the table, she spoke as if through bars to a condemned prisoner.

Her ice cream was rapidly melting in its cup. She ate a few spoonfuls before continuing.

"Melissa says you told her you were an alien. I mean like from outer space. She says she believes you, but between you and me, Melissa believes in elves, too. But I saw you climb the wall at the party. Your mother did the same thing at the Martinez's. I saw her operate on my sister using the most fantastic tools. Then all those bad guys passing out. Your difficulty with English. Your being an alien could explain these things. But aliens? That's science fiction. Fantasy. Hollywood. Outside America, no one believes in flying saucers. So I feel funny asking you. Besides even if you were an alien, you wouldn't tell me, but are you?"

"Am I an alien?"

"Yes."

"I am an alien. Yes."

"Well, I deserved that. How stupid of me to have asked. I don't know what I was thinking. I'm sorry. It's just that when a lot of people are talking about something you can't help but think about it, too. But honestly, Cricket, I don't really care what your explanations are. You and your family are great. I'll try to stop asking questions. Except for one more. I'm sorry, but how did you climb the wall?"

"Our transformation from our original form to human form was incomplete. The microscopic hairs on the palms of our hands and soles of our feet were not resorbed. Each of these hairs branches into smaller hairs around a billionth of an inch in diameter. Van der Waals forces hold these tiny hairs to a surface. We are able to employ them or fold them up at will."

"Would you explain that all again?"

Earnestly I repeated myself, simplifying the vocabulary, though she should have known what Van der Waal's forces were from chemistry.

"Let me see your hands again."

She examined them even more carefully this time.

"You're serious, aren't you?"

35

Cricket

A remarkable thing happened. Clyde Cummings invited us to dinner. Nobody from Immigration and Customs Enforcement would be there he joked awkwardly. He wanted to express his appreciation for what we had done for his girls. Yet we were wary. Up to now Cummings had been nothing but hostile and threatening. Father recited a line from a poem. "Will you walk into my parlor, said the spider to the fly."

But of course we accepted. What was a spider against three hyper vigilant flies from an advanced civilization? At least we tried to think of it this way.

The Cummings family lived in a pink stucco, ranch-style house with a long, low profile. The concrete expanse of front yard enclosed a rectangular area of egg-sized, red river rocks within which grew two barrel cactuses and a prickly pear. Mother looked it over with a discerning eye. From our first day in town, desert front yards intrigued her. Neighbors with humdrum or excessively thirsty yards even came to her for consultation.

Whether due to interest or anxiety, she dawdled.

"The plants are not properly placed. I speak aesthetically."

Ill at ease, Father must have thought better of hurrying her along.

She was kneeling to heft a rock when the front door opened and Cummings stepped out.

"Please help yourself. There's more where they came from." She stood.

"They have a nice look and feel to them."

"Yes," said Cummings. "My wife's idea."

We shook hands with Cummings and he invited us in, the tone of his voice suggesting, to me at least, hospitality and uneasiness in equal measure.

"Claudia's finishing up in the kitchen. Let's sit in the living room for a while. May I get you something to drink? Wine, seltzer water, juice?"

Annie sat in the middle of the living room carpet playing with a baby girl doll and a doll's crib replete with mattress, sheets, blanket, pillow, and dangling rattle. Annie appeared pain free, though her leg was still encased in its plastic cast.

We were seated on a sofa. Cummings took our orders for drinks. We opted for ice water. On his best behavior, Cummings made no facetious comments. Indeed, he returned from the kitchen with his own glass of ice water.

He sat opposite on a small love seat.

"I want to thank you for what you did for Annie. And for what you did for Claudia. And for what you did for everybody by routing that bunch of thugs." We nodded our thanks for his thanks. What could we say?

The walls of the powder blue living room were hung with family photos, a seascape, and a painting of a dozen roses in a round clay pot. Mrs. Cummings appeared relaxed and cheerful in the earlier photos, in which Claudia was eleven and Annie a baby. But in more recent photos, her smile appeared forced.

Cummings' smile seemed none too natural either. He hadn't gotten around to business yet. There was more to the invitation than a thank you. I got down on the floor with Annie.

"How is your baby?"

"She's not my baby. Her leg is broke. I'm the doctor."

She uncovered the doll. The right leg was bandaged.

"You must be a good doctor. The baby's not crying."

She agreed and covered the doll again. "You can hold her if you're careful."

I took the doll in my arms, holding it against my shoulder.

"They were flabbergasted at the hospital," said Cummings. "Why didn't you tell us you were a doctor, Crick?"

This was the first time he'd addressed Mother by her first name. After a pause she answered.

"I don't have a license to practice here."

We sat in the dining room with Annie, as Cummings and Claudia brought food to the table. We'd earlier conveyed our distaste for the flesh of higher animals. With Claudia's assistance, Cummings had prepared a meal of stir-fried broccoli, red pepper, and tofu, with white rice, and a mixed salad.

Cummings thanked us effusively. There could be no doubt about his sincerity. We repeatedly tipped our heads in acknowledgement, adding "you're welcome" from time to time. Eventually there came a lull. Cummings had not touched his food. His tone changed.

"Watson, Crick, Cricket, I find myself in a quandary, a moral quandary. I am deeply indebted to you...But—let's be honest—you're not ordinary people. Listen, I don't want to talk to the police about all this stuff—phony papers, no fingerprints, and all that. But if you're spies how can I not report you? Do you understand what I'm saying?"

"No," said Father, "we do not understand, specifically we do not understand what you wish to do."

"My husband is somewhat dimwitted," said Mother, smiling ironically at Father. How often had he said this of her before her English improved. Claudia appeared embarrassed. Cummings took his first bite of dinner.

"I understand perfectly," continued Mother. "You are grateful for what we've done. You do not wish to reveal our embarrassing, possibly illegal, doings. You would like us to prove to you that we are not spies, Russian or otherwise."

"Dear wife," replied Father peeved. "I knew that. I meant to say that I did not understand what he might accept as proof of our nonspyhood."

"There is no such word as nonspyhood."

"It is a neologism."

"It is not a neologism until it enters the language, which it is highly unlikely to do."

Their underlying tension was being expressed in argument. I disliked them behaving like this.

"Mother. Father. Please."

Cummings took his second bite of dinner. He, too, was ill at ease. We ate in silence for ten minutes before Claudia spoke.

"Dad, they can't be spies. There's nothing out here to spy on. If they wanted to spy on the air force base they would have lived closer to it, don't you think?"

"May I be excused?" asked Annie. "I want to play."

She'd eaten most of her serving.

"Don't you want dessert?" asked Cummings.

"I'll come back when it's ready."

After she'd left the table, Cummings spoke to Claudia though we were his intended audience.

"You saw the...the technology they have. It's out of this world. And I've been thinking about that gang all fainting at once."

He turned from Claudia to us.

"I think you folks are behind that. How, I haven't a clue. Nerve gas or something. Frankly, after what I've seen, I wouldn't be surprised if you had devices that could measure the temperature of a jet's exhaust at forty thousand feet or the temperature of the pilot for that matter. You're right, Crick. I want some kind of concrete reassurance that you're not spies. I don't want to report you. I really and truly don't."

Mother spoke. "Mr. Cummings—"

"Clyde. Call me Clyde."

"Clyde," continued Mother. "What if we told you we were—"

"My dear wife," interrupted Father. "We have not fully discussed this among ourselves. What you have in mind is premature. Prudence. Please, prudence."

"I think Mother should tell."

The Sminth family bickering was less heated than I imagined it would be. Was Father already resigned? Back and forth we went until Mother turned to Cummings.

"Understand this is only a theoretical question, Mr.—I mean Clyde."

"You haven't asked your question."

Father shook his head and began eating. Yes, he was resigned after all.

"Would you believe we were not spies if we were aliens?" said Mother.

"From Mexico or from Russia?" Cummings was either smiling or grimacing. I could not tell which.

"Neither from those nor from any other country. What would you do if I told you we were from another planet?"

"If you told me you were extraterrestrials in other words?"

"Exactly that."

He scratched his bald head. Claudia looked at her father, then at Mother. Father was quiet but shaking his head.

"I invited you here with the best intentions but...All right, I'll be patient. If that's what you told me—theoretically, of course—I would say that interplanetary travel is impossible. The distances are too great."

"But Daddy," said Claudia, flustered, "you're always talking about aliens."

"I'm advertising my business, that's all. You know that."

Claudia was angry. My family's bickering bothered me, but the bickering of another family was just as bad. And I sensed it coming.

"I know what it is, Daddy, and everyone else knows what it is, and no one takes it seriously, but you don't even believe it's possible like they do in Roswell. Advertising is one thing, but if you think it's impossible, that's like dishonest."

"This is not the time or place to discuss my business practices."

"Which aren't working anyway!"

"Claudia!"

"Well, they're not and that alien artifact shop is a total flop. And all that fighting about money. That's why Mom went away."

"She ran off with a Mexican man."

"She did not!" bawled Claudia. "The man just gave her a ride! I talk with her on the phone. She made a mistake. She misses us, but she can't stand the fighting over money and she thinks we're going to lose the house. She made a mistake and wants to come home. Daddy, if you'd just give up the business..."

"We'd really go bust then," he erupted.

As this continued, Mother, Father, and I, despite a loss of appetite, had turned to our food, eating slowly, eyes down, chewing each spoonful excessively. Annie came in crying. "I want my Mommy!" Cummings took her on his lap and held her, rocking her from side to side. The crying stopped, the sniffling continued. Cummings wiped her nose with a napkin. Claudia glowered at him but said no more.

"Sorry about the dirty laundry," said Cummings chagrined. "All happy families are happy in the same way. All unhappy families are unhappy in different ways. Tolstoy."

Here, finally, was some wisdom, I thought. Who was this Tolstoy I wondered? I would scan for her later.

We'd finished the salad and main course without further argument, discussion, or invective. But though silent, we were ruffled. Chocolate ice cream for dessert helped to a degree.

"I forgot where we were," said Cummings. Annie fetched her doll from the living room and returned to Cummings' lap.

"We were discussing a hypothetical question," said Mother, "but I wish to dispense with hypotheticals. Mr. Cumm—Clyde, I began by asking how you would react were I to tell you that we are extraterrestrials. I am now telling you unequivocally that we are indeed extraterrestrials. And as I know you do not believe this, I offer to show you our landing craft which is half buried in the desert north of here."

"Oh, my God," said Claudia.

Cummings scratched his head again and moved his spoon around in his dessert dish though no ice cream remained. He would be interested in seeing what we'd found, but no matter what it might be, he would not believe we were extraterrestrials. In fact, he would be even more suspicious that we were spies.

"That just wouldn't prove anything," he said finally.

Mother appreciated his honesty. We could prove our otherness in numerous other ways she explained. We'd just have to come up with the most convincing.

"I believe them, Daddy," said Claudia. It explains so much. And they don't have to think about what to do to convince you. They can do that right now. Climb a wall, Cricket. You too, Mrs. Sminth, Mr. Sminth. Show him."

Mother looked at Father and me. She spoke in our language. We twittered, chirruped, clicked, and peeped freely, if a bit self-consciously, discussing how to go about this. Cummings, wide-eyed, looked as if he'd heard hoof beats under the table. Annie, beaming with delight, put her doll down on the table. Claudia said, "Wow!"

Committed to proving we were from far far away, there was no need to speak English. And by speaking Sassathan we provided further proof of our far-off origin.

"Do either of you have any objections?" Mother asked us. We had none. "Should we tell him what we are about to do, or should we surprise him?"

"Let us surprise him," I said.

Reverting to English, Mother asked Cummings for permission to remove the family pictures from the wall. Silently, he signaled to continue.

Eagerly Claudia helped. As we removed the pictures, she spoke of her shock at seeing me near the ceiling at Sarah's slumber party. Her father hadn't believed her, nor had anyone else. She was excited that I was going to do it again.

Father and I took off our shoes and socks, Mother her shoes and sheer stockings. Mother choreographed the ascent.

First, Father climbed up three feet, stopped, and began singing the first part of *Ognim in Search of Water*. Annie started laughing. Cummings croaked, "That's impossible."

On the way to the ceiling Mother sang the second voice of *Ognim in Search of Water*. Cummings stiffened in his chair, tightening his hold around Annie.

"Stop, Daddy. That hurts."

Singing the third voice of the harmony, I climbed up to the ceiling and then out to the middle, hanging upside down, my hands and feet firmly attached. When we'd finished the song, we jumped back to the floor, my landing most theatrical. It was a good show. Claudia clapped. Annie giggled.

We returned to our places at the table. Cummings was frozen in place, gripped by a powerful fear. I was surprised to discover in myself sympathy for him. He shuddered, blinked, and swallowed. Annie freed herself and brought me her doll. I took her on my lap.

"That was a beautiful song," said Claudia.

"Sing it again," added Annie.

"Maybe we will later, just for you," said Mother. Cummings, it was clear, did not wish to hear it again. He just sat there like goldilocks finding herself in a cabin with three bears—weird, alien, whistling bears. Though a rotund, heavy man, he gave the impression of fragility. We all felt it, even Annie, who climbed off my lap and went to her father. He unfroze and took her onto his lap again.

The hush in the room was as eerie as a seance. But the spirits from beyond did not manifest themselves as flickering lights or a trembling table.

"Clyde," said Father at length, in the gentlest tone I'd ever heard him use, "may I have a little more ice cream?"

"And some coffee, if you don't mind," added Mother.

Cummings' features began moving like minuscule tectonic plates. We had no standard to gauge the depth of his discomfiture. I feared a convulsion. His breathing had been rapid and shallow, but after gasping like a swimmer surfacing from a long dive, he exploded in laughter, and then abruptly stopped.

"I'm frightened," he said.

"Don't be frightened, Daddy," said Annie. "They're like birds or something. They're nice."

36

Cricket

C ummings, like the father of a newborn baby, smiled so broadly his cheeks must have ached. Over three hundred townspeople walked around the craft, waiting their turn to take a look inside. Most had arrived by nine or ten in the morning. After what they'd heard from people who'd seen the site the previous two days, many planned to stay for hours and had brought their lunches with them.

"Well, Clyde, I owe you an apology," said Pedro Gonzalez, my chemistry teacher. "I thought this was going to be another one of your half-cocked publicity stunts. Sorry. I don't know if it's from outer space or not but it sure is weird. Those wings. That indecipherable inscription over the exit. And there's no engine. It must have glided in. And talk about weird, where is the pilot, the passengers? Could be a drone—except for the seats."

Mr. Gonzalez was right. The engine and fuel tanks had been jettisoned, tumbling into the Indian Ocean. Rocket plane had become glider.

"It's probably from Edwards Air Force Base," said Hoppy Jones. "An experimental glider."

"No. They wouldn't have lost track of something like this,"

objected Ms. Hardy. "And how do you explain the fire damage inside, which seems selective to me?"

The people formed a sort of ellipse around two focal points: Cummings and his "discovery." He was asked the same questions again and again: How did he find it? Why did he think it was an alien craft? How long had he known about it? Could they buy some of that spare aluminum siding he had? And where were the aliens?

"Where do you suppose the aliens are, Watson?" he asked, daring to tease Father, but now firmly allied with him, with the whole family.

"I presume they are safely ensconced in Malibu by this time. A cozy little million dollar shack by the water. Easier to blend in there despite the antennae and bug eyes. But you never know. Maybe *I* am one them." Father made a funny face.

Mother attested to his often acting as if he were from another planet. She was rewarded with laughter.

One might have thought the people would be somber at the scene of a crash. They were not. With the picture taking, the Sunday picnic lunches, the unique airship, the crowd, and Cummings as the barker, it was a carnival. In a few weeks, little shaded stands would dot the area, purveying hot dogs and souvenirs.

But a contingent of county police, National Transportation Safety Engineers, Air Force personnel, and NASA scientists had also begun to assemble. The police ushered people to the periphery, but they kept drifting back towards the plane, approaching from all points.

Cummings could not have wished for a more enthusiastic promoter of his plan than Buddy Gaylord, half owner of the Still Waters Motel. Animated by the occasion and by nips from a hip flask of whiskey, he staggered through the crowd urging everyone to be on their toes.

"They've landed. They're among us now. Maybe they're friendly, maybe not. Time will tell. Time will tell."

Should Buddy stumble or pass out, his sister Miriam followed him at a short distance. Ordinarily his public drunkenness would have exasperated her, but the Still Waters Motel was filling up with UFO enthusiasts from as far away as Los Angeles as well as government agents. If this kept up, she'd have to light the "no vacancy" sign for the first time. She was ecstatic.

Hoppy Jones's gas station was also in much demand as were, for that matter, all the services, restaurants, and shops in town. Some people were offering rooms for rent.

The first person to enter the ship and the last to leave it was Gus Theodorakis, a casually dressed, earnest-looking man from NASA. While he was still inside other officials came and went, among them a test pilot from Edwards Air Force base, a man in a crisp blue uniform. A woman from the National Transportation Safety Board, a plastic identification card hanging from her neck on a lanyard, was clearly annoyed. Scowling, she'd been asking questions of the townspeople, several of whom pointed fingers, some literally, at Mayor Cummings.

After she went back into the craft for a second look, she confronted him.

"It looks like the whole town tramped through that thing. There're even footprints on the wings. That's not right. Why didn't you report this immediately?"

My English was pretty good by now and I can confidently describe Mr. Cummings' explanation as a cock-and-bull story. He was confused he said, didn't know who to call, and when he did try to call, he couldn't get through, connections went dead, had to attend to his kids who were sick, and so on.

An entourage of curious townspeople surrounding her, like iron filings around a magnet, slowed her way to her car.

"What is it?"

"Is it a space shuttle?"

"Did it come from the air force base?"

"Is it one of ours?"

And from my point of view, the most troubling question of all: Were there passengers?

She could not, or did not wish to, answer any of these questions. She only wished to ask them.

Mr. Theodorakis asked questions, too but not about why the crash wasn't reported. He asked what the weather had been like in the desert, whether there'd been any wind storms. He asked if people had noticed anything unusual, anything out of the ordinary. Any footprints?

How had Mr. Cummings discovered the plane, as he referred to it?

"Oh, I just like to get out into nature. Try a different spot each time. Get to know the desert a little. Lots of interesting creatures. Ran across it by accident."

"Well," said Cindy Penny. "Unusual things? Yes. I have just eaten the most delicious fruit. Really, it's out of this world," said Mrs. Penny.

He approached Mother.

"Dr. Sminth?"

"Pardon me."

"You're Dr. Crick Sminth, aren't you?"

"I am Crick Sminth, but I'm not a doctor."

He looked puzzled and squinted at her in the bright sun. He held a notebook in his left hand and shaded his eyes momentarily with his right. He introduced himself and then asked about the fractured leg she'd treated.

"Oh, heavens, how people do exaggerate. I bandaged a sprained ankle, that's all."

Mr. Theodorakis seemed to struggle with himself, but then part of him won the struggle.

"Well, you do treat people's medical problems. Isn't that right?

"Yes. With herbs and things."

"During the past few months have you treated anyone with any unusual injuries?"

Mother mimed an active thinker, tilting her head from side to side, moving her pursed lips, lowering and raising her eyebrows. All this just to say, "Not that I can think of."

"Have you treated any unusual people recently"

"No. I'm sorry. Why do you ask?

Mr. Theodorakis's fruitless questioning was interrupted by a loud, deep thrumming overhead. He looked up, thanked Mother, and walked away.

A dull green helicopter like a monstrous, blurred-winged grasshopper, descended to hover twenty feet over the plane. The sandstorm it kicked up was much more effective in driving back the crowd than had been the orders of officialdom.

Workers wearing dust masks and goggles, bore into the sand under the plane, girding it with bright orange straps. Sets of cables dangling from the helicopter were attached to the straps on either side of the plane forming a sling. The crew scurried to get clear as the helicopter effortlessly lifted the plane and made its way west toward NASA's Jet Propulsion Laboratory at the California Institute of Technology.

————

Tom

A mazing! I was in love with a girl from outer space. Absolutely sounds like a B movie. But it was true. True. True. True. Thank God I never told anyone about the spaceship. I'd like to give myself credit for a wise decision, but the truth is I just couldn't decide what to do. I just kept stewing over it.

There she is!

————

Cricket

T om came to me out of the crowd when the helicopter had left.
"Quite a circus," he said, putting his arm around me.
"Yes."

37

Cricket

W e had lowered the blinds and closed the curtains over our west-facing living room window, and covered it with a Mexican blanket, darkening the room further.

Seated in a circle facing the center of the room were Oscar, Mary, and Tom Martinez on the sofa; Clyde Cummings on the wing chair; and Claudia and my parents on kitchen chairs. I remained standing.

Although he had agreed to it, Father said the idea of complete openness still unsettled him. He did not wish to narrate. Perfectly understandable. But when Mother, whose English was now perfect, said she was insufficiently proficient, I was puzzled. By default, then, I was the designated narrator.

On the floor in the center of the circle lay a perfectly flat silver disc the size of a dinner plate.

"Is it going to levitate?" asked Cummings, humor masking anxiety.

"No," I said. "It won't."

"Is everyone ready?" I asked.

As soon as I'd asked the question it struck me that I myself was not ready. How would I react to the projected holographic video images I had had access to since arrival but never chose to watch?

And in hindsight it seemed that my parents' excuses for not narrating were contrived. Why would they want me to do the talking?

"Fire away," said Oscar Martinez.

Our instantaneous plunge into deep space was orchestrated with the astonished gasps and exclamations of the uninitiated. In the distance before us hung Sassatha, at the moment a marbled basketball surrounded by stars. As it grew larger, smudges of orange and yellow resolved themselves into clouds being torn apart and reforming in a smoky sky.

Tom was first to speak.

"It's like we're in a spaceship, like we're headed toward the planet. What's it called again?"

"Sassatha is as close as we can get to it in English."

"Say it in your language, please," asked Mary Martinez. So I did.

Claudia said, "It's like a snippet of a bird song."

The planet rose to meet us. Twisting dust storms, their columns rising hundreds of feet in the air, veiled the corroded, broken towers of abandoned cities.

"Global warming?" ventured Tom.

"Yes."

"We did not completely recycle the detritus of civilization," added Mother, "and then the warming ground began releasing gases that insulated the planet further."

As we descended below ten thousand feet, a tube city came into view—crisscrossing cylinders running for miles parallel to the surface.

Again the scene changed radically, accompanied by muffled sounds of wonder.

"Unbelievable," said Cummings.

"This is the inside of our home—what was our home, I mean."

Now! What was I feeling, I asked myself? Not homesickness. Some other realization trying to push through into consciousness. I hesitated.

"Shall I continue from here?" asked Mother solicitously.

"No. No. It's all right."

I began walking through the projection.

"Our module is a small section within a sixteen-foot-diameter cylinder that runs partially buried and parallel to the surface for miles. It is not completely underground. A long, narrow window runs along the top." I pointed up at the window.

"You can explore the module. If an object seems to block your way, just walk through it. Everything looks solid but it's only a projection."

I stopped talking and waited.

After a while Tom began walking through the scene. His father joined him.

"You're walking on a flooring of fused sandglass tiles, about five feet above the bottom of the cylinder. Below it are pipes, cables, pumps, and cybernetic arrays of monitors and controls."

Tom pointed to one of the pictures hanging from the wall in what might be thought of as the living room area; three standing Sassathans, the smallest one with its tongue sticking out.

"My mother, father, and me," explained Father. "My excuse for acting juvenile? I was a juvenile at the time."

"He is growing more mature by the day," said Mother.

"As I have no role models, it may take awhile," retorted Father. "That gesture, by the way, is older than speech and evolved independently in your species."

Mother and Father were playfully teasing each other. This confused me.

Claudia asked about a picture of a dark blue meadow punctuated by red and yellow wildflowers under a pastel blue sky.

"This looks like a painting."

I told her it was.

Mother spoke. "Such places had vanished hundreds of years before I painted it. Blue grass like so many others, was an extinct species. All gone."

I looked at the familiar curved, white walls, up at the overhead window, at the pieces of curve-backed furniture nestling against the walls. Although all was shown precisely as it had existed, I could not avoid the thought that something was wrong. Damnation—English curses came easily now—I was feeling something I could not put a name to.

"You can see this single room has separate areas for recreation, study, sleep, eating, and toileting. Note the prominent meters. We were never allowed to ignore how much precious water and electricity we were using."

Everyone was up, examining the appliances, fixtures, desks, and chairs, the style suggesting Danish Modern. Nothing, of course, could be felt.

After a while I asked them to be seated.

"I don't want you to be frightened. I'm going to show you the original me."

"It's going to be like the sculpture you made in art class, isn't it?" asked Claudia.

"You are a smart biscuit."

"Cookie," corrected Father.

Ignoring him, I wondered if Claudia were alarmed. A papier maché figure was one thing, a virtual creature only a few feet away was another.

The original me entered from behind a curtain. What an eerie sight it must have been seeing the two of us facing each other. I, a teenage girl, and I, an upright, slender, faintly iridescent, ochre colored, large-eyed, gecko-like humanoid.

"Oh!" said Mr. Martinez.

"My, oh, my," murmured Mrs. Martinez.

Surprise was also given voice by shifting positions, creaking furniture, the rustle of clothing against cushions, inhalations, puffs of air, a truncated whistle, a nasal "Mmm?"

My former self sang a short song and danced a jig, leaping off the floor.

Similes can only fail to describe their surprise.

"That's you?" asked Tom, "but how...I mean...Are you like that underneath?

Was he asking if a scaly lizard lurked just beneath my skin? His question bothered me. What difference did it make? Or more precisely, what difference did it make to him?

I was relieved to hear Mother respond.

"Your species and ours, remarkable as it may seem, are not that dissimilar, given our evolution under similar circumstances, on similar planets. With the blueprint of the human genome project we were able to dedifferentiate our cells into totipotent cells then redifferentiate them to reshape our bones and other organs. Our scales for example after resorption were replaced with hypodermis, dermis, and epidermis. In other words, no Sassathan body lies beneath this one, though our brains are less modified. Perhaps later, if you are interested we can go into the details."

The bony scaffold of my original oval face was more mammalian than reptilian. My large eyes were centered in even larger, shallow, bowl-like indentations, a low narrow nose running between them. Eyelashes and eyebrows framed my eyes, yet a seemingly unnecessary nictitating membrane flashed back and forth over them. My head was hairless, but adorned with a yellow feathery crest.

My mouth was wide with prominent lips. Silver dollar-sized tympanic membranes were situated just before my small, external, low ears.

"Wow!" blurted Claudia, "You're so different but you're kind of...good-looking. I always thought aliens were ugly."

"You're kind of good looking yourself," I said without malice. Claudia took it as it was meant, and chuckled. The room's tension dropped a notch.

I wore a sort of white jumpsuit decorated—remarkably—with pictures of an extinct species of blue wildflower. Except in the broadest sense—having two eyes, a nose, a mouth—my old face did not resemble the new me.

How profoundly powerful our cybernetic psychology that I'd been prepared to look at my new human face in the mirror and not be aghast. Strange, yet in a way I felt a bittersweet empathy for my previous self. What that poor creature had been through!

"Say goodbye to the former me," I told the audience.

And as I said it the full force of the realization struck me. My parents had contrived my becoming master of ceremonies, so I would be unable to look away from these images.

I would finally see, they hoped, that on Sassatha I had been no less confined than that gecko I'd released from its cage the first day of school. I had rarely seen my friends—and then only as projections—and I barely knew them. Nor were our meetings ever private. I'd been out of our module only a few times in my life and on the surface of the planet only once. Yes, my life on Sassatha had been impoverished.

And I saw it. How immature and obstreperous I had been. What if I'd managed to prevent our exodus? No wonder they lied to me. I turned to them, tears welling up in my eyes. I could not put this off until we were alone. The feelings were too strong. And why not confess publicly in English?

"Mother, Father, please.... forgive me." I wiped my nose on my sleeve. "I have been a thankless, unrelenting pain in the posterior. I have made things so hard on you. I have been miserable to live with. I am so sorry."

"To stand outside, without a mask, without that dreadful suit, it was a miracle. I could never have even dreamed that simply taking a walk could be such a great pleasure."

"At school I was frightened to be in the physical presence of so many people. It was so unnatural, but now I know that always being alone is unnatural. To freely mingle with others, not virtually, but actually, is natural. I have flesh and blood friends here." Again I wiped my nose on a sleeve and struggled against blubbering. In a moment I was surrounded. Mother, Father, and Tom all hugging me with the Martinezes and Cummings' in the outer circle, their arms enveloping us as well.

38

Cricket

The transformation of Prickly Pear from poverty to prosperity was inexorable. As soon as photographs of our scout ship began appearing in newspapers and on the Internet, UFO enthusiasts began arriving to investigate. They hired townspeople as guides to the crash site and to provide first-person accounts of what they had seen. Enterprising individuals sold photographs of the ship.

Many of the buildings along Main Street were sheathed in riveted sheets of shiny aluminum—spaceship mimicry. No matter the type of business, there were always more than enough customers. Real estate prices began to increase. Townspeople bought the ramshackle houses at the edge of town and remodeled them. They could be rented out for the weekends or longer periods. Miriam Gaylord and her brother remodeled the Still Waters Motel and hired back the help.

The photographs in Cummings's souvenir shop displayed more than just our landing craft. The walls were covered with images of the colony ship itself, including details of its inner compartments. Tourists were astounded by the pictures of the suspended animation canisters and of the pilgrims within them. On a counter in the middle of his shop was a scale model of the Colony, with cut-away views of the interior. He'd also borrowed the life-sized papier maché model I'd made at school.

"This is what they look like," he'd tell his customers. "Just like this."

The sophisticated visitors asked who'd done the artwork and made the model. The less sophisticated asked how he'd gotten the photographs and where were the aliens now. He laughed off both questions.

Gus Theodorakis of NASA returned repeatedly, staying at the Still Waters Motel. People got used to seeing him drive out to the crash site, walking around out there for hours, scratching his head. No one told him anything new about the discovery of the strange plane that had made the town famous. Mayor Cummings said the displays in his thriving curio shop were given him by tourists passing through town. He teased Mr. Theodorakis. "You don't really believe in alien visitors, do you?" We avoided the NASA man. He made us nervous.

As happy as Mayor Cummings was with his business and his neighbors' newfound respect for him, nothing matched his joy at the return of his wife.

She asked his forgiveness. She'd simply been unable to believe that his UFO business was worth pursuing and was hurt by their arguments. What puzzled her the most was why, if he'd found this "spaceship," he'd waited so long to announce it.

"Timing," he'd answered. "Timing is everything." This was all he could think of to say.

With money in his pocket, Cummings hired a top-notch immigration attorney for the young kitchen worker who'd been arrested at Rosita's. He'd developed some sympathy for undocumented aliens.

Levi Barker and Billy Bob went to trial. Claudia, Tom, and I testified against them, as did Officer Camacho, and numerous townspeople. The young woman who'd been afraid to testify against Barker now came forward. She'd been in therapy for the trauma and was now a strong and credible witness with an intact rape kit that was damning. Billy Bob surprised us by testifying against Barker, who received a fifteen-year sentence.

The gang never returned after that, though one of them, having shed his leather jacket and driven to town in a car, came back once as a well behaved sightseer. Father told him to leave. He did.

Mother and Father permitted themselves to obtain patents on a few electronic devices. With the sale of these they have enough money to live comfortably. Neither wishes to leave Prickly Pear. Father continues working at the garage, where he dabbles in metallurgy and what can rightly be called "space-age" auto technology. He's also begun shooting pigeons—clay pigeons. Father is a champion skeet shoot. Given the opportunity, Mr. Martinez brags, "I taught him everything he knows." And sometimes adds, "His girl isn't bad either."

Mother continues practicing medicine without a license, tending free of charge everyone in town. She's also begun breeding drought-resistant plants. Cindy Penny, with Mother's blessing, has begun raising rylnin plants. Her stoop is gone, her step bouncy. "I haven't felt this way since I was in high school", she tells everyone. Whether this change in her is from the fruit or because she has something she loves doing, is unclear. She no longer goes to Las Vegas.

Mother and Father are prominent citizens. They serve on the town council and the PTA.

Although we worried that the regrowth of Tom's missing arm would bring unwanted attention, we hid the phenomenon and then did a little camouflage so the limb would be mistaken for a prosthesis.

———

D espite my earlier, unwarranted disdain for them, people are *not* stupid. A lot of them have put two and two together and deduced that Mother, Father, and I are actually extraterrestrials who arrived in the rocket plane that Clyde Cummings found out there in the desert. But no one wants to give us away. We don't frighten them; we've done too much for the town; and people like us. Buddy Gaylord, still ignorant, is writing a fanciful "exposé" called The Aliens of Prickly Pear, but we don't worry too much about that.

Yet the government is more obsessed than ever with arresting undocumented immigrants and that suspicious man from NASA keeps returning to ask questions. So Father has again begun saying, "English, please, even when we think we are alone." And Mother is working on a way for us to grow hair on our heads. Thank goodness for that.

THANK YOU FOR READING

Did you enjoy this book?

We invite you to leave a review at the website of your choice, such as Goodreads, Amazon, Barnes & Noble, etc.

DID YOU KNOW THAT LEAVING A REVIEW...

- Helps other readers find books they may enjoy.
- Gives you a chance to let your voice be heard.
- Gives authors recognition for their hard work.
- Doesn't have to be long. A sentence or two about why you liked the book will do.

_____

Don't miss out on your next favorite teen or new adult read!

_____

Join the Fire & Ice mailing list at
www.fireandiceya.com

Perks include:

- First peeks at upcoming releases.
- Exclusive giveaways.
- News of book sales and freebies right in your inbox.
- And more!

ABOUT THE AUTHOR

Peter J. Manos is married with two daughters. He remains in regular contact with a gecko-like extraterrestrial race that has fled its dying planet to blend into society in the little desert community of Prickly Pear, California. His other books include, *Care of the Difficult Patient: A Nurse's Guide* (with Joan Braun, R.N.); *Lucifer's Revenge*, a novel of magical realism, which takes place in Seattle; and *Dear Babalu: Letters to an Advice Columnist* illustrated by Toby Liebowitz.

www.peterjmanos.com

COPYRIGHTED SONGS NOTED

Earth Angel by The Penguins
Pearly Shells, lyrics by John Kalapana-Leonpobar

ACKNOWLEDGMENTS

For their suggestions and support I would like to thank Ingrid Dinter, Alice Manos, Brigitte Manos, Jesse Paulson, David Strauss, Elizabeth Strauss, Susan Picquelle, Emma Rous, Steve Tanimoto, Gunnel Tanimoto, and Venus Tan.